More ...

THE CHALK MAN

"Readers will undoubtedly be reminded of the kids of *Stand by Me* and even *IT*. . . . [The] first-person narration alternates between past and present, taking full advantage of chapter-ending cliff-hangers. A swift, cleverly plotted debut novel that ably captures the insular, slightly sinister feel of a small village. Children of the 1980s will enjoy the nostalgia."

—*Kirkus Reviews*

"If you can't get enough of psychological thrillers with sharp twists and turns, you need to read *The Chalk Man*."

—HelloGiggles

"[A] promising debut . . . with the nightmarish inevitability of the Grimmest of tales . . . her storytelling prowess is undeniable."

—*Publishers Weekly*

"Imaginative, with an intriguing premise that straddles two fascinating worlds. It's a frenetic ride that's deep and alluring, oozing with suspense. A rollicking good time."

—Steve Berry,
New York Times bestselling author of *The 14th Colony*

"C. J. Tudor knows the twelve-year-old who still lives in all of us, that kid who chills himself to the bone with an intuition of what lurks in the woods, or in his own closet, and *The Chalk Man* walks the haunted bridge between then and now—between sheer childhood terrors and a true crime so grisly and personal its cold hand never leaves the back of your neck. Suburban adolescents on bikes, squeamish love, nascent sexuality meets adult-world obsession and lust and violence . . . and through it all runs an affecting story of friendship, loss, and the inescapable frailties of mind and body."

—Tim Johnston,
New York Times bestselling author of *Descent*

"A cleverly constructed, artfully told tale of secrets, lies, and warped passions—featuring a troubled protagonist, a terrible murder that wasn't what it seemed to be, and a raging monster at the heart of it all."

—John Verdon,
internationally bestselling author of *Think of a Number*
and the Nero Award–winning *Peter Pan Must Die*

"C. J. Tudor's *The Chalk Man* is a stunning debut, a riveting thriller about the powerful grip of the past and the unbreakable bonds of childhood friendship. The ending of this smasher will completely throw you for a loop. Don't miss a word of it!"

—David Bell,
bestselling author of *Bring Her Home* and *Somebody I Used to Know*

"*The Chalk Man* is an intricate and surprising book that will reward the reader who approaches it with the attention it deserves."

—Thomas Perry,
New York Times bestselling author of *The Old Man*

"Tense, skillful storytelling."

—Ali Land,
internationally bestselling author of *Good Me Bad Me*

"Kept me up until five in the morning. Wonderfully written. I loved it!"

—Kimberley Chambers,
bestselling author of *Backstabber* and *The Wronged*

"It's been a while since I've read such an impressive debut. The pace was perfectly judged, the characters superbly drawn, and there's a creeping sense of unease that starts with the prologue and grows throughout the book. And then that ending! It feels so fresh and deserves to be a huge success."

—James Oswald,
bestselling author of the Inspector McLean series

"What an amazing debut! Such an ingenious, original idea. I was engrossed from the very first page. I loved how the 1986 and present-day storylines weaved so skillfully together to create that unforgettable and unexpected ending. Compelling, taut, and so very, very chilling. This book will haunt you!"

—Claire Douglas,
bestselling author of *Last Seen Alive*

"Impossible to put down, cleverly constructed and executed."

—Ragnar Jónasson,
author of the bestselling Dark Iceland series

C. J. TUDOR

CHALK MAN

A NOVEL

B\D\W\Y
BROADWAY BOOKS
NEW YORK

This is a work of fiction. Names, characters, places, and incidents
either are the product of the author's imagination or are used fictitiously.
Any resemblance to actual persons, living or dead, events,
or locales is entirely coincidental.

Published in the United States by Broadway Books, an imprint of the
Crown Publishing Group, a division of Penguin Random House LLC, New York.
crownpublishing.com

Broadway Books and its logo, B \ D \ W \ Y, are trademarks of
Penguin Random House LLC.

Originally published in hardcover in Great Britain by Michael Joseph,
a division of Penguin Random House Ltd., London, and simultaneously
in the United States by Crown, an imprint of the Crown Publishing Group,
a division of Penguin Random House LLC, New York, in 2018.

Excerpt taken from *The Hiding Place* by C. J. Tudor,
which will be published in hardcover by Crown,
an imprint of the Crown Publishing Group, a division of
Penguin Random House LLC, New York, in 2019.

Library of Congress Cataloging-in-Publication Data is available.

ISBN 978-1-5247-6099-1
Ebook ISBN 978-1-5247-6100-4

Printed in the United States of America

Cover design by Josh Smith
Cover photograph by Benot Boucher/EyeEm/Getty Images

10 9 8 7 6 5 4 3 2

First United States Paperback Edition

FOR BETTY. BOTH OF THEM.

THE

CHALK

MAN

PROLOGUE

The girl's head rested on a small pile of orange-and-brown leaves.

Her almond eyes stared up at the canopy of sycamore, beech and oak, but they didn't see the tentative fingers of sunlight that poked through the branches and sprinkled the woodland floor with gold. They didn't blink as shiny black beetles scurried over their pupils. They didn't see anything anymore, except darkness.

A short distance away, a pale hand stretched out from its own small shroud of leaves as if searching for help, or reassurance that it was not alone. None was to be found. The rest of her body lay out of reach, hidden in other secluded spots around the woods.

Close by, a twig snapped, loud as a firecracker in the stillness, and a flurry of birds exploded out of the undergrowth. Someone approached.

They knelt down beside the unseeing girl. Their hands gently caressed her hair and stroked her cold cheek, fingers trembling with anticipation. Then they lifted up her head, dusted off a few leaves that clung to the ragged edges of her neck, and placed it carefully in a bag, where it nestled among a few broken stubs of chalk.

After a moment's consideration, they reached in and closed her eyes. Then they zipped the bag shut, stood up and carried it away.

Some hours later, police officers and the forensic team arrived. They numbered, photographed, examined and eventually took the girl's body to the morgue, where it lay for several weeks, as if awaiting completion.

It never came. There were extensive searches, questions and appeals but, despite the best efforts of all the detectives and all the town's men, her head was never found, and the girl in the woods was never put together again.

2016

Start at the beginning.

The problem was, none of us ever agreed on the exact beginning. Was it when Fat Gav got the bucket of chalks for his birthday? Was it when we started drawing the chalk figures or when they started to appear on their own? Was it the terrible accident? Or when they found the first body?

Any number of beginnings. Any of them, I guess, you could call the start. But really, I think it all began on the day of the fair. That's the day I remember most. Because of Waltzer Girl, obviously, but also because it was the day that everything stopped being normal.

If our world was a snow globe, it was the day some casual god came along, shook it hard and set it back down again. Even when the foam and flakes had settled, things weren't the way they were before. Not exactly. They might have looked the same through the glass but, on the inside, everything was different.

That was also the day I first met Mr. Halloran, so, as beginnings go, I suppose it's as good as any.

1986

"Going to be a storm today, Eddie."

My dad was fond of forecasting the weather in a deep, authoritative voice, like the people on the TV. He always said it with absolute certainty, even though he was usually wrong.

I glanced out of the window at the perfect blue sky, so bright blue you had to squint a little to look at it.

"Doesn't look like there'll be a storm, Dad," I said through a mouthful of cheese sandwich.

"That's because there isn't going to be one," Mum said, having entered the kitchen suddenly and silently, like some kind of ninja warrior. "The BBC says it's going to be hot and sunny all weekend . . . and don't speak with your mouth full, Eddie," she added.

"Hmmmm," Dad said, which was what he always said when he disagreed with Mum but didn't dare say she was wrong.

No one dared disagree with Mum. Mum was—and actually still is—kind of scary. She was tall, with short dark hair, and brown eyes that could bubble with fun or blaze almost black when she was angry (and, a bit like the Incredible Hulk, you didn't want to make her angry).

Mum was a doctor, but not a normal doctor who sewed on people's legs and gave you injections for stuff. Dad once told me she "helped women who were in trouble." He didn't say what kind of trouble, but I supposed it had to be pretty bad if you needed a doctor.

Dad worked, too, but from home. He was a writer for magazines and newspapers. Not all of the time. Sometimes he would moan that no one wanted to give him any work or say, with a bitter laugh, "Just not my audience this month, Eddie."

As a kid, it didn't feel like he had a "proper job." Not for a dad. A dad should wear a suit and tie and go off to work in the mornings and come home in the evenings for tea. My dad went to work in the spare room and sat at a computer in his pajamas and a T-shirt, sometimes without even brushing his hair.

My dad didn't look much like other dads either. He had a big, bushy beard and long hair he tied back in a ponytail. He wore cut-off jeans with holes in, even in winter, and faded T-shirts with the names of ancient bands on, like Led Zeppelin and The Who. Sometimes he wore sandals, too.

Fat Gav said my dad was a "frigging hippie." He was probably right. But back then, I took it as an insult, and I pushed him and he body-slammed me, and I staggered off home with some new bruises and a bloody nose.

We made up later, of course. Fat Gav could be a right penis-head—he was one of those fat kids who always have to be the loudest and most obnoxious, so as to put off the real bullies—but he was also one of my best friends and the most loyal and generous person I knew.

"You look after your friends, Eddie Munster," he once said to me solemnly. "Friends are everything."

Eddie Munster was my nickname. That was because my surname was Adams, like in *The Addams Family.* Of course, the kid in *The Addams Family* was called Pugsley, and Eddie Munster was out of *The Munsters*, but it made sense at the time and, in the way that nicknames do, it stuck.

Eddie Munster, Fat Gav, Metal Mickey (on account of the huge braces on his teeth), Hoppo (David Hopkins) and Nicky. That was our gang. Nicky didn't have a nickname because she was a girl, even though she tried her best to pretend she wasn't. She swore like a boy, climbed trees like a boy and could fight almost as well as most boys. But she still looked like a girl. A really pretty girl, with long red hair and pale skin, sprinkled with lots of tiny brown freckles. Not that I had really noticed or anything.

We were all due to meet up that Saturday. We met most Saturdays and went round to each other's houses, or to the playground, or sometimes the woods. This Saturday was special, though, because of the fair. It came every year and set up on the park, near the river. This year was the first year we were being allowed to go on our own, without an adult to supervise.

We'd been looking forward to it for weeks, ever since the posters went up around town. There were going to be bumper cars and a Round Up and a Pirate Ship and an Orbiter. It looked ace.

"So," I said, finishing my cheese sandwich as quickly as I could, "I said I'd meet the others outside the park at two?"

"Well, stick to the main roads walking down there," Mum said. "Don't go taking any shortcuts or talking to anybody you don't know."

"I won't."

I slid from my seat and headed to the door.

"And take your bumbag."

"Oh, Muuuum."

"You'll be going on rides. Your wallet could fall out of your pocket. Bumbag. No arguments."

I opened my mouth and shut it again. I could feel my cheeks burning. I hated the stupid bumbag. Fat tourists wore bumbags. It would *not* look cool in front of everyone, especially Nicky. But when Mum was like this, there really was no arguing.

"Fine."

It wasn't, but I could see the kitchen clock edging closer toward two and I needed to get going. I ran up the stairs, grabbed the stupid bumbag and put my money inside. A whole £5. A fortune. Then I charged back down again.

"See you later."

"Have fun."

There was no doubt in my mind I would. The sun was shining. I had on my favorite T-shirt and my Converse. I could already hear the faint *thump, thump* of the fairground music, and smell the burgers and candyfloss. Today was going to be perfect.

FAT GAV, HOPPO and Metal Mickey were already waiting by the gates when I arrived.

"Hey, Eddie Munster. Nice fanny pack!" Fat Gav yelled.

I blushed purple and gave him the finger. Hoppo and Metal Mickey both chortled at Fat Gav's joke. Then Hoppo, who was always the nicest, and the peacemaker, said to Fat Gav, "Least it doesn't look as gay as your shorts, penis-head."

Fat Gav grinned, grabbed his shorts at the hems and did this little dance, raising his chunky legs up high, like he was a ballerina. That was the thing with Fat Gav. You could never really insult him because he just didn't care. Or, at least, that's what he made everyone think.

"Anyway," I said, because despite Hoppo's deflection I still felt that the bumbag looked stupid, "I'm not wearing it."

I unclipped the belt, slipped my wallet into my shorts pocket and looked around. A thick hedge ran around the outside of the park. I stuffed the bumbag into the hedge so it couldn't be seen if you were walking past but not so far that I couldn't grab it again later.

"Sure you want to leave it there?" Hoppo asked.

"Yeah, what if your *mummy* finds out?" Metal Mickey said, in the snide, sing-song way he had.

Although he was part of our gang and Fat Gav's best friend, I'd never liked Metal Mickey much. There was a streak running through him that was as cold and ugly as the braces that ran around his mouth. But then, bearing in mind who his brother was, perhaps that wasn't really surprising.

"I don't care," I lied, with a shrug.

"Who does?" Fat Gav said impatiently. "Can we forget the frigging bag and get going? I want to get to the Orbiter first."

Metal Mickey and Hoppo started to move—we usually did what Fat Gav wanted. Probably because he was the largest and loudest.

"But Nicky's not here yet," I said.

"So what?" Metal Mickey said. "She's always late. Let's just go. She'll find us."

Metal Mickey was right. Nicky *was* always late. On the other hand, that wasn't the deal. We were all supposed to stick together. It wasn't safe at the fair on your own. Especially not for a girl.

"Let's give her five more minutes," I said.

"You *cannot* be serious!" Fat Gav exclaimed, doing his best—so pretty bad—John McEnroe impression.

Fat Gav did a lot of impressions. Mostly American. All so terrible they made us crease up with laughter.

Metal Mickey didn't laugh quite as hard as Hoppo and me. He didn't like it if he felt the gang was going against him. But anyway, it didn't matter because we had just about stopped laughing when a familiar voice said, "What's so funny?"

We turned. Nicky walked up the hill toward us. As always, I felt a weird kind of fluttering in my stomach at the sight of her. Like I was suddenly really hungry and felt a bit sick.

Her red hair was loose today, falling in a tangled jumble down her back, almost brushing the edges of her frayed denim shorts. She wore a yellow, sleeveless blouse. It had small blue flowers around the neck. I caught a glint of silver at her throat. A small cross on a chain. She had a large and heavy-looking hessian bag slung around her shoulders.

"You're late," Metal Mickey said. "We were waiting for you."

As if it had been his idea.

"What's in the bag?" Hoppo asked.

"My dad wants me to deliver this crap around the fair."

She pulled a leaflet from the bag and held it out.

Come to St. Thomas's Church and praise the Lord. It's the greatest thrill ride of all!

Nicky's dad was the vicar at our local church. I had never actually been to church—my mum and dad didn't do that type of stuff—but I'd seen him around town. He wore small, round glasses and his bald scalp was covered with freckles, like Nicky's nose. He always smiled and said hello, but I found him just a bit scary.

"Now that is a pile of *stinking* Buckaroo, my man," Fat Gav said.

"Stinking" or "flying Buckaroo" was another one of Fat Gav's favorite phrases, usually followed by saying "my man" in a really posh accent, for some reason.

"You're not really going to, are you?" I asked, suddenly envisioning the whole day being wasted, traipsing around with Nicky while she handed out her leaflets.

She gave me a look. It reminded me a bit of my mum.

"Of course I'm not, you *Joey*," she said. "We'll just take some, scatter them around, like people have thrown them away, and then stuff the rest in a bin."

We all grinned. There's nothing better than doing something you shouldn't and getting one over on an adult while doing it.

We scattered the leaflets, dumped the bag and got down to business. The Orbiter (which really *was* ace), the bumper cars, where Fat Gav rammed me so hard I felt my spine crack. The Space Rockets (pretty exciting last year but now a bit boring), the Helter Skelter, the Round Up and the Pirate Ship.

We ate hot dogs, and Fat Gav and Nicky tried to hook ducks and learned the hard way that a prize every time does not necessarily mean a prize you want, and came away laughing and throwing their crappy little stuffed animals at each other.

By this point, the afternoon was already getting away from us. The thrill and adrenaline were starting to fade, along with the growing realization that I probably only had enough cash left for two or maybe three more rides.

I reached into my pocket for my wallet. My heart leapfrogged into my mouth. It was gone.

"Shit!"

"What?" Hoppo asked.

"My wallet. I've lost it."

"You sure?"

"Of course I'm frigging sure."

But I checked my other pocket just in case. Both empty. Crap.

"Well, where did you have it last?" Nicky asked.

I tried to think. I knew I'd had it after the last ride, because I checked. Plus, we bought hot dogs afterward. I didn't have a go on the Hook a Duck so . . .

"The hot-dog stall."

The hot-dog stall was all the way across the fair, in the opposite direction to the Orbiter and the Round Up.

"Shit," I said again.

"Come on," Hoppo said. "Let's go and look."

"What's the point?" Metal Mickey said. "Someone'll have picked it up by now."

"I could lend you some money," Fat Gav said. "But I haven't got much left."

I was pretty sure this was a lie. Fat Gav always had more money than the rest of us. Just like he always had the best toys and the newest, shiniest bike. His dad owned one of the local pubs, The Bull, and his mum was an Avon lady. Fat Gav was generous, but I also knew he *really* wanted to go on some more rides.

I shook my head anyway. "Thanks. It's okay."

It wasn't. I could feel tears burning behind my eyes. It wasn't just the lost money. It was feeling stupid, it was the spoiled day. It was knowing that Mum would be all annoyed and say, "I told you so."

"You lot go on," I said. "I'll go back and have a look. No point us all wasting our time."

"Cool," Metal Mickey said. "C'mon. Let's go."

They all shambled off. I could see they were relieved. It wasn't their money lost, or their day ruined. I started to trudge back across the fair, toward the hot-dog stall. It was right across from the Waltzers, so I used that as a marker. You couldn't really miss the old carnival ride. Right in the center of the fairground.

Music blared out, distorted through the ancient speakers. Multicolored lights flashed and the riders screamed as the wooden carriages spun round and round, faster and faster on the revolving wooden carousel.

As I got closer, I started looking down, shuffling along more carefully, scanning the ground. Rubbish, hot-dog wrappers, no wallet. 'Course not. Metal Mickey was right. Someone would have picked it up and nicked my money.

I sighed and looked up. I spotted the Pale Man first. That wasn't his name, of course. I found out afterward his name was Mr. Halloran and he was our new teacher.

It was hard to miss the Pale Man. He was very tall, for a start, and thin. He wore stonewashed jeans, a baggy white shirt and a big straw hat. He looked like this ancient seventies singer my mum liked. David Bowie.

The Pale Man stood near the hot-dog stall, drinking a blue slushy through a straw and watching the Waltzers. Well, I thought he was watching the Waltzers.

I found myself looking in the same direction, and that's when I saw the girl. I was still pissed off about my wallet but I was also a twelve-year-old boy with hormones just starting to bubble and simmer. Nights in my room weren't always spent reading comic books by torchlight under my bedcovers.

The girl was standing with a blond friend I vaguely recognized from around town (her dad was a policeman or something), but my mind instantly dismissed her. It's a sad fact that beauty, real beauty, just eclipses everything and everyone around it. Blond Friend was pretty, but Waltzer Girl—as I would always think of her, even after I learned her name—was properly beautiful. Tall and slim, with long, dark hair and even longer legs, so smooth and brown they gleamed in the sun. She wore a rara skirt, and a baggy vest with "Relax" scrawled on it over a fluorescent-green bra top. She tucked her hair behind one ear and a gold hoop earring gleamed in the sun.

I'm slightly ashamed to say I didn't notice her face much at first, but when she turned to talk to Blond Friend I wasn't disappointed. It was heartachingly pretty, with full lips and tilted almond eyes.

And then it was gone.

One minute *she* was there, her *face* was there, the next there was this terrible, eardrum-wrenching noise, like some great beast had bellowed from the bowels of the earth. Later, I found out it was the sound of the slew ring on the ancient Waltzers' axis snapping after too much use and too little maintenance. I saw a flash of silver and her face, or half of it, was sheared away, leaving a gaping mass of gristle, bone and blood. So much blood.

Fractions of a second later, before I even had a chance to open my mouth to scream, something huge and purple and black came tearing past. There was a deafening crash—the loose Waltzer carriage smashing into the hot-dog stall in a hail of flying metal and splinters of wood—and more screaming and yelling as people dived out of the way. I found myself bowled over and knocked to the ground.

Other people fell on top of me. Someone's foot stamped down on my wrist. A knee clipped my head. A boot kicked me in the ribs. I yelped but somehow managed to bundle myself up and roll over. Then I yelped again. Waltzer Girl lay next to me. Mercifully, her hair had fallen over her face, but I recognized the T-shirt and fluorescent bra top, even though both were soaked through with blood. More blood ran down her leg. A second piece of sharp metal had sliced right through the bone, just below her knee. Her lower leg was barely hanging on, tethered only by stringy tendons.

I started to scramble away—she was obviously dead. I couldn't do anything—and that was when her hand reached out and grabbed my arm.

She turned her bloody, ravaged face toward me. Somewhere, within all the red, a single brown eye stared at me. The other rested limply on her ruined cheek.

"Help me," she rasped. "Help me."

I wanted to run. I wanted to scream and cry and be sick all at once. I might have done all three if another, large, firm hand hadn't clamped down on my shoulder and a soft voice hadn't said, "It's okay. I know you're scared, but I need you to listen to me very carefully and do just what I say."

I turned. The Pale Man stared down at me. Only now did I realize that his face, beneath the wide-brimmed hat, was almost as white as his shirt. Even his eyes were a misty, translucent gray. He looked like a ghost, or a vampire, and under any other circumstances I would probably have been scared of him. But right now he was an adult, and I needed an adult to tell me what to do.

"What's your name?" he asked.

"Ed—Eddie."

"Okay, Eddie. You hurt?"

I shook my head.

"Good. But this young lady *is*, so we need to help her, okay?"

I nodded.

"This is what I need you to do . . . hold her leg here, and hold on tight, really tight."

He took my hands and placed them around the girl's leg. It felt hot and slimy with blood.

"Got it?"

I nodded again. I could taste fear, bitter and metallic, on my tongue. I could feel blood seeping between my fingers, even though I was holding on really tight, as tightly as I could . . .

In the distance, a lot farther away it seemed than the sounds actually were, I could hear music pounding and screams of enjoyment. The girl's screams had stopped. She lay motionless and quiet now, just the low rasp of her breathing, and even that was growing fainter.

"Eddie, you have to concentrate. Okay?"

"Okay."

I stared at the Pale Man. He unwound his belt from his jeans. It was a long belt, too long for his skinny waist, and it had extra holes in it where he had made it smaller. Funny, the weird things you notice at the crappiest moments. Like I noticed that Waltzer Girl's shoe had come off. A jelly shoe. Pink and sparkly. And I thought how she probably wasn't going to need it again, what with her leg almost cut in two.

"You still with me, Eddie?"

"Yes."

"Good. Almost there. You're doing great, Eddie."

The Pale Man took the belt and wrapped it around the top of the girl's leg. He pulled hard, really hard. He was stronger than he looked. Almost straightaway I could feel the gush of blood slowing.

He looked at me and nodded. "You can let go now. I've got it."

I took my hands away. Now the tension had gone, they started to shake. I wrapped them around my body, under my arms.

"Is she going to be okay?"

"I don't know. Hopefully, they can save her leg."

"What about her face?" I whispered.

He looked up at me, and something in those pale gray eyes stilled me. "Were you looking at her face before, Eddie?"

I opened my mouth, but I didn't know what to say, or understand why his voice didn't sound so friendly anymore.

Then he looked away again and said quietly, "She'll live. That's the important thing."

And that was when a huge crack of thunder broke overhead and the first drops of rain started to fall.

I guess it was the first time I understood how things can change in an instant. All the stuff we take for granted can just be ripped away. Maybe that's why I took it. To hold on to something. To keep it safe. That's what I told myself anyway.

But like a lot of stuff we tell ourselves, that was probably just a pile of stinking Buckaroo.

THE LOCAL PAPER called us heroes. They got Mr. Halloran and me back together in the park and they took our photo.

Incredibly, the two people in the Waltzer carriage that broke loose suffered only broken bones, cuts and bruises. A few other bystanders caught some nasty gashes that needed stitches, and there were a few more fractures and cracked ribs in the stampede to get out of the way.

Even Waltzer Girl (whose name was actually Elisa) lived. The doctors managed to reattach her leg and somehow save her eye. The papers called it a miracle. They didn't say so much about the rest of her face.

Gradually, as with all dramas and tragedies, interest in it started to fade. Fat Gav stopped cracking bad-taste jokes (mostly about being legless), and even Metal Mickey got bored of calling me "Hero Boy" and asking where I'd left my cape. Other news and gossip took its place. There was a car crash on the A36, and the cousin of one of the kids at school died, and then Marie Bishop, who was in the fifth year, got pregnant. So life, as it tends to, moved on.

I wasn't so bothered. I'd got a bit tired of the story myself. And I wasn't really the sort of kid who likes being the center of attention. Plus, the less I talked about it, the less often I had to picture Waltzer Girl's missing face. The nightmares started to fade away. My secret trips to the laundry basket with soiled sheets became less frequent.

Mum asked me a couple of times if I wanted to visit Waltzer Girl in hospital. I always said no. I didn't want to see her again. Didn't want to look at her ruined face. Didn't want those brown eyes to stare at me accusingly: *I know you were going to run away, Eddie. Until Mr. Halloran grabbed you, you would have left me there to die.*

I think Mr. Halloran visited. A lot. I guess he had the time. He wasn't due to start teaching at our school until September. Apparently, he had decided to move into his rented cottage a few months early so he could settle into the town first.

I supposed it was a good idea. It gave everyone a chance to get used to seeing him around. Got all the questions out of the way before he stepped into the classroom:

What was wrong with his skin? He was an *albino*, the adults explained patiently. That meant he was missing something called a "pigment" that made most people's skin a normal pink or brown color. *And his eyes?* Same thing. They were just missing pigment. *So, he wasn't a freak, or a monster or a ghost?* No. Just a normal man with a medical condition.

They were wrong. Mr. Halloran was many things, but normal was never one of them.

2016

The letter arrives without a flourish or fanfare or even a sense of foreboding. It slips through the letter box, sandwiched between a charity envelope for Macmillan Cancer Support and a flyer for a new pizza shop.

And who the hell sent letters these days, anyway? Even my mother has, at the age of seventy-eight, embraced email, Twitter and Facebook. In fact, she is far more tech savvy than me. I'm a bit of a Luddite. This is of constant amusement to my pupils, whose talk about Snapchat, favorites, tags and Instagram might as well be a foreign language. *I thought I taught English,* I often tell them ruefully. *I haven't got a flying Buckaroo what you lot are talking about.*

I don't recognize the handwriting on the envelope, but then I barely recognize my own these days. It's all keyboards and touch-screens now.

I slit the envelope open and regard the contents while sitting at the kitchen table, sipping a cup of coffee. Actually, that's not quite true. I sit at the table, staring at the contents as a cup of coffee grows cold beside me.

"What's that?"

I start and glance around. Chloe pads into the kitchen, sleep-crumpled and yawning. Her dyed black hair is loose, the choppy fringe stuck up in cowlicks. She wears an old Cure sweatshirt and the remains of last night's makeup.

"This," I say, carefully folding it up, "is what we call a letter. People used to use them as a means of communication in the olden days."

She gives me a withering look, along with her middle finger. "I know you're talking, but all I hear is blah, blah, blah."

"That's the problem with young people these days. They just don't listen."

"Ed, you're barely old enough to be my dad, so why do you sound like my grandfather?"

She's right. I am forty-two and Chloe is somewhere in her late twenties. (I think. She has never said and I am too much of a gentleman to ask.) Not so many years between us, but it often feels like decades.

Chloe is youthful and cool and could pass for a teenager. I am not and could possibly pass for a pensioner. You might kindly call my look "careworn." Although I've found it's not cares that wear you down but worries and regrets.

My hair is still thick and mostly dark, but my laughter lines lost their sense of humor some time ago. Like a lot of tall people, I stoop, and my favored clothes are what Chloe calls "charity-shop chic." Suits, waistcoats and proper shoes. I do own some jeans but I don't wear them to work and—unless I am hunkered down in my study—I'm usually working, often taking on extra tutoring in the holidays.

I could say this is because I love teaching, but nobody loves their job that much. I do it because I need the money. It's also the reason Chloe lives here. She's my lodger and, I like to think, a friend.

Admittedly, we're an odd couple. Chloe is not the type of lodger I would normally take in. But I had just been let down by another would-be tenant and the daughter of an acquaintance knew "this girl" who urgently needed a room. It seems to work, and the rent helps. As does the company.

It might seem strange that I need a lodger at all. I'm relatively well paid, the house I live in was given to me by my mum, and I'm sure most people presume this means a cozy, mortgage-free existence.

The sad truth is that the house was bought when interest rates were in double figures, was remortgaged once to pay for renovations, and then again to pay for my dad's care when his decline became too much to deal with at home.

Mum and I lived here together until five years ago, when she met Gerry, a jovial ex-banker who decided to chuck it all in for a self-sufficient lifestyle in a self-built eco home in the Wiltshire countryside.

I have nothing against Gerry. I have nothing really *for* him either, but he seems to make Mum happy, and that, as we are fond of lying, is the main thing. I suppose, even though I'm forty-two, a part of me doesn't want Mum to be happy with any man other than my dad. This is childish, immature and selfish. And I'm good with that.

Besides, at seventy-eight, Mum, quite frankly, does not give a shit. Those weren't the exact words she used when she told me she had decided to move in with Gerry, but I got the subtext:

"I need to get away from this place, Ed. There are too many memories."

"You want to sell the house?"

"No. I want you to have it, Ed. With a little love, it could be a wonderful family home."

"Mum, I don't even have a partner, let alone a family."

"It's never too late."

I didn't reply.

"If you don't want the house, just sell it."

"No. I just . . . I just want you to be happy."

"So who's your letter from?" Chloe asks, walking over to the coffee machine and pouring out a mug.

I slip it into the pocket of my dressing gown. "No one important."

"Oooh. Mysterious."

"Not really. Just . . . an old acquaintance."

She raises an eyebrow. "Another one? Wow. They're all coming out of the woodwork. Never knew you were so popular."

I frown. And then I remember that I told her about my dinner guest tonight.

"Don't sound so surprised."

"I am. For someone so unsociable, the fact you have any friends is astounding."

"I have friends, here in Anderbury. You know them. Gav and Hoppo."

"They don't count."

"Why?"

"Because they're not really friends. They're just people you've known all your life."

"Isn't that the definition of a friend?"

"No, that's the definition of parochial. People you feel obliged to hang around with out of habit and history rather than any real desire for their company."

She has a point. Sort of.

"Anyway," I change the subject, "I'd better go and get dressed. I have to go into school today."

"Isn't it the holidays?"

"Contrary to popular belief, a teacher's work does not end when school is out for summer."

"Never had you down as an Alice Cooper fan."

"I love her music," I say, deadpan.

Chloe smiles, a quirky lopsided smile that turns her somewhat plain face into something remarkable. Some women are like that. Unusual, even strange-looking, at first glance, but then a smile or a subtle cock of an eyebrow transforms them.

I suppose I have a small crush on Chloe, not that I would ever admit it. I know she sees me more as a protective uncle than as a prospective boyfriend. I would never want to make her feel uncomfortable by letting her think that I view her with anything other than paternal fondness. I am also well aware that, in my position, in a small town, a relationship with a much younger woman could easily be misconstrued.

"When's your other 'old acquaintance' arriving?" she asks as she brings her coffee to the table.

I push back my chair and stand. "Around seven." I pause. "You're welcome to join us."

"Think I'll pass. Don't want to spoil your catch-up."

"Okay."

"Maybe another time, though. From what you've said, he seems an interesting character."

"Yes." I force a smile. "Interesting is one word for it."

THE SCHOOL IS a brisk fifteen-minute walk from my house. On a day like today—a pleasantly warm summer day, a hint of blue beckoning between the thin layer of cloud—it's a relaxing walk. A way to get my thoughts in order before work begins.

In term time, this can be useful. Many of the kids I teach at Anderbury Academy are what we call "challenging." In my day, they would have been called "a bunch of little shits." Some days, I need to mentally prepare myself to deal with them. Other days, the only preparation that helps is a shot of vodka in my morning coffee.

Like many small market towns, Anderbury looks, to the casual eye, like a picturesque place to live. Quaint cobbled streets, tea shops and a semi-famous cathedral. There's a market twice a week, and plenty of pretty parks and riverside walks. It's only a short drive to the sandy beaches of Bournemouth and the open heathland of the New Forest.

Scratch the surface, though, and you'll find the tourist sheen is just that. Much of the work here is seasonal, and unemployment is high. Groups of bored youths hang around the shops and in the parks. Teenage mums wheel screaming babies up and down the high street. This is not new, but it does seem to have become more prevalent. Or maybe that's just my perception. Often, what comes with age is not wisdom but intolerance.

I reach the gates to Old Meadows Park. My teenage stomping ground. It has changed a lot since my day. Obviously. There's a new skate park, and the playground where our gang used to hang out has been usurped by a new, modern "recreation area" at the other end of the park. There are rope swings and a huge tunnel slide, zip-wires and all manner of cool stuff that we couldn't even have dreamed of when we were young.

Strangely, the old play area remains, abandoned and derelict. The climbing frame has rusted, the swings are tangled over the tops of the bars and the once bright paint on the wooden roundabout is blistered and flaking, daubed with ancient graffiti by people who have long forgotten why *Helen is a bitch* or why on earth they *hearted* Andy W.

I stand for a moment, staring at it, remembering.

The faint squeak of the baby swing, the biting chill of the early-morning air, the crispness of white chalk on black tarmac. Another message. But this one was different. Not a chalk man . . . something else.

I turn abruptly. Not now. Not again. I won't be drawn back in.

MY WORK AT school doesn't take long. I'm finished by lunchtime. I gather my books, lock up and walk back toward the town center.

The Bull stands on the corner of the high street, the last of the remaining "locals." Anderbury used to have two other pubs, The Dragon and The Wheatsheaf, then the chains moved in. The old locals closed and Gav's parents were forced to cut prices, host ladies' nights, do happy hours and "welcome families" in order to survive.

Eventually, they had had enough. They moved to Majorca, where they now run a bar called Britz. Gav, who had worked part-time in the pub since he turned sixteen, took over the beer pumps and has been there ever since.

I push open the heavy old door and step inside. Hoppo and Gav sit at our usual table, in the corner by the window. From the waist up, Gav is still bulky, large enough to remind me why we used to call him Fat Gav. But now the bulk is more muscle than flab. His arms are tree trunks, veins standing out like taut blue wires. His face is chiseled, his shorn hair gray and sparse.

Hoppo has hardly changed at all. In his plumbers' overalls, if you squinted slightly, he could still be mistaken for a twelve-year-old boy playing dress-up.

The two of them are deep in conversation. Their barely touched pints sit on the table. Guinness for Hoppo and a Diet Coke for Gav, who rarely drinks.

I order a Taylor's Mild from a surly-looking girl behind the bar who frowns at me, then frowns at the pump as though it has mortally offended her.

"Need to change the barrel," she mutters.

"Okay."

I wait. She rolls her eyes.

"I'll bring it over."

"Thanks."

I turn and walk across the pub. When I glance back she still hasn't moved.

I sit down on a rickety stool, next to Hoppo.

"Afternoon."

They look up, and straightaway I can tell that something is wrong. Something has happened. Gav wheels himself out from behind the table. The muscles in his arms are in stark contrast to the wasted limbs that rest idly in his wheelchair.

I turn on my stool. "Gav? What—"

His fist flies toward my face, my left cheek explodes with pain, and I topple backward onto the floor.

He stares down at me. "How long have you known?"

1986

Despite being the biggest, and our gang's unspoken leader, Fat Gav was actually the youngest.

His birthday was at the beginning of August, at the start of the school holidays. We were all pretty jealous of this. Me in particular. I was the oldest. My birthday was also in the holidays, three days before Christmas. It meant, instead of getting two proper presents, I nearly always got one "big" present, or two not so good ones.

Fat Gav always got loads of presents. Not just because his mum and dad were loaded but also because he had a million relatives. Aunts and uncles and cousins and grandparents and great-grandparents.

I was a bit jealous of this, too. I only had my mum and dad and my gran, who we didn't see very often because she lived miles away, and also because she was going a "bit dippy," as Dad put it. I didn't really like visiting her. Her living room was always too hot and smelly, and she always had the same stupid film playing on the TV.

"Wasn't Julie Andrews beautiful?" she would sigh, misty-eyed, and we all had to nod and say "yes" and eat soft digestives out of this rusty old biscuit tin that had dancing reindeer all around the side.

Fat Gav's mum and dad threw a big party for him every year. This year, they were having a barbecue. There was going to be a magician and even a disco afterward.

My mum rolled her eyes when she saw the invitation. I knew she didn't really like Fat Gav's mum and dad. I heard her once tell Dad that they were "often-contagious." When I got older, I realized she'd actually said "ostentatious," but for years I thought she meant that they harbored some strange disease.

"A disco, Geoff?" she said to my dad in an odd tone of voice. I couldn't decide if it was good or bad. "What d'you think of that?"

Dad moved over from where he was doing the washing-up and glanced at the invite. "Sounds like fun," he said.

"You can't come, Dad," I said. "This is a kids' party. You're not invited."

"Actually, we are," Mum said, and pointed at the invitation. "'Mums and Dads welcome. Bring a sausage.'"

I looked at it again and frowned. Mums and dads at a kids' party? I didn't think that was a good idea. Not a good idea at all.

"SO WHAT ARE you getting Fat Gav for his birthday?" Hoppo asked.

We were sitting in the park on the climbing frame, swinging our legs and sucking on cola ice pops. Murphy, Hoppo's old black Labrador, lay on the ground beneath us, dozing in the shade.

This was around the end of July, almost two months after the terrible day at the fair and a week before Fat Gav's birthday. Things were starting to get back to normal, and I was glad. I wasn't really a kid who liked excitement or unexpected drama. I was—and have remained—someone who likes routine. Even at twelve, my sock drawer was always neatly arranged and my books and tapes were stored in alphabetical order.

Perhaps it was because everything else in our house was kind of chaotic. It wasn't fully built, for a start. Again, this was typical of the difference between my mum and dad and other parents I knew.

Aside from Hoppo, who lived with his mum in an old terraced house, most of the kids at school lived in nice, modern houses with neat, square gardens that all looked the same.

We lived in this ugly old Victorian house which seemed to be constantly surrounded by scaffolding. Out back, it had a big, overgrown garden that I had never managed to fight my way to the end of, and upstairs, at least two rooms where you could see the sky through the ceiling.

Mum and Dad had bought it as a "fixer-upper" when I was really small. That was eight years ago and, as far as I could tell, there was still a lot more *fixing-upping* required. The main rooms were all liveable-ish. But the hallway and kitchen had bare plaster on the walls, and nowhere had any carpet.

Upstairs, we still had the old bathroom. A prehistoric enamel bath with its own resident house spider, a sink that leaked and an ancient loo with a long chain flush. And no shower.

As a twelve-year-old kid, I found it mortally embarrassing. We didn't even have an electric fire. Dad had to chop logs outside, bring them in and light a fire. Like it was the frigging Dark Ages.

"When are we going to finish getting the house built?" I would ask sometimes.

"Well, building work takes time and money," Dad would say.

"Haven't we got any money? Mum's a doctor. Fat Gav says doctors make loads of money."

Dad sighed. "We've discussed this before, Eddie. Fa— *Gavin* does not know everything about everything. And you have to remember, my work isn't as well paid as some, or as regular."

More than once I almost blurted out, "Why can't you just go and get a proper job, then?" But that would upset my dad and I didn't like to do that.

I knew Dad often felt guilty about money because he didn't earn as much as Mum. In between the stuff he wrote for magazines he was trying to write a book.

"Things will change when I'm a bestselling author," he would often say, with a laugh and a wink. He pretended he was joking, but secretly I think he believed that, one day, it would actually happen.

It never did. He got close. I know he submitted manuscripts to agents and even had some interest from one for a while. But somehow, nothing ever came of it. Perhaps, if he hadn't started to get ill, he might have eventually made it. As it was, when the illness started to eat away at his mind, the first thing it swallowed was the thing he loved the most. His words.

I sucked harder on my ice pop. "I haven't really thought about a present," I said to Hoppo.

A lie. I *had* thought about it, long and hard. That was the problem with Fat Gav. He had pretty much everything and buying him a present he liked was really difficult.

"What about you?" I asked.

He shrugged. "Dunno yet."

I changed tack. "Is your mum coming to the party?"

He pulled a face. "I'm not sure. She might be working."

Hoppo's mum worked as a cleaner. You'd often see her trundling around the streets in her rusty old car, the boot piled high with mops and buckets.

Metal Mickey called her "a gyppo" behind Hoppo's back. I thought that was a bit cruel, but it's true that she did look a bit like a gypsy, with her straggly gray hair and shapeless dresses.

I'm not sure where Hoppo's dad was. Hoppo never really spoke about him, but I got the impression he had left when Hoppo was small. Hoppo had an older brother, too, but he'd gone to join the army or something. Thinking back, I guess one of the reasons our gang all hung out together was that none of our families was exactly "normal."

"Are your mum and dad coming?" Hoppo asked.

"Think so. Just hope they don't make it really boring."

He shrugged. "It'll be okay. And there *is* gonna be a magician."

"Yeah."

We both grinned, then Hoppo said, "We could go down the shops now, if you like, look for something for Fat Gav?"

I hesitated. I liked hanging out with Hoppo. You didn't have to act clever all the time. Or be on guard. It was just easy.

Hoppo wasn't the brightest kid but he was one of those kids who just knew how to be. He didn't try to be liked by everyone, like Fat Gav, or change his face to fit in, like Metal Mickey, and I kind of respected him for that.

That's why I felt a bit bad now when I said, "Sorry, I can't. I have to get back, to help Dad with some stuff in the house."

That was usually my get-out clause. No one could doubt that there was plenty of "stuff" that needed doing in our house.

Hoppo nodded, finished his ice pop and chucked the wrapper on the floor. "Okay. Well, I'm gonna walk Murphy."

"Okay. See you later."

"See you."

He ambled away, floppy bits of fringe swinging in his face, Murphy loping by his side. I chucked my ice-pop wrapper in the bin and headed off in the opposite direction, toward home. And then, when I was sure I was out of sight, I made a U-turn and started walking back into town.

I didn't like lying to Hoppo, but there are some things you can't share, even with your best friends. Kids have secrets, too. More so than adults, sometimes.

Out of our gang, I knew I was the nerdy one; studious, slightly square. I was the sort of kid who liked to collect stuff—stamps, coins, model cars. Other stuff, too: shells, bird skulls from the woods, keys. Surprising how often you would find a lost key. I liked the idea that I could sneak into people's houses, even if I didn't know who the keys belonged to or where the people lived.

I was pretty precious about my collections. I hid them well and kept them safe. I suppose, in a way, I liked the feeling of control. Kids don't have a lot of control over their lives, but only I knew what was in my boxes, and only I could add stuff or take it away.

Since the fair, I had been collecting more and more. Stuff I found, stuff people left lying around. (I had started to notice how careless people were; like they didn't realize how important it was to hold on to things or they could be gone forever.)

And sometimes—if I saw something I absolutely *had* to have—I took stuff I really should have paid for.

ANDERBURY WAS NOT a big town but it got really busy in summer with coachloads of tourists, most of them American. They hobbled around, cluttering up the narrow pavements in their flowered sundresses and baggy shorts, squinting at maps and pointing up at buildings.

As well as the cathedral, there was a market square with a big Debenhams, a lot of small tea shops and one posh hotel. The high street had mostly boring shops like a supermarket and a chemist's and a bookshop. However, it also had a huge Woolworths.

As kids, Woolworths—or "Woolies," as everyone called it—was our absolute favorite shop. It had everything you could ever want. Aisle upon aisle of toys, from big, expensive ones to loads of cheap plastic crap which you could buy a ton of and still have change left for the pick-and-mix counter.

It also had a really mean security guard called Jimbo who we were all pretty scared of. Jimbo was a skinhead and I'd heard that beneath his uniform he had a load of tattoos, including a huge swastika on his back.

Fortunately, Jimbo was pretty useless at his job. He spent most of his time loitering outside, smoking and leering at girls. That meant, if you were smart and quick, it was dead easy to avoid Jimbo's attention by just waiting until he was distracted.

Today my luck was in. A group of teenage girls was hanging around the phone box just down the street. It was warm, so they were wearing miniskirts or shorts. Jimbo was leaning against the corner of the store, a cigarette dangling from his fingers, tongue scraping the floor, even though the girls were only a couple of years older than me, and he was like *thirty* or something.

I scooted across the road and waltzed straight through the entrance. The store spread out in front of me. Rows of sweets and the pick-and-mix counter to my left. To my right, tapes and records. Straight ahead, the toy aisles. I felt a flutter of anticipation. But I couldn't savor it. Or linger. One of the staff might notice.

I walked purposefully toward the toys, scanning the rows and assessing my options. Too expensive. Too big. Too cheap. Too lame. Then I saw it. A Magic 8 Ball. Steven Gemmel had one. He'd brought it into school one day and I remember thinking it was ace. I was also pretty sure that Fat Gav didn't have one. That alone made it special. As did the fact that it was the last one on the shelf.

I picked it up and glanced around. Then, in one swift move, I slipped it into my rucksack.

I sauntered back toward the sweets. The next bit took nerve. I could feel the weight of my illicit plunder banging against my back. I grabbed a pick-and-mix bag and forced myself to take my time, choosing a selection of fizzy cola bottles, white mice and flying saucers. Then I walked up to the till.

A fat woman with a huge, very curly perm weighed the sweets and smiled at me. "43p, love."

"Thanks."

I counted out some change from my pocket and handed it over.

She started to chuck it into the till then frowned. "You're 1p short, love."

"Oh."

Crap. I fumbled in my pocket again. I didn't have anything else.

"I, erm, I'd better put something back," I said, cheeks burning, hands sweating, the bag on my back feeling heavier than ever.

Perm Lady looked at me for a moment and then she leaned forward and gave me a wink. Her eyelids were all crinkly, like wrinkled-up paper. "Don't worry, love. Pretend I counted wrong."

I grabbed the bag of sweets. "Thank you."

"Go on. Get out of here."

I didn't need telling twice. I scurried back out into the sunshine, past Jimbo, who was only just finishing his cigarette and barely gave me a second glance. I walked quickly down the street, faster and faster, the exhilaration and excitement and sense of achievement growing until I broke into a run and sprinted almost all the way back home, an insane grin plastered over my face.

I'd done it, and not for the first time. I like to think I wasn't a bad kid in any other way. I tried to be kind, not to rat out my friends or bitch behind their backs. I even tried to listen to my mum and dad. And, in my defense, I never took money. If I found someone's wallet on the floor, I'd give it back with all the cash inside (but maybe something like a family photo missing).

I knew it was wrong but, like I said, everyone has secrets, things they know they shouldn't do but do anyway. Mine was taking stuff—*collecting* things. The crappy thing was, it was only when I tried to take something back that I really screwed up.

IT WAS HOT the day of the party. It seemed like every day that summer was hot. I'm sure it wasn't. I'm sure a weatherman—a proper one, not like my dad—would say that there were loads of rainy, overcast and downright miserable days, too. But memory is weird and time works differently when you're a kid. Three hot days in a row is like a month of hot days to an adult.

Fat Gav's birthday was definitely hot. Clothes sticking to your body, car seats burning your legs, tarmac melting on the hot pavement.

"Won't need a barbecue to cook the food at this rate," Dad joked as we left the house.

"I'm surprised you're not telling us to pack raincoats," Mum said, locking the door and giving it a few hard tugs just to check.

She looked pretty that day. She was wearing a plain blue sundress and Roman sandals. Blue suited her, and she'd put a little sparkly clip in the side of her dark fringe, pulling it off her face.

Dad looked, well, like Dad, in cut-off denim shorts, a T-shirt with "Grateful Dead" scrawled across it and leather sandals on his feet. Mum had at least given his beard a trim.

Fat Gav's house was on one of the newest estates in Anderbury. They'd only moved there last year. Before that, they'd all lived above the pub. Even though the house was almost new, Fat Gav's dad had extended it, so it had lots of extra bits that didn't quite match the original house and these big white pillars outside the front door, like in pictures of ancient Greece.

Today they had lots of balloons with "12" on tied to them, and there was a big, sparkly banner across the door that read, "Happy Birthday, Gavin."

Before Mum could make a comment, snort or even ring the bell, the door swung open and Fat Gav stood there, resplendent in Hawaiian shorts, a neon-green T-shirt and a pirate's hat. "Hi, Mr. and Mrs. Adams. Hi, Eddie."

"Happy Birthday, Gavin," we all chorused, although I had to catch myself not to say, "Fat Gav."

"Barbecue's out the back," Fat Gav told Mum and Dad, and then he grabbed my arm. "Come and see the magician. He's *awesome.*"

Fat Gav was right. He *was* awesome. The barbecue was pretty good, too. There were also loads of games and two big buckets filled with water and water pistols. After Fat Gav had opened his presents (and said the Magic 8 Ball was "ace"), we had a massive water fight with some other kids from school. It was so hot, you were dry almost as soon as you got soaked.

Halfway through, I realized I needed the toilet. I padded back up the garden, dripping slightly, past the adults, who were all standing around in small groups, clutching plates and drinking beer out of bottles and wine out of plastic cups.

Nicky's dad had come, which surprised everyone. I didn't think vicars did things like going to parties or having fun. He was wearing his white collar. You could spot him a mile off, with it gleaming under the sun. I remember thinking he must be bloomin' hot. Maybe that was why he was drinking so much wine.

He was talking to Mum and Dad, which also surprised me, as they weren't really into church stuff. Mum spotted me and smiled. "You okay, Eddie?"

"Yeah, Mum. Great."

She nodded, but she didn't look very happy. As I wandered past, I heard my dad say, "I'm not sure this is a subject we should be discussing at a children's party."

Reverend Martin's reply faded in my ears. "But it's the lives of children we're talking about."

It didn't make any sense to me; just adult stuff. Besides, I was already distracted by something else. Another familiar figure. Tall and skinny, covered up in dark clothes, despite the blistering heat, and wearing a large, floppy hat. Mr. Halloran. He stood at the far end of the garden, near a statue of a little boy peeing into a birdbath, chatting to some other mums and dads.

I thought it was a bit odd that Fat Gav's parents had invited a teacher to his party, especially one who hadn't even started at school yet, but maybe they were just trying to make him feel welcome. They were like that. Plus, Fat Gav once told me: "My mum makes sure she knows everyone. That way, she knows everyone's business, too."

In that weird way where you always *feel* when someone is staring at you, Mr. Halloran glanced around, saw me and raised a hand. I half raised my hand back. It was a bit awkward. We might have saved Waltzer Girl's life together, but he was still a teacher and it wasn't cool to be seen waving at a teacher.

Almost like he knew what I was thinking, Mr. Halloran gave a small nod and turned away again. Gratefully—and not just because of my bulging bladder—I hurried across the patio and through the French doors.

Inside the living room, it was cool and dark. I let my eyes adjust. Presents were strewn everywhere. Dozens and dozens of toys. Toys I had on my wish list for *my* birthday but knew I would never get. I looked around enviously . . . and that's when I saw it. A medium-sized box sitting right in the center of the room, wrapped up in Transformers wrapping paper. Unopened. Someone must have arrived late and left it. No way would Fat Gav have left a present unopened otherwise.

I did what I needed to do in the bathroom then looked at the present again on my way back through the living room. After a moment's hesitation, I grabbed it and took it outside with me.

Groups of kids were scattered about. Fat Gav, Nicky, Metal Mickey and Hoppo were all sitting together in a semicircle on the grass, drinking pop, looking red and sweaty and happy. Nicky's hair was still a bit wet and tangled. Drops of water glistened on her arms. She was wearing a dress today. It suited her. It was long and had flowers on. It covered some of the bruises on her legs. Nicky always had bruises. I don't remember ever having seen her without a brown or purple mark somewhere. Once, she even had a black eye.

"Hey, Munster!" Fat Gav said.

"Hey, guess what?"

"You've finally stopped being such a wanker?"

"Ha ha. I found a present you haven't opened yet."

"No way, José. I opened everything."

I held the box out.

Fat Gav grabbed it. "Awesome!"

"Who's it from?" Nicky asked.

Fat Gav shook it, studied the wrapping paper. No tag.

"Who cares?" He started to rip the paper open, then his face fell. "What the hell?"

We all stared at the present. A big bucket full of multicolored chalks.

"Chalks?" Metal Mickey snickered. "Who bought you chalks?"

"Dunno. There's no tag, genius," Fat Gav said. He took the top off the bucket and pulled out a couple of chalks. "What am I going to do with this shit?"

"It's not that bad," Hoppo started to say.

"It's a pile of stinking Buckaroo, my man."

I thought that was a bit harsh. After all, someone had still gone to the trouble of buying the present and wrapping it and stuff. But Fat Gav was kind of hyped on sun and sugar by this point. We all were.

He threw the chalks down in disgust. "Forget it. Let's get some more water pistols."

We all started to get up. I let the others go first then quickly crouched down, picked up a piece of chalk and slipped it into my pocket.

I'd barely straightened when I heard a crash and a scream. I spun around. I'm not sure what I expected to see. Perhaps someone had dropped something or fallen over.

What I saw took a while to sink in. Reverend Martin lay on his back amid a scattered mess of cups, plates, broken sauce bottles and relishes. He was clutching his nose and making an odd moaning noise. A tall, disheveled figure in shorts and a torn T-shirt loomed over him, one fist raised. My dad.

Holy crap. *My dad* had laid out Reverend Martin.

I stood, paralyzed by shock, as he said in a harsh, guttural voice, "If you ever speak to my wife again, I swear I'll . . ."

But what he swore was lost as Fat Gav's dad pulled him away. Someone helped Reverend Martin to his feet. He was red-faced and his nose was bleeding. His white collar had spots of blood on it.

He pointed at my mum and dad. "And God will be thy judge."

Dad started to lunge again, but Fat Gav's dad had him in a firm grip. "Just leave it, Geoff."

I caught a flash of yellow and realized Nicky had run past me and up to Reverend Martin. She took his arm. "C'mon, Dad. Let's go home."

He shrugged her off, so roughly I saw her stumble a little. Then he took out a tissue, dabbed his nose and said to Fat Gav's mum, "Thank you for inviting me," and walked stiffly back inside the house.

Nicky glanced back toward the garden. I like to think that her green eyes met mine, that some current of understanding flowed between us, but actually I think she was just looking to see who had noticed the commotion—*everyone,* of course—before she turned and followed him.

For a moment, it seemed like everything stopped. Movement, conversation. Then Fat Gav's dad clapped his hands together and said in a big, hearty voice: "So who's for more of my giant sausages?"

I don't think anyone really was, but people nodded and smiled and Fat Gav's mum turned the music up, just a touch.

Someone thumped me on the back. I jumped. It was Metal Mickey. "Whoah. I can't believe your dad just punched a vicar."

Neither could I. I felt my face flush fire red. I looked at Fat Gav. "I'm really sorry."

He grinned. "You *cannot* be serious. That was ace. This is the best birthday party ever!"

"Eddie." My mum walked over. She gave me an odd, strained smile. "Your dad and I are going to head home now."

"Okay."

"You can stay, if you want to."

I did want to, but I also didn't want the other kids looking at me like I was some kind of freak, and Metal Mickey going on and on about it, so I said, sulkily, "No, it's okay." Even though it wasn't. "I'll come, too."

"Okay." She nodded.

I had never heard my parents apologize until that day. You don't. As a kid, you're always the one saying sorry. But that afternoon they both said sorry lots of times to Fat Gav's mum and dad. Fat Gav's mum and dad were nice and all that, and told them not to worry, but I could tell they were a bit pissed off. Still, Fat Gav's mum gave me a goodie bag, with cake and some Hubba Bubba and other sweets in it.

As soon as the front door closed behind us I turned to my dad. "What happened, Dad? Why did you hit him? What did he say to Mum?"

Dad wrapped an arm around my shoulder. "Later, Eddie."

I wanted to argue, to shout at him. After all, it was *my* friend's party that had just been ruined. But I didn't. Because, when it came down to it, I loved my mum and dad and something in their faces told me that this was not the time.

So I let Dad hug me, and Mum took my other arm, and we all walked down the street together. And when Mum said, "Fancy getting some chips for tea?" I forced a grin and said, "Yeah. Ace."

Dad never did tell me. But I found out eventually. After the police came round to arrest him for attempted murder.

2016

"Two weeks," I say. "He sent me an email. I'm sorry."

Hoppo offers me his hand. I accept it and collapse heavily back down onto my stool. "Thanks."

I should have told Gav and Hoppo that Mickey was back in Anderbury. It should have been the first thing I did. I'm not sure exactly why I didn't. Curiosity, perhaps. Or because Mickey asked me not to. Maybe I just wanted to find out what he was up to myself.

I'd already known a little of our old friend's backstory. I looked him up a few years ago. Boredom coupled with too much wine. His was not the only name I'd typed into Google, but it was the only one that gleaned any results.

He has done pretty well for himself. He works for an advertising agency—the type that has unnecessary umlauts in its name and an aversion to capital letters. There were pictures of him with clients, at product launches, clutching glasses of champagne, smiling the type of smile that ensures a dentist's comfortable retirement.

None of this came as much of a surprise. Mickey was the sort of kid who would always get by on his wits. He was also good at being creative. Usually with the truth. Which must come in useful in his line of work.

His email had mentioned a project he was working on. Something that could be "mutually beneficial." I'm pretty sure he isn't arranging a school reunion. The fact is, I can think of only one reason why Mickey might want to talk to me after all this time. And that is because he is about to plunge a blunt knife into a rusty and buckled can of rotting worms.

I don't say this to Gav and Hoppo. I rub at my cheek, which is throbbing, and glance around the pub. It's only a quarter full. The few patrons glance quickly away, back into pints and newspapers. Well, who are they going to complain to? It's not like Gav is going to throw himself out of his own pub for causing a scene.

"How did you find out?" I ask.

"Hoppo saw him," Gav says. "On the high street, plain as day and twice as ugly."

"Right. I see."

"He even had the nerve to say hello. Said he was visiting you. Was surprised you hadn't mentioned it."

I feel my own anger notch up. Good old Mickey, stirring it like he always did.

The barmaid brings my pint over and sets it down carelessly on the table. Drink sloshes over the side.

"Nice girl," I say to Gav. "Lovely temperament."

Gav smiles reluctantly.

"I'm sorry," I say to him again. "I should have told you."

"Fucking right," he mutters. "We're supposed to be friends."

"Why didn't you?" Hoppo asks.

"He asked me not to. Until we had talked."

"And you agreed?"

"I suppose I wanted to give him the benefit of the doubt."

"I shouldn't have hit you," Gav says, and takes a sip of his Diet Coke. "I was out of order. It's just, the thought of him being here, it brought it all back."

I stare at him. None of us is what you would call a fan of Mickey Cooper. But Gav hates him more than any of us.

We were seventeen. There was a party. I didn't go, or wasn't invited. I can't quite recall. Mickey got off with a girl Hoppo was seeing. There was an argument. Then Gav got really shitfaced and

Mickey was persuaded to drive him home . . . except they never made it because Mickey veered off a completely straight road and crashed into a tree.

Incredibly, Mickey suffered nothing more than a concussion and some cuts and bruises. Fat Gav, well, Fat Gav crushed several vital vertebrae in his spine. Beyond repair. He's been in the wheelchair ever since.

It turned out Mickey was over the limit, by a fair amount, despite his protestations that he'd drunk nothing but Diet Coke all night. Fat Gav and Mickey never spoke again. And both Hoppo and I knew better than to bring it up.

There are some things in life you can alter—your weight, your appearance, even your name—but there are others that wishing and trying and working hard can never make any difference to. Those things are the ones that shape us. Not the things we can change, but the ones we can't.

"So," Gav says. "Why is he back?"

"He didn't say exactly."

"What did he say?"

"He mentioned a project he was working on."

"That's all?" Hoppo asks.

"Yes."

"That's not the real question, though, is it?" Gav says. He looks at us both, blue eyes blazing. "The real question is, what are we going to do about it?"

THE HOUSE IS empty when I return. Chloe has either gone out to meet friends or maybe she's at work. I lose track a little. Chloe works at some alternative clothing shop in town and her days off vary. She probably told me, but my memory is not as good as it once was. This worries me, more than it should.

My dad's memory started to fail him in his late forties. Small things, things we all tend to dismiss. Forgetting where he had put his keys, or putting things in odd places, like the remote control in the fridge and a banana in the sideboard where we kept the remotes. Losing track of sentences halfway through or mixing words up. Sometimes I would see him struggle for the right word only to replace it with something similar.

As the Alzheimer's got worse, he would mix up days of the week and, finally, and the one that really frightened him, he couldn't recall what came after Thursday. The final working day of the week totally eluded him. I still remember the look of panic in his eyes. Losing something so basic, something that we all know from childhood, that was when he was finally forced to admit that he was not just absentminded. It was far more serious.

I am probably a bit of a hypochondriac about it. I read a lot to keep my mind sharp, and do sudoku, even though I do not particularly enjoy it. The fact is, Alzheimer's is often hereditary. I have seen what the future holds, and I would do anything to avoid it, even if it means cutting my life shorter than it might otherwise be.

I throw my keys onto the rickety old hall table and glance in the small, dusty mirror hanging above it. There's a faint bruise blooming on the left side of my face, but it's mostly lost in the hollow of my cheek. Good. I could do without explaining that a man in a wheelchair beat me up.

I walk into the kitchen, debate making a coffee, then decide I'm still a little too full of fluid from lunchtime. Instead, I head upstairs.

My parents' room is now Chloe's, I sleep in my old room at the back and my dad's study is, along with the other spare room, a place where I store stuff. A lot of stuff.

I don't like to think of myself as a hoarder. My "collectables" are stored neatly in boxes, carefully labeled and stacked on shelving units. But they do fill most of the rooms upstairs, and it is true that, without the labels, I would have forgotten much of what I have accumulated.

I run a finger along a few of the labels: Earrings. Porcelain. Toys. There are several boxes of the latter. Retro ones from the eighties, some from my own childhood, some purchased—at generally extortionate prices—on eBay. On another shelf there are a couple of boxes labeled "Photos." Not all of these are of my own family. Another box contains shoes. Sparkly, glittery women's shoes. There are half a dozen boxes of pictures. Watercolors and pastels scavenged from car-boot sales. Many boxes are lazily labeled "Miscellaneous." Even under interrogation, I probably couldn't say what's inside these. There's only one box I know the contents of by heart—sheets of typed paper, a pair of old sandals, a dirty T-shirt and an unused electric razor. This one is labeled simply "Dad."

I sit down at the desk. I'm pretty sure Chloe isn't at home and won't be back anytime soon, but I've locked the door, anyway. I open the envelope I received this morning and look at its contents again. There's no writing. But the message is very clear. A stick figure with a noose around its neck.

It's drawn in crayon, which is wrong. Perhaps that's why, as an added reminder, the sender has included something else. I tip up the envelope and it falls to the desk in a small cloud of dust. A single piece of white chalk.

1986

I hadn't seen Mr. Halloran properly since the day at the fair. The "terrible day at the fair," as I had come to think of it. I mean, I'd *seen* him—when the papers took our photo, around the town, at Fat Gav's party—but we hadn't really spoken.

That might seem a bit weird, bearing in mind what happened. But just because we got stuck in some horrible situation didn't mean we were suddenly bound by an incredible bond. At least, I didn't think we were, not then.

I was wheeling my bike through the park, on my way to meet the others at the woods, when I spotted him. He was sitting on a bench, a sketch pad on his lap, a small tray of pencils or something next to him. He wore black jeans, chunky boots, and a flowing white shirt with a skinny black tie. As always, a large hat was perched on his head to keep off the sun. Still, I was amazed he wasn't melting. I was hot, and I was only wearing a vest, shorts and my old trainers.

I hovered for a moment, uncertain. I didn't really know what to say to him, but I couldn't just walk past and ignore him either. As I dithered, he looked up and saw me.

"Hi, Eddie."

"Hi, Mr. Halloran."

"How are you?"

"Err, fine thanks, sir."

"Good."

There was a pause. I felt like I should say something else, so I asked, "What are you drawing?"

"People." He smiled. His teeth always looked a bit yellow because his face was so white. "Want to look?"

I didn't really, but that would sound rude, so I said, "Okay."

I laid my bike down, walked over and perched on the bench next to him. He turned the pad around so I could see what he had been drawing. I let out a little gasp.

"Wow. That's really good."

I wasn't bullshitting (although I would have felt like I had to say it was good even if it hadn't been). Like he said, they were sketches of people in the park. An older couple on a nearby bench, a man with his dog, and a couple of girls sitting on the grass. It doesn't sound like much, but something about them was pretty awesome. Even as a kid I could tell that Mr. Halloran was really talented. There's something about pictures done by someone with talent. Anyone can copy something and make it look like the thing they're copying, but it takes something else to bring a scene, to bring people, to life.

"Thanks. Want to see some more?"

I nodded. Mr. Halloran flicked back a few pages. There was a picture of an old man in a raincoat with a cigarette (you could almost smell the curls of whisper-gray smoke); a group of women gossiping on one of the cobbled streets near the cathedral; a picture of the cathedral itself, which I didn't like as much as the people and . . .

"But I don't want to bore you," Mr. Halloran said, suddenly moving the pad away before I could get a proper look at the next picture. I just caught a glimpse of long, dark hair and one brown eye.

"You're not," I said. "I really like them. Will you be teaching us art at school?"

"No. I'll be teaching English. Art, well, that's just a hobby."

"Okay." I wasn't really into drawing that much, anyway. I sometimes doodled pictures of my favorite cartoon characters, but they weren't very good. I could write, though. English was my best subject.

"What are you drawing with?" I asked.

"These." He held up the packet of what looked like chalks. "These are pastels."

"They look like chalk."

"Well, they're the same sort of thing."

"Fat Gav got some chalks for his birthday, but he thought they were pretty lame."

An odd little flicker crossed his face. "Did he now?"

For some reason, I felt like I had said the wrong thing.

"But Fat Gav can be a bit, you know—"

"Spoiled?"

Although it felt disloyal, I nodded. "Kind of. I guess."

He considered. "I remember having chalks as a kid. We used to draw on the pavement outside our house."

"Really?"

"Yeah? You never do that?"

I thought. I didn't think I ever had. Like I said, I wasn't much into drawing.

"You know what else we used to do? My friends and me, we made up these secret symbols and we'd use them to leave messages for each other, all over the place, that only we understood. Like I would draw a symbol for wanting to go to the park in chalk outside my best friend's house and he'd know what it meant."

"Couldn't you just knock on his door?"

"Well, I could, but that wouldn't have been as much fun."

I thought about this. I could see the appeal of the idea. Like clues on a treasure hunt. A secret code.

"Anyway," Mr. Halloran said when—thinking about it later—he had given me just enough time for the idea to settle but not enough for me to dismiss it. He closed his drawing pad and shut the lid of his pastels. "I should get going. I have someone I have to go and see."

"Okay. I should get going, too. I'm meeting my friends."

"Good to see you again, Eddie. Stay brave."

It was the first time he had made any reference to the day at the fair. I liked him for that. A lot of adults, it would have been the first thing they'd gone on about. *How are you? Are you okay?* All that stuff.

"You too, sir."

He smiled his yellow smile again. "I'm not brave, Eddie. I'm just a fool."

He cocked his head at my puzzled expression. "Fools rush in where angels fear to tread. Ever heard that saying?"

"No, sir. What does it mean?"

"Well, the way I see it, it means it's better to be a fool than an angel."

I thought about it. I wasn't quite sure how that worked. He tilted his hat at me. "See you, Eddie."

"Bye, sir."

I jumped from the bench and got on my bike. I liked Mr. Halloran, but he was definitely weird. *Better to be a fool than an angel.* Weird, and just a little bit scary.

THE WOODS SKIRTED the edge of Anderbury, where suburbia melted away into farmland and fields. Although not for long. The town was spreading this way. A large area of land had already been razed to gravel and earth. Bricks, cement and scaffolding erupted from the ground.

"Salmon Homes," a sign read in large, cheery writing. "Building homes and winning hearts for thirty years." A high wire fence ran around the site. Behind it I could see the hulking shapes of huge machinery, like great big mechanical dinosaurs, but inactive at the moment. Burly men in orange waistcoats and jeans stood around, smoking and drinking from mugs. A radio blared out Shakin'

Stevens. A few signs had been stuck to the fence. KEEP OUT. DANGER.

I cycled around the edge of the site, then along a narrow track that ran beside more fields. Eventually, I reached a small wooden fence with a stile. I hopped off my bike and slung it over first, then climbed into the woods' cool embrace.

They weren't huge woods, but they were dense and dark. Formed in a natural hollow, they dipped into low folds and rose again around the sides, trees straggling away to low scrub and chalky white rock. I half wheeled, half carried my bike as I walked deeper in. I could hear the trickling whisper of a small stream. Sunlight peeked through the canopy of leaves.

A little farther ahead I heard the murmur of voices. Caught a glimpse of blue and green. A flash of a silver spoke. Fat Gav, Metal Mickey and Hoppo were crouched down in a small clearing, shielded by foliage and shrubbery. They had already constructed about half of a pretty impressive den from intertwining branches tied around a natural overhang made by a broken bough.

"Hey!" Fat Gav called out. "It's Eddie Munster, whose dad's a big puncher."

This was Fat Gav's new thing to entertain us with this week. Rhyming everything.

Hoppo looked up and waved. Metal Mickey didn't bother. I picked my way through the undergrowth and slung my bike down next to their racers, conscious that, out of all of them, it was the oldest and rustiest.

"Where's Nicky?" I asked.

Metal Mickey shrugged. "Who cares? Probably playing with her dolls." He snickered at his own joke.

"Not sure she's coming," Hoppo said.

"Oh."

I hadn't seen Nicky since the party, although I knew she'd been down the shops with Hoppo and Metal Mickey. I was starting to feel she might be avoiding me. I'd been hoping to see her today, hoping things could be right again.

"Her dad's probably just got her doing some chores," Hoppo said, as if he guessed what I was thinking.

"Yeah, or she's still really pissed off at you because your dad laid hers out. *Wham!*" This from Metal Mickey again, who could never resist an opportunity to stir things up.

"Well, he probably deserved it," I said.

"Yeah," Hoppo said. "And he did seem pretty wasted."

"I didn't think vicars drank," I said.

"Maybe he's a secret drinker." Fat Gav tipped his head back, made a *glug, glug* motion and then rolled his eyes, slurring, "My name's Reverend Martin. Praise the Lorrrd. Hic."

Before anyone could answer, the undergrowth rustled and a flock of birds exploded out of the trees. We jumped like a pack of startled rabbits.

Nicky stood at the edge of the hollow, holding the handlebars of her bike. Somehow I got the feeling she'd been standing there a while.

She looked around at us. "So what are you all sitting here for? I thought we were building a den?"

WITH FIVE OF us, it didn't take long to finish the den. It was pretty wicked. Big enough so we could all squeeze in, even if you did have to huddle over a bit. We even constructed a door of leafy branches to cover the entrance. Best of all, you could barely see it until you got right up close.

We sat cross-legged outside. Hot, scratched to ribbons, but happy. Hungry, too. We started to unpack our sandwiches. Nicky hadn't said anything about the party so I didn't either. We just carried on as normal. That's how it is when you're kids. You can let things go. It gets harder as you get older.

"Didn't your dad pack you any?" Fat Gav asked Nicky.

"He doesn't know I'm here. I had to sneak out."

"Here," Hoppo said. He took a couple of his cheese sandwiches out of their cling-film wrapping and handed them over.

I liked Hoppo, but just then I really hated him, because he got there first.

"You can have my banana, too," Fat Gav said. "I don't really like them."

"And you can share my juice," I said quickly, not wanting to be left out.

Metal Mickey stuffed a peanut-butter sandwich in his face. He didn't offer Nicky anything.

"Thanks," Nicky said, but shook her head. "I should get back. My dad'll notice if I'm not there for lunch."

"But we've only just built the den," I said.

"Sorry. I can't."

She pushed up her sleeve and rubbed at her shoulder. It was only then I noticed she had a massive bruise on it.

"What did you do to your shoulder?"

She pulled her sleeve down again. "Nothing. Bumped into a door." She stood up quickly. "I've got to go."

I stood up, too. "Is this because of the party?" I asked.

She shrugged. "Dad's still pretty pissed off about it. But he'll get over it."

"I'm sorry," I said.

"Don't be. He deserved it."

I wanted to say something else, but I wasn't sure what. I opened my mouth.

Something hit the side of my head. Hard. My world wavered. My legs buckled. I fell to my knees. Clutched at my head. My fingers came away all sticky.

Something else whizzed through the air, narrowly missing Nicky's head. She screamed and ducked. Another large lump of rock hit the ground in front of Hoppo and Metal Mickey, causing an explosion of peanut butter and bread. They squawked and scurried backward, toward the cover of the woods.

More missiles rained down. Stones and rocks, bits of brick. I could hear hollering and whooping from the steep slope above the wooded hollow. I looked up and could just make out three older boys at the top of it. Two with dark hair. One taller and blond. I knew who they were right away.

Metal Mickey's brother, Sean, and his mates Duncan and Keith.

Fat Gav grabbed my arm. "You okay?"

I felt dizzy and a bit sick. But I nodded. He shoved me toward the trees. "Get under cover."

Metal Mickey turned and yelled up at the older boys. "Leave us alone, Sean!"

"Leave us alone. Leave us alone," the blond boy—his brother—called back in a high-pitched girly voice. "Why? You gonna cry? You gonna go and tell Mummy?"

"Maybe."

"Yeah. Try it with a broken nose, Shit-for-brains!" Duncan yelled.

"You're in our woods!" Sean shouted.

"They're not your woods!" Fat Gav yelled back.

"Yeah? Then we'll fight you for them."

"Shit," Fat Gav muttered.

"C'mon. Let's get 'em!" Keith shouted.

They began to make their way down the slope, still bombarding us with missiles.

Another big chunk of rock flew through the air and hit Nicky's bike with a crunch.

She shrieked, "That's my bike, you spastics!"

"Hey, it's Copper-top."

"Copper-top, got any copper pubes yet?"

"Piss off, benders."

"Bitch."

A lump of brick crashed through the canopy and struck her on the shoulder. She yelped and staggered.

Anger rose up in my chest. You didn't hit girls. You didn't throw bricks at them. I forced myself to my feet and broke cover. Grabbed the heaviest missile from the ground and lobbed it up the slope as hard as I could.

If it hadn't been so heavy, carried by the weight of its own momentum, if Sean hadn't been halfway down the slope and not right at the top, then I would probably have missed by a mile.

Instead I heard a cry. Not a jeering cry. A scream of pain. "*Fuck.* My eye. *Fucking* hit me in the *fucking* eye."

There was a pause. One of those moments where time seems to stand still. Fat Gav, Hoppo, Metal Mickey, Nicky and I stared at each other.

"You little shits!" one of the other voices yelled. "We are *so* going to get you for that!"

"Let's get out of here," Hoppo said.

We ran for our bikes. I could already hear scrabbling and panting sounds as the gang scrambled down the steep slope.

It would take them some time to make it. But we were at a disadvantage, having to wheel our bikes out of the woods before we could hit the path. We jogged along, shoving the bikes clumsily through the undergrowth. I could hear swearing and rustling behind us. Not far enough behind us. I tried to pick up my pace. Hoppo and Metal Mickey were out in front. Nicky was fast, too. Fat Gav was surprisingly quick for a big kid and he'd got a head start on me. My legs were the longest but I was hopelessly uncoordinated and rubbish at running. Dimly, I remembered an old joke my dad used to tell about outrunning a lion. Didn't matter if you outran the lion. You just needed to outrun the slowest person. Unfortunately, I was the slowest person.

We burst out of the shade of the woods into the blistering sun and onto the narrow path. I could see the stile ahead. I glanced behind. Sean was already out of the woods behind us. His left eye was swollen and red. Blood streaked down his cheek. It didn't seem to be slowing him down any. If anything, the anger and pain seemed to be giving him extra speed. His face twisted into a snarl. "I'm gonna kill you, Shitface."

I turned back, heart thumping so hard and fast now it felt like it might explode. My head throbbed. Sweat streamed down my forehead, salt stinging my eyes.

Hoppo and Metal Mickey reached the stile and threw their bikes over, vaulting after them. Nicky followed, bundling her bike over and clambering behind like an agile monkey. Fat Gav climbed up and hefted his bike and body over. I was next. I lifted my bike up, but it was older and more cumbersome than the others. It stuck. The wheel lodged on the stile. A bit of wood caught on the spoke.

"Shit."

I wrestled with the bike, but it just stuck more firmly. I tried to heave it up, but I was small and the bike was heavy and I was already tired from den-building and running.

"Leave it!" Fat Gav shouted.

Which was all right for him, with his shiny racer. My bike probably looked like a bucket of junk.

"I can't," I gasped. "It was a birthday present."

Fat Gav turned; Hoppo and Nicky ran back. After a split second, Metal Mickey followed. They tugged from the other side. I pushed. A spoke bent and it was free. Fat Gav staggered backward and the bike thudded to the ground. I swung my leg over the stile and felt someone yank me backward by my T-shirt.

I almost fell but just managed to grab hold of the fence post. I turned. Sean loomed behind me. He held a bunch of my T-shirt in one fist. He grinned through streaks of blood and sweat, teeth eerily white against the red. His one good eye burned with feverish fury. "*You're fucking dead, Shitface.*"

Out of sheer gut panic, I kicked back with one foot as hard as I could. It connected with the lean muscle of his stomach, and he buckled, grunted in pain. The grip on my T-shirt loosened. I flung my other leg over the stile and leapt. I heard a tear as the T-shirt ripped. But that didn't matter. I was free. The rest were already on their bikes. As I scrambled to my feet, they started to pedal away. I grabbed my bike from the ground and wheeled it along, running along at the side then throwing myself into the saddle at a sprint and pedaling as fast as I could. This time I didn't look back.

. . .

THE PLAYGROUND WAS empty. We sat on the roundabout, bikes slung on the ground. Now the adrenaline was fading, my head throbbed. My hair was sticky with blood.

"You look like crap," Nicky told me bluntly.

"Thanks."

Her arm was all scraped up and her T-shirt streaked with dirt. Bits of twig and fern had lodged in her auburn curls.

"So do you," I said.

She looked down at herself. "Shit." She stood up. "Now my dad really is gonna kill me."

"You could come and clean up back at mine?" I suggested.

Before she could answer, Fat Gav interrupted. "Nah, my house is closer."

"I guess," Nicky said.

"But what are we gonna do then?" Metal Mickey whined. "The whole day sucks now."

We all looked at each other, kind of downcast. He was right, although I felt like pointing out that it was *his* stupid brother's fault that it sucked. But I didn't. Instead, something pinged in the back of my mind and I suddenly heard myself saying, "I've got a cool idea for something we can do."

2016

I am no cook. I take after my mother in that regard. But living alone does necessitate a basic knowledge of the kitchen. I can rustle up a decent roast chicken and potatoes, steak, pasta and varieties of fish. My curry I am still working on.

I have reasoned that Mickey probably eats in good restaurants. In fact, his first suggestion was to meet at a restaurant in town. But I wanted to see him on my home turf. And have him on the back foot. An invitation to dinner is hard to refuse without seeming rude, even though I am sure he accepted reluctantly.

I decide on spaghetti bolognese. It's easy, homely. Everyone likes it, usually. I've got a decent bottle of red wine to go with it and a stick of garlic bread in the freezer. I'm preparing the mince and sauce when Chloe walks back in just before six. Mickey is due at seven.

She inhales deeply. "Mmmmm, you'll make someone a lovely wife someday."

"Unlike you."

She feigns offense, clutching at her chest. "And all I ever wanted was to be a homemaker."

I smile. Chloe usually manages to make me smile. She's looking, well, pretty isn't exactly the word. She's looking very Chloe this evening. Her dark hair is in two pigtails. She is wearing a black sweatshirt with a picture of Jack Skellington on, a pink miniskirt over black leggings, and para boots with multicolored laces. On some women this would look ridiculous. But Chloe carries it.

She wanders over to the fridge and grabs a bottle of beer.

"Going out this evening?" I ask.

"Nope, but don't worry, I'll make myself scarce while your friend is here."

"There's no need."

"No, it's fine. Besides, I'll just feel like a spare part while you two talk about old times."

"Okay."

And actually it is. The more I think about it, the more I think it might be better if Chloe isn't here. I'm not sure how much she knows about Mickey and our history in Anderbury, but the story has been pretty well covered in the press over the years. It's one of those crimes that always provokes people's interest. It has everything, I suppose. The weird protagonist, the creepy chalk drawings and the gruesome murder. We have made our mark in history. A small, chalk-man-shaped mark, I think bitterly. Of course, the facts have been embellished over time, the truth gradually worn away at the edges. History itself is only ever a story, told by the ones who survive it.

Chloe swigs her beer. "I'll be upstairs, in my room, if you need me."

"Want me to put you aside some spaghetti?"

"Nah, you're fine. I had a late lunch."

"Okay." I wait.

"Oh, go on, then. I might be peckish later."

Chloe eats more than I would have deemed humanly possible for someone who could comfortably disappear behind a lamp post. She also eats at odd hours. I've often found her in the kitchen, snacking on pasta or sandwiches or, on one occasion, a full fry-up in the early hours of the morning. But then I suffer from insomnia, and occasionally I sleepwalk, too, so I am not one to call someone up on their odd nocturnal habits.

At the door, Chloe pauses. She has on her concerned face.

"Seriously, though, if you need a get-out I can give you a call on your mobile if you like—fake an emergency?"

I stare at her. "This is an old friend coming for dinner, not a blind date."

"Yeah, but 'old' is the operative word. You haven't seen this guy in decades."

"Thanks for rubbing it in."

"Point is, you guys haven't exactly kept in touch, so how d'you know you're going to have anything to talk about?"

"Well, after all that time we've got a lot to catch up on."

"But if you had anything worth saying you'd have spoken before now, right? There must be a reason he wants to come and visit you after all this time?"

I see where she's going, and it's making me feel uncomfortable.

"There doesn't always have to be a reason for everything."

I reach for the glass of wine I poured to savor while I was cooking and gulp down half the glass. I can feel her watching me.

"I do know what happened thirty years ago," she says. "The murder."

I concentrate on stirring the bolognese. "Right. I see."

"The four kids who found her body. You were one of them."

I still don't look up. "So, you've done your research."

"Ed, I was coming to lodge with a strange, single man in a big, spooky old house. Of course I asked a few people about you."

Of course. I relax a little. "You just never mentioned it."

"Never saw the need to. I guessed it wasn't something you wanted to talk about."

I turn and manage a smile. "Thank you."

"No problem."

She tips back her beer and finishes it.

"Anyway," she says now, depositing the empty bottle in the recycling box near the back door. "Have fun. Don't do anything I wouldn't do."

"Again, it's not a date."

"Yeah, because a date really would be something to write home about. I think I might even hire a plane and have them fly a banner across the sky—ED HAS A DATE."

"I'm happy as I am, thank you."

"Just saying, life is short."

"If you tell me to seize the day I'm confiscating all the beer."

"Not the day, just some booty." She winks and sashays out of the kitchen and up the stairs.

Against my better judgment, I pour myself some more wine. I'm feeling nervous, which I suppose is natural. I'm not sure what to expect from this evening. I glance at the clock. 6:30 p.m. I should try to make myself vaguely presentable, I suppose.

I plod upstairs, have a quick shower and then change into gray cords and a shirt I deem suitably casual. I drag a comb through my hair. My hair springs back even more roughly. As hair goes, mine has a stubborn resistance to all methods of styling, from the humble comb, to waxes and gels. I've shorn it almost to the bone and it has miraculously gained several unruly inches overnight. Still, at least I have hair. From the photos I've seen of Mickey, he hasn't been so fortunate.

I leave the mirror and head back downstairs. Just in time. The doorbell rings, followed by a heavy *rat-a-tat-tat* on the door knocker. Imaginary hackles rise along my back. I hate it when people ring the doorbell *and* use the knocker, implying that I must be incapable of hearing or that their need to enter is so urgent it requires a full frontal assault on the exterior of my property.

I compose myself and walk down the hallway. I pause for just a moment and then I open the door . . .

THESE MOMENTS ARE always more dramatic in books. Reality is disappointing in its banality.

I see a small, wiry middle-aged man. His hair has all but gone, clippered to a close grade one all round. He wears an expensive-looking shirt, a sports jacket and dark blue jeans, teamed with shiny loafers, no socks. I've always thought men look ridiculous wearing shoes without socks. Like they got dressed in a hurry, in the dark, with a hangover.

I know what *he* sees. A thin, taller-than-average man in a threadbare shirt and baggy cords with wild hair and a few more lines than a forty-two-year-old should rightly bear. But then, some lines you have to earn.

"Ed. It's good to see you."

I can't in all honesty say the same, so I just nod. Before he can stick out a hand and I am forced to shake it, I move to one side and hold out my arm. "Please, come in."

"Thanks."

"Just through here."

I take his jacket and hang it on the hall coat-stand then indicate the way to the living room, even though I'm pretty sure Mickey remembers where it is.

I am struck, perhaps in comparison to the pristine sheen of Mickey, at how shabby and dark it seems. A tired, dusty room occupied by a man who doesn't really care much about decor.

"Can I get you a drink? I've got a nice bottle of Barolo open, or there's beer, or—"

"Beer would be good."

"Okay. I've got Heineken—"

"Anything. I'm not much of a drinker."

"Right." Another thing we don't have in common. "I'll just grab a bottle out of the fridge."

I walk back into the kitchen, take out a Heineken and open it. Then I reach for my wineglass and take a deep swig before refilling it from the bottle, which is already half empty.

"You've done a good job with this old place."

I jump. Mickey stands in the doorway, looking around. I wonder if he saw me gulp and refill my wine. I wonder why I should care.

"Thanks," I say, even though we both know that I have done very little with "this old place."

I hand him his beer.

"An old house like this must eat money, though?" he says.

"It's not too bad."

"I'm surprised you don't sell up."

"Sentimental reasons, I guess."

I take a sip of my wine. Mickey sips his beer. The moment lingers a fraction too long, drifting from a natural pause into an awkward silence.

"So," Mickey says, "I hear you're a teacher?"

I nod. "Yes, for my sins."

"Enjoy it?"

"Most of the time."

Most of the time I love my subject. I want to share that love with my pupils. I want them to enjoy their lessons and to go away having learned something.

Others days I'm tired, hungover and I'd give anyone an A* just to shut the hell up and leave me alone.

"Funny." Mickey shakes his head. "I thought you'd end up being a writer, like your dad. You were always good at English."

"And you were always good at making stuff up. Guess that's why you're in advertising."

He laughs, a little uneasily. Another pause. I make a pretense of checking the spaghetti.

"I've just rustled up a bit of spag bol. Hope that's okay?"

"Yeah, great." I hear the scrape of a chair as he sits down. "Thanks for going to all the effort. I mean, I was happy to stump up for a meal at the pub."

"Not The Bull, though?"

His face tightens. "I guess you told them about my visit."

By "them," I presume he means Hoppo and Gav.

"Actually, no. But Hoppo said he ran into you in town the other day, so—"

He shrugs. "Well, I wasn't keeping it a secret."

"So why ask me not to tell them?"

"I'm a coward," he says. "After the accident, everything that happened . . . I just didn't think either of them would want to hear from me."

"You never know," I say. "People change. It was a long time ago."

This is also a lie, but it seems a better thing to say than: *You're right. They still hate your guts, especially Gav.*

"I suppose." He tips up his beer and takes several deep gulps. For someone who doesn't drink much he's putting on a good show.

I fetch him another one from the fridge and settle at the table opposite him. "What I'm saying is, we all did things we probably weren't proud of back then."

"Except you."

Before I can reply there's a spitting sound behind me. The spaghetti is boiling over. I quickly turn the gas down.

"Want a hand with anything?" Mickey asks.

"No. It's fine."

"Thanks." He raises the beer. "I'd like to talk to you about a proposition."

And there it is.

"Oh?"

"You're probably wondering why I'm back?"

"My legendary cooking?"

"It will be thirty years this year, Ed."

"I'm aware of that."

"There's already media interest."

"I don't really pay attention to the media."

"Probably wise. Most of it is misinformed bullshit. That's why I think it's important for someone to tell the real story. Someone who was actually here."

"Someone like you?"

He nods. "And I'd like your help."

"With what exactly?"

"A book. Maybe TV. I have contacts. And I've already done a lot of background research."

I stare at him. Then I shake my head. "No."

"Just hear me out."

"I'm not interested. I don't need to drag it all up again."

"But I do." He throws back the bottle. "Look, for years I've tried not to think about what happened. I've been avoiding it. Shutting it away. Well, I've decided it's time to look all that fear and guilt in the eye and deal with it."

Personally, I have found that it is much better to take your fears, lock them up in a nice, tightly shut box and shove them into the deepest, darkest corner of your mind. But each to their own.

"And what about the rest of us? Have you thought about whether we want to face our fears, go back over everything that happened?"

"I get what you're saying. Really I do. That's why I want you involved—and not just with the writing."

"Meaning?"

"I haven't been back to this place for over twenty years. I'm a stranger. But you still live here. You know people, they trust you—"

"You want me to smooth things over with Gav and Hoppo?"

"You wouldn't be doing it for free. There would be a share of the advance. Royalties."

I hesitate. Mickey takes my hesitation for continued reticence.

"And there's something else."

"What?"

He smirks, and I realize, in an instant, that everything he said about coming back and facing his fears was just crap, just a pile of stinking Buckaroo.

"I know who really killed her."

1986

The summer holidays were drawing to a close.

"Just six more days," Fat Gav had said despondently. "And that includes the weekend, which doesn't count, so really, it's only four days."

I shared his despondency, but I was trying to put the thought of school out of my head. Six days was still six days, and I was clinging on to that for more reasons than one. So far, Sean Cooper had not made good on his threat.

I'd seen him around town but had always managed to duck out of vision before he could spot me. His right eye sported a great big bruise and a nasty-looking cut. The sort of cut that would probably have stayed with him into adulthood—if Sean had actually made it all the way into adulthood.

Metal Mickey reckoned he had forgotten about me, but I didn't think so. Avoiding him during the school holidays was one thing. The town was big enough, as cowboys say, for the both of us. But once we were all back at school, avoiding him every day—at lunchtime, in the playground, on the way to school and home—was going to be far more difficult.

I was worried about other stuff, too. People think kids' lives are worry free. But that's not the case. Kids' worries are bigger because we're smaller. I was worried about Mum. She had been kind of sharp and snappy recently and even quicker to get cross than usual. Dad said it was because she was stressed about the opening of the new clinic.

Mum used to travel to work in Southampton. But now there was going to be this new clinic, in Anderbury, near the technology college. The building used to be something else. I forget what, but it was a forgettable kind of building. I think that was the point. There wasn't even a sign. In fact, you'd have probably walked straight past without even noticing it was there if it hadn't been for the people hanging around outside.

I was cycling back from the shops when I saw them. There was a group of about five. They marched in a circle, holding up signs, singing and chanting stuff. Their signs said things like "CHOOSE LIFE," "STOP KILLING BABIES" and "SUFFER THE LITTLE CHILDREN."

I recognized a few. A woman who worked in the supermarket and Waltzer Girl's blond friend from the fair. Incredibly, Blond Friend hadn't been hurt at all that day. A small part of me—not a very pleasant part—thought that was a bit unfair. She wasn't as pretty as Waltzer Girl, and she obviously wasn't as nice. She carried one of the signs and marched behind the other person I knew. Reverend Martin. He chanted the loudest and walked with an open Bible, reciting stuff.

I paused on my bike and watched them. After the fight at Fat Gav's party Dad had had a bit of a chat with me, and I knew a bit more about what happened at Mum's clinic. But still, at twelve, you can't really grasp the enormity of a subject like abortion. I just knew that Mum helped women who couldn't look after their babies. I don't think I wanted to know more than that.

However, even as a kid, I could sense the anger—the *venom*—of those protesters. Something about their eyes, the spittle that exploded from their mouths, the way they brandished their banners like weapons. They were chanting a lot of stuff about love but they seemed full of hate.

I cycled home more quickly. The house was quiet, aside from

Dad sawing something somewhere. Mum was upstairs, working. I took out the shopping and put it away, left the change on the side. I wanted to talk to them about what I'd seen, but they were both busy. I wandered aimlessly outside through the back door. That's when I noticed the chalk drawing on the driveway.

We'd been drawing the chalk figures, and other chalk symbols, for a while by then. Ideas, when you're a kid, are a bit like seeds scattered in the wind. Some don't make it; they get carried away on the breeze, forgotten about and never mentioned again. Others take root. They dig their way down, they grow and they spread.

The chalk drawings were one of those weird ideas that everyone got, almost right away. I mean, obviously, one of the first things we did was draw a load of stick men with huge cocks in the playground and write "Fuck off" a lot. But once I'd floated the idea of using them to leave secret messages between us, well, I guess that's when the chalk men grew legs of their own.

We each had our own color of chalk, so we knew who had left the message, and different drawings meant different things. Like a stick figure with a circle meant meet me at the playground. A load of lines and triangles meant the woods. There were symbols for meeting at the shops and the rec. We had warning signs for Sean Cooper and his gang. I admit we also had signs for swear words, too, so we could write "Fuck off" and worse outside the houses of people we didn't like.

Did we become a bit obsessed with it all? I guess. But then that's what kids do. Get obsessive over things for a few weeks or months, then wear that idea down into the ground until it's no good and can't be played with ever again.

I remember going into Woolies one day to buy more chalk, and Perm Lady was behind the till. She looked at me a bit oddly and I wondered if she suspected I also had another pack of chalk hidden in my rucksack. But she said, "You kids like these chalks, don't you? You're the third one in today. And I thought it was all Donkey Kong and Pac-Man now."

The message on the driveway was drawn in blue chalk, which meant it was from Metal Mickey. A stick man next to a circle, and an exclamation mark (which meant come quickly). It crossed my mind briefly that it was unusual for Mickey to call for me. He usually chose Fat Gav or Hoppo first. But I didn't feel like hanging around the house that day, so I put any doubts aside, yelled through the door that I was going to meet Mickey, and headed back out on my bike.

THE PLAYGROUND WAS empty. Again. That wasn't unusual. It was nearly always empty. There were lots of families in Anderbury and lots of little toddlers who, you would have thought, would like to be pushed on the baby swings. But most mums and dads took their kids to another playground farther away.

According to Metal Mickey, the reason no one hung around the playground was because it was haunted. Apparently, some girl was found murdered there years ago:

"They found her on the roundabout. Her throat was cut, so deep her head was almost falling off. And he'd slit open her stomach, too, so all her insides were spilling out like sausages."

Metal Mickey could tell a story, you had to give him that; usually, the gorier, the better. But that's all they were. Stories. He was always making stuff up, although sometimes there was a tiny bit of truth in there somewhere.

There was definitely something a bit "off" about the playground. It was always dark , even on sunny days. Of course, that was probably more to do with the overhanging trees than anything supernatural, but I'd often feel a slight shiver when I sat on the roundabout or get this strange urge to check behind me, like someone was looking over my shoulder, and I never normally went there on my own.

Today, I pushed open the creaky gate, feeling annoyed that Metal Mickey wasn't here yet. I propped my bike against the fence. I felt the first stirrings of unease. Metal Mickey wasn't usually late.

Something was wrong. And that's when I heard the gate creak again, and a voice said, from behind me: "Hey, Shitface."

I looked round and a fist smacked me in the side of the head.

I OPENED MY eyes. Sean Cooper stared down at me. His face was in shadow. I could only make out his silhouette, but I was pretty sure he was smiling, and not in a good way. None of this was good.

"Been avoiding us?"

Us? From my position flat on my back on the ground, I tried to twist my head left and right. I could just make out two pairs of dirty Converse trainers. I didn't need to see faces to guess that they belonged to Duncan and Keith.

The side of my head throbbed. Panic clawed at my throat. Sean's face loomed close. I felt his hand grab my T-shirt, pulling it tight around my throat. "You threw a brick in my fucking eye, Shitface." He shook me again. My head banged against the tarmac. "I don't hear you saying sorry?"

"I'm . . . suh-reee." The words came out all weird and slurry. I was finding it hard to breathe.

Sean yanked me forward so my head rose off the ground. My T-shirt tightened around my neck.

"*Suh-reee?*" He put on a whining, high-pitched voice. He glanced toward Duncan and Keith, who I could see now, lounging against the climbing frame. "D'you hear that? Shitface is *suh-reee*."

The pair grinned. "Doesn't sound very *suh-reee*," Keith said.

"Nah. Sounds like a little shitface," Duncan agreed.

Sean leaned closer. I could smell cigarettes on his breath. "I don't think you mean it, Shitface."

"I . . . I do."

"Nah. But that's okay. Cos we're going to make you *suh-reee*."

I felt my bladder loosen. I was glad it was a hot day and I'd been sweating because if I'd had an ounce of excess water in my body it would have just gushed out into my pants.

Sean yanked me by my T-shirt to my feet. I scrabbled with my trainers to get purchase on the tarmac so I wouldn't choke. Then he shoved me backward, pushing me toward the climbing frame. My head spun. I almost lost my footing, but his tight grip kept me upright.

I stared desperately around the playground, but it was empty aside from Sean and his gang and their shiny BMX racers, discarded carelessly by the swings. You could always recognize Sean's. It was bright red with a black skull painted down the side. Across the road, one lone blue car sat in the small car park outside the Spar. No sign of the driver.

And then I saw something: a figure in the park. I couldn't quite make them out, but it looked like . . .

"Are you listening to me, Shitface?"

Sean rammed me hard against the bars of the climbing frame. My head banged against metal and my vision clouded. The figure disappeared; everything disappeared for a moment. Thick gray curtains swished in front of my eyes. My legs wobbled. A yawning chasm of darkness beckoned. I felt a hard slap across my cheek. Then another. My head whipped sideways. My skin stung. The curtains swished open again.

Sean's face grinned into mine. I could see him properly now. The thick blond hair. The small scar above his eye. Bright blue eyes like his brother's. But they glittered with a different kind of light. *Dead light,* I thought. Cold, hard, crazy.

"Good. Now I have your full attention."

His fist struck me in the stomach. All the air whooshed out of me. I doubled over. I couldn't even cry out. I'd never been hit properly before and the pain was immense, huge. It felt like all my insides were on fire.

Sean grabbed me by the hair and yanked my head back up. My eyes and nose streamed water and snot.

"Aww, did I hurt you, Shitface? Here's the deal: I won't hit you again if you show us how *suh-reee* you are?"

I tried to nod, even though it was pretty impossible, because Sean was holding me so tight by my hair the roots were screaming.

"D'you think you can do that?"

Another hair-wrenching nod.

"Okay. Get on your knees."

I didn't have much choice, as he forced me down by my head. Duncan and Keith stepped forward to grab my arms.

My knees scraped against the rough tarmac of the playground. It stung, but I didn't dare cry out. I was too scared for that. I stared down at Sean's white Nike trainers. I heard the sound of a buckle, a zip, and suddenly I knew where this was going and fear and panic and revulsion ripped through me all at once.

"No." I struggled, but Duncan and Keith held me tight.

"Show me how *suh-reee* you are, Shitface. Suck my dick."

He yanked my head back. I found myself staring at his cock. It looked massive. All kind of pink and swollen. It smelled, too. Of sweat, and something strange and sour. Curly blond pubes were tangled and matted around the base.

I clenched my teeth tight and tried to shake my head again.

Sean pressed the tip of his cock against my lips. The rancid smell drifted up my nostrils. I clenched my jaw together harder.

"Suck."

Duncan grabbed my arm and twisted it high up my back. I screamed. Sean pushed his cock into my mouth.

"*Suck*, you little fuck."

I couldn't breathe; I gagged. Tears and snot mixed their way down my chin. I thought I was going to throw up. And then, distantly, I heard a man's voice shout:

"*Hey!* What do you think you're doing?"

I felt the grip on my head slacken. Sean stepped back, pulling his cock from my mouth and stuffing it quickly back into his jeans. My arms were released.

"I asked you lot what the hell you're doing!"

I blinked rapidly. Through blurry tears I could see a tall, pale man standing at the edge of the playground. Mr. Halloran.

He hopped over the playground fence and strode toward us. He was wearing his usual uniform of a big, baggy shirt, tight jeans and boots. A gray hat today, white hair streaming out of the back. Beneath it, his face was like stone, marble. Those barely there eyes seemed to burn from within. He looked angry, and scary as hell, like some avenging angel from a comic book.

"Nothing. We weren't doing nothing," I heard Sean say, less cocky now. "Just messing around."

"Just messing around?"

"Yes, sir."

Mr. Halloran's eyes fell on me. They softened. "Are you all right?"

I scrambled to my feet and nodded. "Yeah."

"And is it true that you were just messing around?"

I glanced over at Sean. He shot me a look. I knew what that look meant. If I said anything now, my life was over. I could never step outside the house again. If I kept quiet, maybe, just maybe, this was it. My ordeal and punishment done.

I nodded again. "Yes, sir. Just messing around."

He continued to stare at me. I dropped my eyes, feeling cowardly and stupid and small.

Eventually, he turned away. "Okay," he said to the other boys. "I don't know exactly what I saw going on here, and that's the only reason I'm not marching you straight down to the police station. Now get out of here, before I change my mind."

"Yes, sir," they mumbled in unison, suddenly as meek and mild as little kids.

I watched as they climbed on to their bikes and sped away. Mr. Halloran continued to gaze after them. For a moment I thought he'd forgotten I was even there. Then he turned back to me. "So, are you really all right?"

Something about his face, his eyes, even his voice, made it impossible to lie again. I shook my head, feeling tears threaten.

"I thought not." His lips thinned. "There's nothing I hate more than bullies. But you know the thing about bullies?"

I shook my head. I didn't really know anything about anything right then. I felt weak and shaken. My stomach and head hurt and shame engulfed me. I felt like I wanted to wash my mouth out with detergent and scrub myself until my skin felt raw.

"They are cowards," Mr. Halloran said. "And cowards always get their comeuppance. Karma. Know what that is?"

I shook my head again, half wishing now that Mr. Halloran would go away.

"It means, what you sow, you reap. You do bad things and they'll come back eventually and bite you on the backside. That boy will get his one day. You can be sure about that."

He rested a hand on my shoulder, gave it a squeeze. I managed a small smile.

"That your bike?"

"Yes, sir."

"You okay to ride it home?"

I wanted to say yes but, actually, just standing upright felt exhausting. Mr. Halloran gave me a sympathetic smile.

"My car's just over there. Grab your bike. I'll give you a lift."

We walked across the road to his car. A blue Princess. There was no shade in the Spar car park; when he opened the door, fierce heat poured out. Fortunately, the seats were fabric, not plastic like in Dad's car, and I didn't scorch my legs when I climbed inside. Still I felt my T-shirt cling-film itself to my skin.

Mr. Halloran climbed into the driver's seat.

"Phew. Bit warm, isn't it?"

He wound down the window. I did the same on my side. A faint breeze washed through as we pulled off.

Even so, in the enclosed, hot space, I felt horribly aware of the overpowering smell of sweat on me and the dirt and blood and everything else.

Mum was going to kill me, I thought. I could already picture her face:

"*What on earth happened, Eddie? Did you get into a fight? You're filthy—and look at your face. Did someone do this to you?*"

She'd want to find out who did it, and then she'd go round there and it would all be a huge mess. I felt my stomach slowly sink into my toes.

Mr. Halloran glanced over. “Are you all right?”

“My mum,” I muttered. “She’s going to be really mad.”

“But what happened wasn’t your fault.”

“It doesn’t matter.”

“If you tell her—”

“No, I can’t.”

“Okay.”

“She’s under a lot of stress at the moment, with stuff.”

“Ah.” He said it in a way like he knew what the stuff was. “Tell you what. Why don’t we go back to my house and clean you up a bit?”

He slowed for the junction and signaled, but instead of turning left toward my road he turned right. We took another couple of turns and pulled up outside a small whitewashed cottage.

He smiled. “Come on, Eddie.”

THE COTTAGE WAS cool and dark inside. All the curtains were drawn closed. The front door opened straight into a small living room. There wasn’t much furniture. Just a couple of armchairs, a coffee table and a small TV on a stool. It smelled a bit, too, of something herby and weird. An ashtray sat on the coffee table with a couple of small white butts in it.

Mr. Halloran snatched it up. “I’ll just get rid of this. Bathroom’s at the top of the stairs.”

“Okay.”

I walked up the narrow stairs. At the top of the landing was a tiny bathroom with a green suite and floor. Pale orange mats lay neatly beside the bath and around the bottom of the loo. A small mirrored cabinet was fixed to the wall above the sink.

I closed the bathroom door and faced myself in the mirror. Snot crusted my nose and dirt streaked my cheeks. I felt grateful my mum wouldn't see me like this. I would have been looking forward to spending the rest of the holidays confined to my room and the back garden. I started to dab at my face with the flannel by the sink, bathing it in warm water that turned murky as I washed the dirt away.

I looked at myself again. Better. Almost normal. I dried myself off with a large, prickly towel and then I stepped out of the bathroom.

I should have gone straight downstairs. If I had, everything would have been okay. I could have gone home and forgotten all about this visit. Instead, I found myself staring at the two other doors upstairs. Both closed. I found myself wondering what lay behind them. Just one little peek. I turned the handle and pushed open the closest one.

It wasn't a bedroom. There was no furniture at all. An easel stood in the center of the room, the painting on it covered with a dirty sheet. Around the rest of the room, propped up against the walls, were loads of other pictures. Some in chalk, or whatever Mr. Halloran had called them, but others in proper thick, heavy paint.

Most of the paintings seemed to be of just two girls. One was pale and blond, a lot like Mr. Halloran. She was pretty but she looked sort of sad, like someone had told her something she didn't really want to hear but she was putting a brave face on it.

The other girl I recognized right away. It was Waltzer Girl. In the first painting, she was sitting sideways in a white gown near a window. You could only see her in profile but I could still tell it was her and she still looked beautiful. The next one was slightly different. She was sitting in a garden in a pretty, long sundress and looking a little more toward the painter. Her silky brown hair fell in waves over her shoulders. You could see the smooth line of her jaw and one large, almond eye.

The third picture showed even more of her face, or rather the side of her face that the shard of flying metal had sliced away. It didn't look so terrible anymore, though, because Mr. Halloran had softened all the scars so they looked more like a pretty patchwork of different colors and her hair half covered her damaged eye. She almost looked beautiful again, just in a different way.

I looked at the canvas on the easel. I found myself walking toward it. I raised a corner of the sheet. And that was when I heard the creak of a floorboard.

"Eddie? What are you doing?"

I spun round, shame crippling me for the second time that day.

"I'm sorry. I was just . . . I just wanted to look."

For a moment I thought Mr. Halloran was going to tell me off, then he smiled. "It's okay, Eddie. I should have shut the door."

I almost opened my mouth to say that he had. But then I realized. He was giving me a get-out.

"They're really good," I said.

"Thank you."

"Who's that?" I asked, pointing at the picture of the blond girl.

"My sister. Jenny."

That explained the resemblance.

"She's very pretty."

"Yes, she was. She died. A few years ago. Leukemia."

"I'm sorry."

I didn't know what I was apologizing for, but that was what people always said when someone died.

"It's okay. In a way, the paintings help me keep her alive . . . I suppose you recognize Elisa?"

Waltzer Girl. I nodded.

"I've visited her a lot, in hospital."

"Is she okay?"

"Not really, Eddie. But she will be. She's strong. Stronger than she realizes."

I stayed quiet. I got the feeling Mr. Halloran wanted to say something else.

"I'm hoping the paintings will help her with her convalescence. A girl like Elisa, her whole life she's been told she's beautiful. And when you take that away it can feel like there's nothing left. But there is, on the inside. I want to show her that beauty. I want to show her there's still something worth holding on to."

I looked back at the picture of Elisa. I kind of got it. She didn't look like she used to. But he had brought out a different kind of beauty, a special kind. I understood about holding on to things, too. About making sure they weren't lost forever. I almost told him that. But when I turned back Mr. Halloran was staring at the painting, like he had forgotten I was even there.

That was when I understood something else. He was in love with her.

I liked Mr. Halloran but, even then, I felt uncomfortable. Mr. Halloran was an adult. Not an old adult (later, we found out he was thirty-one) but still an adult, and Waltzer Girl, well, she wasn't a schoolgirl or anything but she was still way younger than him. He couldn't love her. Not without there being trouble. Lots of it.

Suddenly he seemed to snap back and realize I was still in the room.

"Anyway, here I am, rambling. That's why I don't teach art. No one would ever get anything done." He smiled his yellow smile. "Ready to go home?"

"Yes, sir."

More than anything.

MR. HALLORAN PULLED up at the end of my road.

"I thought you might not want your mum to ask questions."

"Thanks."

"Want a hand getting your bike out of the boot?"

"No, it's okay, I can manage. Thank you, sir."

"You're welcome, Eddie. Just one thing?"

"Yes, sir."

"I'll do you a deal. I won't tell anyone about what happened today if you don't. Especially about the paintings. They're sort of private."

I didn't have to think twice. I didn't want anyone to know what had happened today.

"Yes, sir. I mean, deal."

"Good. Bye, Eddie."

"Bye, sir."

I grabbed my bike, wheeled it down the street and up the driveway. I propped it by the front door. There was a parcel on the step outside. It had a label stuck to it: Mrs. M. Adams. I wondered why the postman hadn't knocked on the door, or perhaps he had and Mum and Dad hadn't heard him.

I picked the box up and carried it indoors.

"Hi, Eddie," Dad called out from the kitchen.

I quickly checked myself in the hall mirror. I still had a bit of a bruise on my forehead and my T-shirt was a bit dirty, but it would have to do. I took a deep breath and walked into the kitchen.

Dad was sitting at the table, drinking a big glass of lemonade. He looked at me and frowned.

"What happened to your head?"

"I, err, fell off the climbing frame."

"Are you okay? You don't feel sick, do you? Dizzy?"

"No, I'm fine."

I put the parcel down on the table. "This was on the step."

"Oh, right. I didn't hear the bell." He stood and called upstairs, "Marianne . . . parcel for you."

Mum called back, "Okay, just coming."

"Want some lemonade, Eddie?" Dad asked.

I nodded. "Thanks."

He went to the fridge and grabbed a bottle out of the door. I sniffed. There was a funny smell in the room.

Mum walked into the kitchen. She had her glasses pushed back in her hair and looked tired.

"Hi, Eddie." She glanced at the parcel. "What's this?"

"Search me," Dad said.

She sniffed. "Can you smell something?"

Dad shook his head but then reconsidered. "Well, maybe a bit."

Mum looked at the parcel again and then she said in a slightly tighter voice, “Geoff, can you get me some scissors?”

Dad passed her some from the drawer. She sliced through the brown tape sealing the parcel and pulled it open.

Mum wasn’t fazed by much, but I saw her recoil. “Jesus!”

Dad leaned over. “Christ!”

Before he could snatch the box away, I peered inside. Something small and pink and covered in slimy goo and blood (later, I would learn it was a pig fetus) nestled at the bottom of the box. A slim knife was sticking out from the top, skewering a piece of paper with just two words printed on it:

“BABY KILLER.”

2016

Principles are nice things. If you can afford them. I like to think I am a principled man, but then, most men do. The fact is, we all have a price, we all have buttons that can be pressed to make us do things that are not entirely honorable. Principles do not pay the mortgage, or clear our debts. Principles are actually pretty useless currency in the daily grind of life. A principled man is generally a man who has everything he wants, or absolutely nothing to lose.

I lie awake for a long time, and not just because an excess of wine and spaghetti has given me indigestion.

"I know who really killed her."

A great cliffhanger. Mickey knew it would be. And, of course, he would not elaborate.

"I can't tell you now. I just need to get a few things straight first."

Bullshit, I thought. But I had nodded, numb with shock.

"I'll let you sleep on it," Mickey had said as he left. He hadn't brought his car and wouldn't let me book him a cab. He was staying in a Travelodge on the outskirts of town.

"The walk will do me good," he said.

I wasn't so sure, bearing in mind how unsteady on his feet he looked. But I concurred. After all, it wasn't that late and he was a grown man.

After he had gone, I loaded the dishes in the dishwasher and retired to the living room with a large bourbon to think about his proposal. I may have closed my eyes for a moment, or several. The after-dinner nap—the curse of the middle-aged.

I started awake to the sound of floorboards creaking above me, footsteps on the old staircase.

Chloe poked her head around the door. "Hey."

"Hello."

She had changed into nightwear. A baggy T-shirt over men's pajama bottoms and slouchy socks. Her dark hair was loose. She looked sexy and vulnerable and disheveled all at the same time. I buried my nose in my bourbon.

"How'd it go?" she asked.

I considered. "Interesting."

She walked in and perched on the arm of the sofa. "Do tell."

I took a swig of my drink. "Mickey wants to write a book, maybe a television script, about what happened. He wants me to work on it with him."

"The plot thickens."

"Doesn't it?"

"And?"

"And what?"

"Well, you said yes, I presume."

"I haven't said anything yet. I'm not sure I want to do it."

"Why not?"

"Because there are a lot of things to consider—how people in Anderbury feel about digging up the past, for one thing. Gav and Hoppo. Our families."

And Nicky, I thought. Had he spoken to Nicky?

Chloe frowned. "Okay. I get that. But what about you?"

"Me?"

She sighed and looked at me like I was a particularly slow toddler. "It could be a great opportunity. And I'm sure the money wouldn't hurt either."

"That's not really the point. Besides, this is all hypothetical. Projects like this fall by the wayside all the time."

"Yes, but you have to take a chance sometimes."

"Do you?"

"*Yes.* Otherwise you never get anywhere in life. You just end up sitting around and fossilizing, instead of actually living."

I raised my glass. "Well, thanks for that. Sage advice from someone who is really living on the edge, working part-time in a crappy clothes shop. You're *really* pushing the limits."

She stood and huffed to the door. "You're drunk. I'm going back to bed."

Regret washed over me. I was an idiot. A grade-A, with-honors-and-a-diploma idiot.

"I'm sorry."

"Forget it." She offered a sour smile. "But then, you probably won't remember it in the morning anyway."

"Chloe—"

"Sleep it off, Ed."

SLEEP IT OFF. I turn on my side and then onto my back. That would be good advice. If I could sleep.

I try to prop myself on my pillows, but it's no good. My stomach is a tight, nagging ache. I think I might have some antacids somewhere. Perhaps in the kitchen.

Reluctantly, I swing my legs from the bed and pad downstairs. I flick on the harsh kitchen light. It scours my sore eyeballs. I squint and fumble in one of the junk drawers. Sticky tape, Blu-Tack, pens, scissors. Unfathomable keys and screws and a pack of ancient playing cards. Eventually, I find the antacids, lurking right at the back, along with a nail file and an old bottle opener.

I take them out to find there is only one left in the packet. It will do. I chuck it in my mouth and crunch down. It's supposed to taste of fruit, but it just tastes of chalk. I walk back out into the hallway, which is when I notice something. Well, two things, actually: there's a light on in the living room, and there's a strange smell coming from somewhere. Kind of sweet, yet sickly stale. Rotten. Familiar.

I take a step forward and tread in something gritty. I look down. Black earth trails across the hall floor. Footsteps. Like something has shuffled, shedding dirt, across the hallway. Something that has dragged itself from the depths of somewhere cold and dark and full of beetles and worms.

I swallow. No. No, not possible. It's just my mind playing tricks. Dredging up an old nightmare, dreamed up by a twelve-year-old kid with a hyperactive imagination.

Lucid dreaming. That's what they call it. A dream that feels incredibly real. You may even perform activities within the dream that contribute to the illusion of reality, like holding conversations, making food, running a bath . . . or other things.

This is not real (despite the very real feeling of dirt between my toes and the chalky tablet in my mouth). All I need to do is wake up. *Wake up. Wake up!* Unfortunately, wakefulness, just like the oblivion I previously sought, seems equally hard to come by.

I walk forward and place a hand on the living-room door. Of course I do. It's a dream, and dreams like these (*bad* ones) follow a somewhat inevitable path; a twisting, narrow path, through the deep, dark woods, right into the gingerbread cottage at the bottom of our psyche.

I push the door open. It feels cold in here, too. Not normal cold. Not the slight chill of a house at nighttime. This type of cold wraps itself around your bones and sits like a lump of ice in your intestines. Fear-cold. And the smell is stronger. Overpowering. I can barely breathe. I want to back out of the room. I want to run. I want to scream. Instead, I turn the light on.

He sits in my armchair. White-blond hair clings to his scalp like sticky strands of spiderweb, parts of bone and brain visible beneath. His face is a skull, loosely draped with shreds of rotting skin.

As always, he wears a baggy shirt and skinny jeans with heavy black boots. The clothes are ragged and torn. The boots scuffed and crusted with dirt. His battered hat sits on the arm of the chair.

I should have realized. The time for my childhood bogeyman has gone. I'm an adult now. Time to face the Chalk Man.

Mr. Halloran turns toward me. His eyes are gone, but there's something within those sockets, some semblance of understanding or recognition . . . and something else that makes me not want to look into them too deeply, for fear I might never drag the whole of my mind back out again.

"Hello, Ed. Long time no see."

CHLOE IS ALREADY up, drinking coffee and munching on toast in the kitchen when I emerge downstairs, feeling distinctly unrested, at just gone eight.

She has retuned the radio and, instead of Radio 4, it is pumping out something that sounds like a man screaming in agony while trying to kill himself by thrashing a guitar over his head.

Suffice to say, it does nothing to alleviate the pounding in my head.

She turns and appraises me briefly. "You look like shit."

"I feel it."

"Good. Serves you right."

"Thanks for the sympathy."

"Self-inflicted pain does not merit sympathy."

"Again, thanks . . . and any chance you could turn down the angry white man with daddy issues."

"It's called rock music, Grandpa."

"That's what I just said."

She shakes her head but nudges the volume down a fraction.

I walk over to the coffee machine and pour a black coffee.

"So how long did you stay up after I went to bed?" Chloe asks.

I sit down at the table. "Not long. I was pretty drunk."

"No kidding."

"I'm sorry."

She waves a pale hand. "Forget it. I shouldn't have got on your case. Really, it's none of my business."

"No, well, I mean, you're right. What you said. But sometimes things aren't so clear-cut."

"Fine." She sips her coffee, then says, "Are you sure you didn't stay up long?"

"Yes."

"And you didn't get up again?"

"Well, I did come down to get some antacids."

"And that's all?"

A fragment of a dream flits across my memory: *"Hello, Ed. Long time no see."*

I push it away. "Yes. Why?"

She gives me an odd look. "Let me show you something."

She gets up and walks out of the kitchen. Reluctantly, I rise from my seat and follow her.

She pauses at the living-room door. "I just wondered if things might have been preying on your mind, after your chat with your friend?"

"Just show me, Chloe."

"Okay."

She pushes open the door.

One of the few renovations I had made to the house was to replace the old fireplace with a new wood-burning stove and a slate hearth.

I stare at it. The hearth is covered in drawings. Standing out stark white against the gray slate. Dozens and dozens, drawn on top of each other, as if in some kind of frenzy. White chalk men.

1986

A policeman came round to our house. We'd never had a policeman in the house before. Up until that summer, I don't think I'd ever seen one up close.

This one was tall and thin. He had a lot of dark hair and a face that was sort of square. He looked a bit like a giant piece of Lego, except he wasn't yellow. His name was PC Thomas.

He peered in the box, took it away in a bin bag and put it in his police car. Then he came back and perched awkwardly in the kitchen while he asked Mum and Dad questions and wrote things down in a small, spiral-bound notebook.

"And your son found the parcel outside?"

"That's right," Mum said, and looked at me. "Isn't it, Eddie?"

I nodded. "Yes, sir."

"What time was this?"

"4:04 p.m.," Mum said. "I checked my watch before I came downstairs."

The policeman scribbled more notes.

"And you didn't see anyone leaving the house or on the street, hanging around?"

I shook my head. "No, sir."

"Okay."

More scribbling. My dad shifted in his chair.

"Look, all of this is pointless," he said. "We all know who left that parcel."

PC Thomas gave him an odd look. It wasn't very friendly, I thought. "Do we, sir?"

"Yes. One of Reverend Martin's little gang. They're trying to intimidate my wife and my family, and it's about time someone put a stop to it."

"Do you have any evidence?"

"No, but it's obvious, isn't it?"

"Perhaps we should leave the unfounded allegations for now."

"Unfounded?" I could tell my dad was getting mad. Dad didn't get mad often, but when he did—like at the party—he really blew.

"There is no law against peaceful protest, sir."

And that was when I got it. The policeman wasn't on Mum and Dad's side. He was on the side of the protesters.

"You're right," Mum said calmly. "Peaceful protest is not illegal. But intimidation, harassment and threats most certainly are. I hope you will be taking this matter seriously?"

PC Thomas snapped his notebook shut. "Of course. If we can find the culprits, you can be sure they will receive the appropriate punishment."

He stood up, the chair squeaking noisily across the tiled floor. "Now, if you'll excuse me."

He walked out of the kitchen. The front door slammed.

I turned to Mum. "Doesn't he want to help?"

Mum sighed. "Yes. Of course he does."

Dad snorted. "Maybe he'd want to help more if his daughter wasn't one of the protesters."

"Geoff," Mum said. "Just leave it."

"Fine." He stood up, and he didn't look like Dad for a moment. His face looked all hard and angry. "But if the police don't deal with this, then I will."

. . .

BEFORE SCHOOL STARTED, we all got together properly for the last time. We met up at Fat Gav's house. We usually did. He had the biggest bedroom and the best garden, with a rope swing and a tree house, and his mum always kept us well stocked with fizzy pop and crisps.

We lolled on the grass, talking crap and taking the piss out of each other. Despite my deal with Mr. Halloran, I told them a little about my encounter with Metal Mickey's brother. I had to, because if he knew about the chalk men that meant our secret game was ruined. Of course, in my version, I fought heroically and got away. I was a bit worried Sean might have told Metal Mickey, who would take great delight in contradicting me, but it seemed that Mr. Halloran had put enough of the frighteners on Sean for him not to say anything either.

"So your brother knows about the chalk men?" Fat Gav said, giving Metal Mickey an unpleasant look. "You're a real blabbermouth."

"I didn't tell him," Metal Mickey whined. "He must have just worked it out on his own. I mean, we drew loads. He probably saw us."

He was lying, but I didn't really care how Sean had found out. The fact was, he had, and that changed everything.

"I suppose we could always come up with some new messages," Hoppo said, but he didn't sound very enthusiastic.

I knew how he felt. Now someone else knew—*especially Sean*—the whole thing was spoiled.

"It was a pretty stupid game, anyway," Nicky said, flicking her hair.

I stared at her, feeling hurt and a bit annoyed. She was being weird today. Sometimes she got like that. All kind of moody and argumentative.

"Nah, it wasn't," Fat Gav said. "But I guess there's no point doing it anymore if Sean knows. Besides, it's school tomorrow."

"Yeah."

A collective sigh ran around the group. Everyone was a bit subdued that afternoon. Even Fat Gav wasn't coming out with his usual bad accents. The blue sky had faded to a murky gray. Clouds shifted restlessly, like they were getting impatient for a really big downpour.

"I should probably get going," Hoppo said. "Mum wants me to chop some logs for the fire."

Like us, Hoppo and his mum had a crappy real fire in their old terraced house.

"Me, too," Metal Mickey said. "We're going to tea at my gran's tonight."

"You lot are bringing me down, maaaan," Fat Gav said, but it was kind of halfhearted.

"I should probably get back, too," I admitted. Mum had bought me some new school stuff and wanted me to try it on before tea, in case any of it needed adjusting.

We stood and, after a pause, Nicky stood, too.

Fat Gav collapsed dramatically onto the grass. "Go on then, go. You're all killing me."

Looking back, I think that was the last time we were all together like that. Relaxed, friends, still a gang, before things started to splinter and crack.

Hoppo and Metal Mickey headed off in one direction. That left Nicky and me to head off in the other. The vicarage wasn't that far from our house and sometimes Nicky and I would walk back together. Not often. Usually, Nicky was the first to leave. Because of her dad, I guess. He was pretty strict about timekeeping. I got the idea that he didn't really approve of Nicky hanging around with us at all. I guess we didn't think too much about it, though. He was a vicar and, in our eyes, that was explanation enough. I mean, vicars didn't really approve of anything, did they?

"So, erm, you all sorted for school?" I said as we crossed at the lights and walked back past the park.

She gave me one of her grown-up looks. "I know."

"Know what?"

"About the parcel."

"Oh."

I hadn't told the others about the parcel. It was too complicated and messy, and felt kind of disloyal to Mum and Dad.

As far as I could see, nothing much had happened about it, anyway. The policeman didn't come back and I hadn't heard about anyone being arrested. Mum's clinic had opened and the protesters continued to circle outside, like vultures. "The police came to talk to Dad."

"Oh."

"Yeah."

"I'm sorry," I started to say.

"What are you sorry for? My dad's the arsehole."

"He is?"

"Everyone is so frigging scared to say anything because he's a vicar—even the policeman. It was pathetic—" She broke off and looked down at her fingers, four of which were wrapped in plasters.

"What happened to your hand?"

She took a long while to reply. For a moment I thought she wasn't going to. Then she said, "Do you love your mum and dad?"

I frowned. It wasn't what I had expected her to say. "Of course. I guess."

"Well, I hate my dad. Really, really *hate* him."

"You don't mean that."

"Yes, I do. I was glad when your dad punched him. I wish he'd hit him harder." She stared at me, and something in her gaze made me feel a little cold inside. "I wish he'd killed him."

Then she flicked her hair over her shoulder and stalked off, walking in a quick, determined way that left me in no doubt that she didn't want me to follow her.

I waited until her red hair had disappeared around the corner and then I trudged wearily down the road. The heaviness of the day seemed like it was squatting on my shoulders. I just wanted to get home.

When I walked in, Dad was making tea; my favorite, fish fingers and chips.

"Can I go and watch some telly?" I asked.

"No." He caught my arm. "Your mum's in there with someone. Go wash up and come and have your dinner."

"Who's she with?"

"Just go wash up."

I walked out into the hall. The living-room door was ajar. Mum was sitting on the sofa with some blond girl. The girl was crying and Mum was hugging her. The girl looked kind of familiar, but I couldn't quite place her.

It wasn't till I'd used the toilet and washed my hands that I realized. She was Waltzer Girl's blond friend, the one I had seen protesting outside the clinic. I wondered what she was doing here and why she was crying. Perhaps she had come to say sorry to Mum. Or she was in some kind of trouble.

As it turned out, it was the latter. But not the sort of trouble I imagined.

THEY FOUND THE body on a Sunday morning, three weeks after school started.

Although none of us would admit it, going back to school after the summer holidays wasn't as bad as we made out. Six weeks of holidays was great. But having fun, finding stuff to do, could get a bit exhausting.

And this summer holiday had been a strange one. In a way, I was glad to put it behind me and get back to some normality. The same routine, the same classes, the same faces. Well, apart from Mr. Halloran.

He wasn't my teacher, which was kind of a shame but also a relief. I knew a bit too much about him. Teachers should be nice and friendly, but they should also be a bit apart. Mr. Halloran and I shared a secret now and, although that was cool in one way, it also made me feel awkward around him, like we had seen each other naked or something.

We saw him around the school, obviously. He was there at dinner and sometimes he would be on break duty, and one day he taught our class when Mrs. Wilkinson, our usual English teacher, was off sick. He was a good teacher. Funny, interesting and really good at making the lessons not boring. So much so that pretty soon you forgot how he looked, although that didn't stop the kids giving him a nickname from day one: Mr. Chalk or the Chalk Man.

This Sunday, nothing much in particular was going on. Which was fine by me. It felt good to just be bored, like normal. Mum and Dad seemed a bit more relaxed, too. I was upstairs in my room, reading, when the doorbell rang. Right away, like you do sometimes, I knew that something had happened. Something bad.

"Eddie?" Mum called upstairs. "Mickey and David are here."

"Coming."

A bit reluctantly, I padded downstairs to the front door. Mum disappeared into the kitchen.

Metal Mickey and Hoppo stood, with their bikes, on the doorstep. Metal Mickey was red-faced and bursting with excitement. "Some kid has fallen in the river."

"Yeah," Hoppo said. "There's an ambulance and police there with tape and all sorts of shit. Wanna come look?"

I'd like to say that, at the time, I thought their enthusiasm to see some poor dead kid was ghoulish and wrong. But I was twelve. *Of course* I wanted to look.

"Okay."

"C'mon, then," Metal Mickey said impatiently.

"I just have to get my bike."

"Hurry," Hoppo said. "Or there won't be anything left to see."

"See what?" Mum poked her head back out of the kitchen.

"Nothing, Mum," I said.

"You seem in a big hurry to see nothing."

"It's just some cool new stuff in the playground," Metal Mickey lied. He was always a good liar.

"Well, don't be long. I want you back for lunch."

"Okay."

I grabbed my bike and we sped off down the street.

"Where's Fat Gav?" I asked Metal Mickey, who usually called for him first.

"His mum said she'd sent him to the shops," he said. "His loss."

Although, as it turned out, it wasn't. It was Metal Mickey's.

THERE WAS A cordon around part of the riverbank and a policeman stopping people getting too close. Grown-ups stood in groups, looking concerned. We stopped our bikes near a small crowd of onlookers.

Actually, it was a bit disappointing. As well as the cordon, the police had put up this big green tent-type thing. You couldn't really see anything.

"D'you think the body is behind that?" Metal Mickey asked.

Hoppo shrugged. "Probably."

"I bet he's all bloated and green and fish have eaten his eyeballs."

"Gross." Hoppo made a gagging noise.

I tried to push the image Metal Mickey had created out of my mind, but it refused to budge.

"This is crap," he sighed. "We're too late."

"Wait," I said. "They're bringing something out."

There was some movement. The policemen were carefully shifting something from behind the green screen. Not a body. A bike. Or at least what was left of it. It was twisted and buckled, covered in slimy weeds. But the moment we saw it we knew. We all knew.

It was a BMX racer. Bright red with a black skull painted on it.

. . .

EVERY SATURDAY AND Sunday morning Sean and his BMX racer could be seen—if you were up early enough—tearing around the town, delivering papers. However, this Sunday morning, when Sean had gone outside to get on his bike, he found it was gone. Someone had stolen it.

The year before, there had been a spate of bike thefts. Some older kids from the college had been nicking them and chucking them in the river, just for fun, for a prank.

Perhaps that's why it was the first place Sean went to look. He loved that racer. More than anything. So when he saw the handlebars sticking out of the river, caught on some broken tree branches, he decided to wade in and try to get it, even though everyone knew that the current was really strong and Sean Cooper was a pretty weak swimmer.

He almost made it. He had just about got the bike out of the tree branches when the weight caused him to stagger and fall backward. Suddenly the water was up to his chest. His jacket and jeans were weighing him down and the current was so strong, like dozens of hands trying to drag him under. And it was cold, too. So frigging cold.

He grabbed at the tree branches. He cried out, but it was still early and not even a lone dog-walker was passing by. Maybe that's when Sean Cooper started to panic. The current wrapped itself around his limbs and began to pull him away, downstream.

He kicked out hard to try to make it back to the shore, but the shore was getting farther away and his head kept going under, and instead of inhaling air he was inhaling stinking brown water . . .

I DIDN'T ACTUALLY know any of this. Some I found out later. Some I imagined. Mum always told me I had a really vivid imagination. It got me good grades in English, but it also gave me some pretty full-on nightmares.

I didn't think I'd sleep that night, despite the hot milk Mum made me before bed. I kept picturing Sean Cooper all green and bloated and covered in slimy weeds, like his bike. Something else kept going around in my head, too, something Mr. Halloran had said: Karma. What goes around comes around.

"You do bad things and they'll come back eventually and bite you on the backside. That boy will get his one day. You can be sure about that."

But I wasn't sure. Sean Cooper might have done bad things. But were they *that* bad? And what about Metal Mickey? What had he done?

Mr. Halloran hadn't seen Metal Mickey's face when he realized the bike was his brother's or heard the awful, wailing cry he made. I never wanted to hear that sound again.

It took both me and Hoppo to stop him from running over to the tent. Eventually, he was making such a scene that one of the policemen came up to us. When we explained who Metal Mickey was he wrapped an arm around him and half walked, half carried Metal Mickey to his car. After a few minutes they drove off. I was pretty relieved. Seeing Sean's bike was bad. Seeing Metal Mickey like that, all crazy and screaming, was worse.

"You okay, Eddie?"

Dad pulled up my covers and sat on the edge of my bed. His weight felt heavy and reassuring.

"What happens when we die, Dad?"

"Whoah. Well, that's a big one, Eddie. I guess nobody really knows, not for sure."

"So we don't go to heaven or hell?"

"Some people think we do. But a lot of other people don't think heaven or hell exist."

"So it doesn't matter if we've been bad, then?"

"No, Eddie. I don't think how you act in this life makes any difference after you die. Good or bad. But it does make a big difference while you're alive. To other people. That's why you should always try to treat them well."

I thought about that, and nodded. I mean, I suppose it was a bit of a bummer if you spent all your life being good and you didn't go to heaven, but I was glad about the other one. Much as I hated Sean Cooper, I didn't like the thought of him burning in hell forever.

"Eddie," Dad said, "what happened to Sean Cooper was really sad. A tragic accident. But that's all it was. An accident. Sometimes things happen and there is no reason. That's just how life is. Death, too."

"I guess."

"So do you think you're ready to go to sleep?"

"Yeah."

I didn't, but I didn't want Dad to think I was a baby.

"Okay, Eddie. Lights off, then."

Dad leaned over and kissed me on the forehead. He hardly ever did that now. Tonight I felt glad of the tickly, musty brush of his beard. Then he flicked off my main light and the room filled with shadows. I'd got rid of my night light years ago, but that night I kind of wished I still had it.

I laid my head down on the pillow and tried to get comfortable. Distantly, an owl hooted. A dog howled. I tried to think about happy stuff and not about dead, drowned boys. Stuff like riding my bike and ice cream and Pac-Man. My head sank farther into the pillow. Thoughts drifted into its soft folds. After a while I wasn't thinking about anything at all. Sleep crept up and pulled me into darkness.

SOMETHING WOKE ME again, suddenly and sharply. A *rat-a-tat-tat* kind of noise, like a shower of rain or hailstones. I frowned and rolled over. It came again. Stones, at my window. I hopped out of bed, crossed the bare floorboards and pulled aside my curtains.

I must have been asleep for a while. It was properly dark outside. The moon was a slash of silver, like a paper cut in the charcoal sky.

It provided just enough illumination for me to see Sean Cooper.

He stood on the grass, near the edge of the patio. He was dressed in jeans and his blue baseball jacket, which was torn and dirty. He wasn't green or bloated and fish hadn't eaten his eyes, but he was very pale, and very dead.

A dream. It had to be. *Wake up,* I thought. *Wake up, wake up, WAKE UP!*

"Hey, Shitface."

He smiled. My stomach rolled. I realized, with an awful, sickening certainty, that this wasn't a dream. It was a nightmare.

"Go away," I hissed under my breath, fists clenched, nails digging into my palms.

"I've got a message for you."

"I don't care," I called down. "Go away."

I tried to sound defiant. But fear had a tight grip on my throat and the words came out more like a high-pitched squeak.

"Listen, Shitface, if you don't come down, I'll have to come up there and get you."

A dead Sean Cooper in the garden was bad but a dead Sean Cooper in my bedroom was even worse. And this was still a dream, right? I just had to go with it till I woke up.

"Okay. Just . . . just give me a minute."

I grabbed my trainers from the bottom of the bed and tugged them on with trembling hands. I crept over to the door, gripped the handle and pulled it open. I didn't dare put a light on, so I felt my way along the wall toward the stairs and inched down sideways like a crab.

Eventually, I reached the bottom. I crossed the hall, into the kitchen. The back door hung open. I stepped outside. The night air nipped at my skin through the thin cotton of my pajamas; a faint breeze teased my hair. I could smell something damp and sour and rotten.

"Stop sniffing the air like a fucking dog, Shitface."

I jumped, turned. Sean Cooper was standing right in front of me. Up close he looked worse than he had from my bedroom. His skin had a weird bluey tinge. I could see tiny veins running underneath it. His eyes looked yellow and sort of deflated.

I wondered if there was a place you reached where you simply couldn't be any more afraid. If so, I thought I had reached it.

"What are you doing here?"

"*Told you. Got a message for you.*"

"What is it?"

"*Look out for the chalk men.*"

"I don't understand."

"*And you think I do?*" He took a step toward me. "*You think I want to be here? You think I want to be dead? You think I want to stink like this?*"

He pointed at me with an arm that hung strangely in its socket. In fact, I realized, it wasn't in its socket. It was torn out at the top. White bone gleamed in the misty moonlight.

"*I'm only here because of you.*"

"Me?"

"*This is your fault, Shitface. You started it all.*"

I took a step back toward the door.

"I'm sorry . . . I'm really sorry."

"*Really.*" His lips twisted into a snarl. "*Well, why don't you show me how* suh-reee *you are?*"

He grabbed my arm. Warm urine ran down my leg.

"*Suck my cock.*"

"NOOO!"

I yanked my arm away, just as the driveway was flooded with bright white light from the landing window.

"EDDIE, ARE YOU UP? WHAT ARE YOU DOING?"

Sean Cooper stood there for a moment, illuminated like some awful Christmas decoration, the light blazing through him. And then, in the way of all good monsters set free from the darkness, he slowly crumbled and floated to the ground in a small cloud of white dust.

I looked down. Where he had stood there was now something else. A drawing. Stark white against the dark driveway. A stick figure, half submerged in crude waves, one arm raised like he was waving. *No,* I thought. *Drowning. Not waving.* And not a stick figure—*a chalk man.*

A shudder rippled through me.

"*Eddie?*"

I darted back inside and closed the door as softly as I could.

"'S'okay, Mum. Just wanted a drink of water."

"Did I hear the back door?"

"No, Mum."

"Well, have your drink and go back to bed. School tomorrow."

"Okay, Mum."

"Good boy."

I locked the door, fingers shaking so hard it took me several attempts to twist the key in the lock. Then I padded back upstairs, peeled off my wet pajama bottoms and stuffed them in the laundry basket. I pulled on a fresh pair and climbed into bed. But I didn't sleep, not for a long while. I lay there, waiting to hear more stones against the window, or maybe the slow tread of wet footsteps up the stairs.

AT SOME POINT, just as the birds in the trees outside began to chatter and tweet, I must have drifted off. Not for long. I woke early. Before Mum and Dad. I immediately charged downstairs and flung open the back door, hoping against hope that it was all a dream. There was no dead Sean Cooper. There was no . . .

The chalk man was still there.

Hey, Shitface. Fancy a dip? Come on in—the water's deadly.

I could have left it. Maybe I should have done. Instead, I grabbed Mum's washing-up bowl from under the sink and filled it with water. Then I emptied the bowl out, drowning the chalk man again in cold water and the remnants of soapy suds.

I tried to tell myself that one of the others must have drawn it. Fat Gav maybe, or Hoppo. Some sort of sick joke. It wasn't until I was halfway to school that it struck me. We all had our own colors of chalk. Fat Gav was red, Metal Mickey blue, Hoppo green, Nicky yellow and I was orange. None of our gang used white.

2016

My mum rings just before lunch. She usually manages to call at the most inconvenient moment, and today is no exception. I could let it go to voicemail, but my mum hates voicemail and it will only make her annoyed when I next talk to her so, reluctantly, I press "accept."

"Hello."

"Hello, Ed."

I make an awkward exit from the classroom into the corridor.

"Is everything okay?" I ask.

"Of course. Why wouldn't it be?"

Because Mum has never been one for purely social calls. If Mum is calling, there's a reason for it.

"I don't know. Are you okay? How's Gerry?"

"Very good. We've just been on a raw-juice detox, so we're both feeling pretty vital at the moment."

I'm sure Mum never used to use words like "vital" or would ever have considered a raw-juice detox a few years ago. Not when Dad was alive. I blame Gerry.

"Great. Look, Mum. I'm actually in the middle of something, so—"

"You're not at work are you, Ed?"

"Well—"

"It's supposed to be the school holidays."

"I know, but that's a bit of an oxymoron these days."

"Don't let them work you too hard, Ed." She sighs. "There are other things in life."

Again, Mum would never have said that years ago. Work used to *be* her life. But then Dad got ill and looking after him became her life instead.

I understand that everything she is doing now—including Gerry—is her way of claiming those lost years back. I don't blame her. I blame myself.

If I'd married and had a family, perhaps she would have other things to fill her days with, instead of raw-juice bloody detoxes. And perhaps I would have other things to fill my days with instead of work.

But this is not what Mum wants to hear.

"I know," I say to her. "You're right."

"Good. You know, you should try Pilates, Ed. It's good for your core."

"I'll think about it."

I won't.

"Anyway, I won't keep you if you're busy. I just wondered if you could do me a small favor?"

"O-kay—"

"Gerry and I are thinking of going away in the camper van for a week or two."

"Very nice."

"But our usual cat-sitter has let us down."

"Oh, no."

"Ed! You're supposed to be an animal lover."

"I am. Mittens just happens to hate me."

"Nonsense. He's a cat. He doesn't hate anyone."

"He's not a cat, he's a furry sociopath."

"Can you look after him or not?"

I sigh. "Yes. I can. Of course."

"Good. I'll bring him round tomorrow morning."

Oh. Good.

I end the call and walk back into the classroom. A skinny teenager with black hair hanging over his face in a lank fringe reclines in a chair, DMs propped up on the desk, tapping away at his smartphone and chewing gum.

Danny Myers is in my class for English. He's a bright kid, or so everyone tells me: our head, and Danny's parents, who, funnily enough, happen to be friends with our head and several members of the Board of Governors. I don't doubt it, but I've yet to see anything in his work that reflects this.

That is not what his parents or our head want to hear, of course. They believe that Danny needs special attention. Danny is being let down by the "one size fits all" state education system. He is too bright, too easily distracted, too sensitive. Blah, blah, blah.

So Danny is now in what we call "intervention." This means that he is wheeled in for extra tutoring during the school holidays and I am supposed to inspire him, bully him and cajole him into achieving the grades his parents believe he really should be getting.

Sometimes these interventions produce results, with kids who have ability but don't do so well in the classroom. Other times, they are a waste of both my time and the pupil's. I don't like to think I am a defeatist. But I am a realist. I am no Mr. Chips. When it comes down it, I want to teach pupils who want to learn. Pupils who are interested and engaged. Or at least pupils who want to try. Better a hard-won D than a couldn't-give-a-crap C.

"Phone and feet. Both off," I say as I sit down at my desk.

He swings his legs from the table but continues to tap away at his phone. I pop my glasses back on and find the place in the text we were just discussing.

"When you've finished, perhaps *Lord of the Flies* could recapture your attention?"

More tapping.

"Danny, I would hate to have to suggest to your parents that an embargo on all social media might just be the boost your grades are looking for . . ."

Danny stares at me for a moment. I smile politely back. He would like to argue, like to push me, but on this occasion he turns the phone off and slips it back into his pocket. I do not consider this a victory, more like he's letting me have this one.

That's fine. Whatever makes these two hours go more easily is fine by me. Sometimes I enjoy these mind games with Danny. And there is indeed a feeling of satisfaction when I get him to actually turn in a half-decent piece of schoolwork. But today is not the day for it. I feel tired from my broken night's sleep, and on edge. Like I am waiting for something to happen. Something bad. Something irretrievable.

I try to concentrate on the text. "Okay, so we were talking about what the main characters represent, Ralph, Jack, Simon—"

He shrugs. "Simon was a waste of space from the start."

"Why's that?"

"Deadweight. A sap. He deserved to die."

"*Deserved* it? How?"

"All right. He was no loss, okay? Jack was right. If they were going to survive on the island, they had to forget all that civilized crap."

"But the whole point of the novel is that if we resort to savagery society falls apart."

"Maybe it should. It's all fake, anyway. That's what the book's really saying. We're all just pretending to be civilized, when, deep down, we're not."

I smile, even though I can feel a knot of discomfort building inside. Probably just indigestion again. "Well, it's an interesting viewpoint."

My watch beeps. I always set an alarm to mark the end of our session.

"Okay. Well, that's all for today." I gather up my textbooks. "I shall look forward to reading more about this theory in your next essay, Danny."

He stands and picks up his duffel bag. "Later, sir."

"Same time next week."

As he saunters from the classroom, I find myself saying, "And I suppose in your new version of society you would be one of the survivors, Danny?"

"'Course." He gives me an odd look. "But don't worry, sir. You would be, too."

THE PARK IS the longer route back from school; it isn't even a particularly warm day, but I decide to take a detour, anyway. A little stroll down memory lane.

The riverside walk is pretty, with rolling fields to one side and, past this, a distant view of the cathedral, although it's currently half shrouded in scaffolding, as it has been for several years. It took four hundred years to build the famous spire from scratch, with no proper tools or machinery. I can't help thinking it will take longer, using the wonders of modern technology, to restore it.

Despite this picturesque setting, whenever I walk by the river I find my eyes drawn to the fast-flowing, brown water. Thinking about how cold it must be. How unforgiving the currents are. Mostly, I still think about Sean Cooper, slipping beneath the surface as he tried to reach his bike. The bike that no one ever claimed responsibility for stealing.

To my left is the new recreation area. A couple of boys clatter skateboards up and down the skate park; a mum pushes a giggling toddler on a merry-go-round; and a solitary teenage girl sits on the swings. Her head is down and her hair falls over her face in a shiny curtain. Brown hair, not red. But the way she sits there, locked in her own hard shell of self-composure, reminds me momentarily of Nicky.

I remember another day, that summer. A small moment, almost lost in the jumbled haze of other memories. Mum had sent me into town to pick up some shopping. I was walking back through the park when I spotted Nicky in the playground. She sat alone on the swings, staring down at her lap. I almost called out to her: *Hey, Nicky!*

But something stopped me. Perhaps the way she was just silently rocking, back and forth. I stole closer. She held something in her hand. It glinted silver in the sunlight—and I recognized the small crucifix she normally wore around her neck. I watched as she raised it up . . . and then jabbed it into the soft flesh of her thigh. Again and again and again.

I backed away and hurried home. I never told Nicky, or anyone, what I saw that day. But it stayed with me. The way she drove the crucifix into her leg. Over and over. Probably drawing blood. But she never made a sound, not even a whimper.

The girl in the park looks up, tucks her hair behind one ear. Multiple silver hoops glint in the lobe, and a large metal ring protrudes from her nose. She is older than I first thought, probably at college. Still, I am acutely aware that I am a middle-aged man, rather eccentric in his appearance, staring at a teenage girl in a child's playground.

I put my head down and walk on, more briskly. My phone buzzes in my pocket. I pull it out, expecting it to be my mum. It isn't. It's Chloe.

"Yes?"

"Nice greeting. You should work on your telephone manner."

"Sorry. I'm just a bit . . . Sorry, what is it?"

"Your mate left his wallet here."

"Mickey?"

"Yeah, found it under the hall table just after you left. Must have fallen out of his jacket."

I frown. It's lunchtime. Surely Mickey must have realized his wallet is missing by now. But then, he was pretty drunk last night. Maybe he's still sleeping it off at his hotel.

"Right. Well, I'll give him a call, let him know. Thanks."

"Okay."

Then something occurs to me.

"Can you get Mickey's wallet and look inside?"

"Hang on."

I hear her moving about and then she comes back to the phone.

"Okay. Cash—about twenty quid—credit cards, bank cards, receipts, driving license."

"His hotel-room key card?"

"Oh, yeah. That, too."

His key card. The card he needed to get into his room. Of course, I'm sure a member of staff would have been happy to issue another one, if he had some form of ID on him . . .

As if echoing my thoughts, Chloe says, "Does this mean he didn't get back to his hotel last night?"

"I don't know," I say. "He could have slept in his car, I suppose."

But why didn't he call me? And even if he didn't want to bother me last night, why hasn't he called this morning?

"Hope he's not lying in a ditch somewhere," Chloe says.

"Why the hell would you say that?"

I immediately regret snapping. I can almost hear her bristle at the other end of the phone.

"What *is* it with you this morning? Did you get out of the side of bed marked 'Twatsville'?"

"I'm sorry," I say. "I'm just tired."

"Fine," she says in a tone which tells me it most certainly is not. "What are you going to do about your friend?"

"I'll give him a call. If I can't get hold of him, I'll drop the wallet round to the hotel. Check he's okay."

"I'll leave it on the hall table."

"You're going out?"

"Bingo, Sherlock. My incredible social life, remember?"

"Okay, well, I'll see you later."

"I sincerely hope not."

She ends the call and I'm left wondering if that was a joke about staying out late or a genuine expression of her desire not to see such a bad-tempered loon as me ever again.

I sigh, and try Mickey's number. It goes straight to voicemail: "Hi, this is Mickey. I can't get to the phone right now, so do what you need to do after the beep."

I don't bother to leave a message. I retrace my steps, out of the park, and take the shorter route back home, trying to ignore the vague disquiet rumbling in the pit of my stomach. It's probably nothing. Mickey probably stumbled back to the hotel, persuaded the staff to give him a new key card and is just sleeping off his hangover. By the time I get there, he'll be tucking into lunch. Absolutely, perfectly, bloody fine.

I tell myself this several times, with more and more conviction.

And each time, I believe it less and less.

THE TRAVELODGE IS an ugly building squatting next door to a rundown Little Chef. I would have thought Mickey could have afforded to stay somewhere better, but I guess it's convenient.

I try Mickey's number twice more on the way. Both times, his phone goes to voicemail. My bad feeling gradually notches up.

I park and walk into reception. A young man with ginger hair in a bristly ponytail and gaping holes in his ears stands behind the desk, looking uncomfortable in a too-tight shirt and badly done-up tie. A badge pinned to his lapel informs me that his name is "Duds," which seems less of a name and more an admission of a chronic fault.

"Hello. Checking in?"

"Actually, no. I'm here to meet a friend of mine."

"Right."

"Mickey Cooper. I believe he checked in yesterday?"

"Okay."

He continues to look at me vaguely.

"So," I labor on, "would you be able to check if he's here?"

"Can't you call him?"

"He's not answering, and the thing is—" I pull the wallet out of my pocket. "He left this at my house last night. It's got his room key card and all his credit cards in."

I wait for the significance of this to dawn. Moss grows around my feet. Glaciers form and melt.

"I'm sorry," he says eventually. "I don't understand."

"I'm *asking* if you could check that he got back here okay last night. I'm worried about him."

"Oh, well, I wasn't on last night. That was Georgia."

"Right. Well, would there be anything on the computer?" I nod to the ancient-looking PC squatting on an untidy desk in one corner. "He would have had to ask for a new room key card. There must be some record?"

"Well, I suppose I could check."

"I suppose you could."

The sarcasm drips right over his head. He plonks himself down at the desk and taps a few keys.

Then he turns. "No. Nothing."

"Well, could you call Georgia?"

He debates this with himself. I sense that getting Duds to do anything even slightly outside of his job remit is a gargantuan effort. To be honest, it looks as if even breathing is a gargantuan effort for Duds.

"Please?" I say.

A deep sigh. "Okay."

He picks up the phone. "Hello. George?"

I wait.

"Last night, did some bloke called Mickey Cooper come back without his key card? You might have had to replace it? Right. Okay. Thanks."

He puts down the phone and walks back to the desk.

"And?" I prompt.

"Nah. Your mate didn't come back here last night."

1986

I'd always imagined funerals were held on gray, rainy days with people in black huddled under umbrellas.

The sun shone on the morning of Sean Cooper's funeral—at least for the start of it. And no one wore black. His family had asked that people wear blue or red. Sean's favorite colors. The colors of the school football team. Quite a few kids came in the school kit.

Mum chose me a new pale blue shirt, with a red tie and dark trousers.

"You still need to look smart, Eddie. To pay your respects."

I didn't really want to pay my respects to Sean Cooper. Didn't really want to go to his funeral at all. I had never been to a funeral before. Not that I remembered. Apparently, my mum and dad had taken me to my grandad's, but I was just a baby then and, besides, Grandad was old. You expected old people to die. They even smelled a bit like they were already half dead. Kind of musty and stale.

Death happened to other people, not kids like us, not people we knew. Death was abstract and distant. Sean Cooper's funeral was probably the first time I understood that death is only ever a cool, sour breath away. His greatest trick is making you think he isn't there. And death has a lot of tricks up his cold, dark sleeve.

. . .

THE CHURCH WAS only a ten-minute walk from our house. I wished it was longer. I dragged my feet, pulled at my shirt collar. Mum wore the same blue dress she had worn to Fat Gav's party, but with a red jacket on top. Dad wore long trousers for once, which I was thankful for, and a shirt with red flowers on (which I wasn't).

We reached the gates to the churchyard at the same time as Hoppo and his mum. We didn't see Hoppo's mum often. Not unless she was out in her car, cleaning. Today she had pulled her straggly hair into a bun. She wore a shapeless blue dress and these really old, ratty-looking sandals on her feet. It sounds horrible to say, but I was glad she wasn't my mum, looking like that.

Hoppo wore a red T-shirt and blue school trousers with black shoes. His thick dark hair had been slicked to one side. He looked different for Hoppo. Not just the hair and smart clothes. He looked tense, worried. He held Murphy on a lead.

"Hello, David. Hello, Gwen," Mum said.

I never knew Gwen was Hoppo's mum's name. Mum was always good with names. Dad not so much. He used to joke, before the Alzheimer's got too bad, that forgetting people's names was nothing new, even before he started going loopy.

"Hello, Mr. and Mrs. Adams," Hoppo said.

"Hello," his mum said, in a faint, weedy voice. She always spoke like she was apologizing for something.

"How are you?" Mum asked, in the polite tone she used when she didn't really want to know.

Hoppo's mum didn't get the hint. "Not so good," she said. "I mean, this is all so terrible, and then Murphy's been ill all night."

"Oh dear," Dad said, with genuine feeling.

I bent down to fuss Murphy. He gave a tired wag and sank to the ground. He seemed as reluctant to be here as the rest of us.

"Is that why you've brought him along?" Dad asked.

Hoppo nodded. "We didn't want to leave him at home. He'll just start messing. And if we put him in the garden he gets over the fence and gets out. So we thought we'd tie him up out here."

Dad nodded. "Well, that seems like a good idea." He patted Murphy on the head. "Poor old fella. Getting old, aren't you?"

"So," Mum said, "I suppose we'd better go in."

Hoppo bent down and hugged Murphy. The old dog ran a big, wet tongue up his face.

"Good boy," he whispered. "Bye."

We all filed through the church gate toward the entrance. More people were milling about outside, some smoking furtively. I spotted Fat Gav and his parents. Nicky stood at the entrance to the church, alongside Reverend Martin. She held a thick sheaf of papers. Hymn sheets, I guessed.

I felt myself tense. It was the first time that Mum and Dad and Reverend Martin had come face to face since the party, and the parcel. As he saw us, the reverend smiled.

"Mr. and Mrs. Adams, Eddie. Thank you for coming on this terribly sad day."

He held out a hand. Dad didn't shake it. The smile remained on the reverend's face, but I could see a flash of something less pleasant in his eyes.

"Please, take a hymn sheet and find a seat inside."

We took the hymn sheets. Nicky gave me a small, mute nod, and we walked slowly into the church.

It was cold inside, cold enough to make me shiver a little. Dark, too. It took my eyes a moment to adjust. A few people were already seated. I knew some of the kids from school. A few teachers, too, and Mr. Halloran. Impossible to miss, with his shock of white hair. Today, he wore a red shirt for a change. His hat sat on his lap. As he saw me enter with Mum and Dad, he gave me a small smile. Everyone's smiles were small and weird that day, like no one really knew what to do with their faces.

We sat and waited, and then the reverend and Nicky walked in and music started to play. It was a tune I had heard but couldn't quite place. Not a hymn or anything. A modern song, a slow one. Somehow, even though it was modern, I wasn't sure it was right for Sean, who liked to listen to Iron Maiden.

We all bowed our heads as they brought the coffin in. Metal Mickey and his mum and dad walked behind it. It was the first time we had seen Metal Mickey since the accident. His mum and dad had kept him off school, and then they went away, to stay with his grandparents.

Metal Mickey didn't look at the coffin. He stared straight ahead, his whole body rigid. The effort of walking, breathing and not crying seemed to take all his concentration. He was about halfway down the church when he just stopped. The man behind him almost walked into his back. There was a moment of confusion, and then Metal Mickey turned and ran out of the church.

Everyone looked at each other, except his mum and dad, who barely seemed to notice he had gone. They continued to shuffle forward like zombies, cocooned in their own hard shell of grief. No one went after Metal Mickey. I glanced at Mum, but she just gave a small shake of her head and squeezed my hand.

I think that's what got to me. Seeing Metal Mickey so upset again, about a boy most of us hated but who was still his brother. Maybe Sean wasn't always a mean bully all the time. Maybe when he was little he played with Metal Mickey. Maybe they went to the park together, shared Lego bricks and bathtime.

And now he was lying in a cold, dark coffin covered with flowers that smelled too strong while someone played music he would have hated, and he couldn't tell them because he would never tell anyone anything ever again.

I swallowed down a hard lump in my throat and blinked fast. Mum nudged my arm, and we all sat down. The music stopped and Reverend Martin stood up and said stuff about Sean Cooper and God. Most of it didn't make much sense. Stuff about heaven having another angel and how God wanted Sean Cooper more than the people on Earth did. Looking at his mum and dad leaning against each other and crying so hard they looked like they might just break into pieces, I didn't think so.

Reverend Martin had almost finished when there was a big bang and a rush of air that caused a few hymn sheets to flutter to the floor. Most of the people in the church turned, including me.

The church doors swung open. To start with, I thought Metal Mickey had come back. But then I realized that, haloed in the light, I could make out two figures. As they walked farther into the church, I recognized them: Waltzer Girl's blond friend and the policeman who had come to our house, PC Thomas. (Later I would learn her name was Hannah and that PC Thomas was her dad.)

For a moment, I wondered if the blond girl was in trouble. PC Thomas held her arm tightly and half marched, half dragged her down the aisle. A murmur ran around the church.

Metal Mickey's mum whispered something to his dad. He stood up. His face looked hard and angry. From the pulpit, Reverend Martin said, "If you are here to pay your respects to the deceased, we are about to proceed to the graveside."

PC Thomas and the blond girl stopped. He looked around the church at the rest of us. No one met his gaze. We all sat, hushed and curious, yet not wanting to seem it. The blond girl just stared down at the ground, as if wishing it would swallow her up, like it was about to do to Sean Cooper.

"Respects?" PC Thomas said slowly. "No. I don't think I'll be paying my respects." Then he spat on the floor, right in front of the coffin. "Not to the boy who *raped* my daughter."

The gasp rose from the pews right up to the church rafters. I think a small noise even escaped my own mouth. *Raped?* I didn't know much about what "rape" meant (I guess, in many ways, I was pretty naïve for twelve), but I knew it was about making a girl do something she didn't want to do, and I knew it was bad.

"*You lying bastard!*" Metal Mickey's dad cried.

"A bastard?" PC Thomas snarled. "I'll tell you what's a bastard." He pointed back at his daughter. "That child she's carrying."

Another gasp. Reverend Martin's face looked like it was about to slide right off his skull. He opened his mouth, but before he could say anything there was this huge roar and Metal Mickey's dad charged forward and launched himself at PC Thomas.

Metal Mickey's dad wasn't big, but he was stocky and fast and he caught PC Thomas off guard. The policeman swayed but managed to keep his balance. The pair of them wobbled back and forth, grappling in each other's arms like they were doing some awful, weird dance. Then PC Thomas pulled away. He aimed a blow at Metal Mickey's dad's head. Somehow, Metal Mickey's dad dodged it and threw his own fist back. This one connected, and PC Thomas staggered backward.

I could see what was about to happen an instant before it actually did. I think most of the mourners saw it, too. There were screams, and someone shouted, "*Noooo!*," just as PC Thomas crashed into Sean Cooper's coffin, dislodging it from its place in front of the pulpit and sending it crashing to the stone floor.

I'm not sure if I imagined the next bit, because surely the lid of the coffin must have been securely fastened? I mean, it wasn't like they wanted it to slide off when they were putting it in the grave. But just as the coffin hit the ground with a horrible, splintering crunch that reminded me a bit too much that Sean Cooper's bones were rattling around inside, the lid shifted slightly and I caught a fleeting glimpse of one pale white hand.

Or maybe I didn't. Maybe it was my crazy, stupid imagination again. It all happened so quickly. Almost as soon as the coffin hit the floor, screams echoing around the church, several men rushed over to pick it up and put it back on its plinth.

PC Thomas stood up unsteadily. Metal Mickey's dad looked just as unsteady. He raised his arm like he might just hit PC Thomas again, then instead turned and threw himself on to the coffin and began to cry. Great, heaving, bellowing sobs.

PC Thomas looked around. He seemed a bit dazed, like he was waking from some terrible dream. His fists clenched and unclenched. He ran a hand through his dark hair, which was all sweaty and disheveled. A bruise bloomed by his right eye.

"Dad, please?" A small whisper from the blond girl.

PC Thomas looked at her, then grabbed her hand again and pulled her back up the church aisle. At the end he turned. "This is not over," he croaked. And then they were gone.

The whole incident could only have taken three or four minutes, but it felt like much longer. Reverend Martin cleared his throat loudly, but you could still only just hear him over Metal Mickey's dad wailing.

"I am so terribly sorry for that interruption. We will now proceed outside for the rest of the service. If the mourners could please stand."

There was more music. Some of Metal Mickey's family dragged his dad away from the coffin, and we all had to walk outside again, to the graveyard.

I had barely stepped out of the church when I felt the first drop of water on my head. I looked up. The blue had been scoured from the sky by Brillo-gray clouds, now starting to drip rain on to the coffin and the mourners.

People hadn't brought umbrellas, so we all huddled, in our bright red and blue, shoulders hunched against the rapidly increasing drizzle. I shivered slightly as the coffin was lowered slowly into the ground. They had taken away the flowers. As if to say that nothing bright and alive should be lowered into that deep, dark hole.

I thought the fight inside had been the worst bit of the funeral, but I was wrong. This was the worst bit. The rattle and scrape of earth on the wooden coffin lid. The smell of damp dirt under the waning warmth of the September sun. Looking into that gaping chasm in the ground and knowing there was no coming back from this. No excuses, no get-out clause, no note your mum could write to the teacher. Death was final and absolute and there was nothing anyone could do to change it.

Eventually, it was over and we all began to file away from the graveside. The church hall had been booked for people to eat sandwiches and drink afterward. "A wake," it was called, my mum said.

We had almost reached the gate when someone Mum and Dad

knew stopped to talk to them. Fat Gav and his family were just behind them, talking to Hoppo's mum. I could see Metal Mickey's family, but not Metal Mickey. I guess he must have been somewhere around.

I found myself standing, a little lost, on the edge of the graveyard.

"Hello, Eddie."

I turned. Mr. Halloran walked over. He'd put his hat on to keep off the rain and held a packet of cigarettes in his hand. I'd never seen him smoke, but I remembered the ashtray in his cottage.

"Hello, sir."

"How are you feeling?"

I shrugged. "I don't know really."

He had this knack, that most adults don't, of making you answer him honestly.

"That's okay. You don't have to feel sad."

I hesitated. I wasn't quite sure what to say to that.

"You can't feel sad about everyone who dies." He lowered his voice. "Sean Cooper was a bully. Just because he's dead, it doesn't change that. It doesn't mean what happened to him isn't tragic either."

"Because he was just a kid?"

"No. Because he never got the chance to change."

I nodded, then asked, "Is it true what the policeman said?"

"About Sean Cooper and his daughter?"

I gave a small nod.

Mr. Halloran looked at his cigarettes. I think he really wanted to light one but probably didn't think he should in the churchyard. "Sean Cooper was not a nice young man. What he did to you—some people would give that the same name."

I felt my cheeks redden. I didn't want to think about that. As if sensing this, Mr. Halloran continued, "But did he do what the policeman accused him of? No, I don't believe that's true."

"Why?"

"I don't believe that young lady was Sean Cooper's type."

"Oh." I wasn't quite sure what he was saying.

He shook his head. "Forget it. But don't worry about Sean Cooper anymore. He can't hurt you now."

I thought about stones at my window, bluey-gray skin in moonlight.

"Hey, Shitface."

I wasn't so sure.

But I said, "No, sir. I mean, yes, sir."

"Good boy." He smiled and walked away.

I was still trying to digest all of this when someone grabbed my arm. I spun around. Hoppo stood in front of me. His hair had already fallen out of its combed-back style and his shirt was half untucked. He held Murphy's lead and collar. But there was no Murphy.

"What's happened?"

He stared at me, wild-eyed. "Murphy. He's gone."

"He slipped his collar?"

"I don't know. He never has before. It's not loose or anything . . ."

"D'you think he'll run home?" I asked.

Hoppo shook his head. "I don't know. He's old and his sight and smell aren't so good." I could see he was trying not to panic.

"But he's slow," I said. "So he can't have gone far."

I looked around. The adults were still talking, Fat Gav was too far away to get his attention. I still couldn't see Metal Mickey . . . but I saw something else.

Drawn on a flat memorial stone near the church gates. Already starting to fade and blur in the rain, but it caught my attention, because it was wrong. Out of place, yet also familiar. I walked closer. My limbs prickled with goosebumps and my scalp felt too tight for my skull.

A white chalk man. Arms raised, a small "o" for his mouth, like he was crying out. And he wasn't alone. Next to him, someone had drawn a crude, white chalk dog. I suddenly had a bad feeling. A very bad feeling.

Look out for the chalk men.

"What is it?" Hoppo asked.

"Nothing." I stood up quickly. "We should go and find Murphy. Now."

"David, Eddie. What's wrong?" Mum and Dad walked up, along with Hoppo's mum.

"It's Murphy," I said. "He's . . . run off."

"Oh, no!" Hoppo's mum raised a hand to her face.

Hoppo just clenched the leash tighter.

"Mum, we have to go and look for him," I said.

"Eddie—" Mum started to say.

"*Please?*" I pleaded.

I saw her thinking about it. She didn't look happy. She looked pale and tense. But then, I guess it *was* a funeral. Dad laid a hand on her arm and gave a small nod.

"Okay," Mum said. "You go and look for Murphy. You can meet us at the church hall when you've found him."

"Thanks."

"Go on. Off you run."

We scuttled off down the road, calling out Murphy's name, which was probably pointless, because Murphy was pretty deaf.

"Should we check your house first, just in case?" I asked.

Hoppo nodded. "I guess."

Hoppo lived on the other side of town, on a narrow street of terraced houses. It was the sort of street where men sat on their front steps drinking cans of lager, kids in nappies played on the curb and there was always a dog barking. I never really thought about it at the time, but perhaps that was why we never hung out at Hoppo's much. The rest of us all lived in pretty okay houses. Mine might have been a bit ramshackle and old-fashioned, but it was still on a nice road with verges and trees and stuff.

It would be kind to say Hoppo's was one of the better houses on the street, but it wasn't. Yellowed net curtains hung in the windows, the paint had all but peeled off the front door and an assortment of broken pots, garden gnomes and an old deckchair cluttered the tiny front yard.

Inside was just as chaotic. I remember thinking, for a cleaner, Hoppo's mum didn't keep their own house very clean. There was stuff piled everywhere, and all in odd places: discount boxes of cereal piled on top of the TV in the living room, loo rolls forming a small mountain in the hall, industrial tubs of bleach and boxes of slug pellets stacked on the kitchen table. It smelled really bad of dog, too. I loved Murphy, but the way he smelled was not his finest point.

Hoppo ran down the side of the house to the back garden and then out again, shaking his head.

"Okay," I said. "Well, let's check the park. He might have gone there instead."

He nodded, but I could see that he was fighting back tears. "He's never done this before."

"It'll be all right," I told him, which was a stupid thing to say, because it wasn't going to be. It was going to be about as far from all right as it could be.

WE FOUND HIM curled up under a bush, not far from the playground. I guess he must have tried to find some shelter. The rain was coming down really hard now. Hoppo's hair hung in thick wet tendrils, like seaweed, and my shirt was plastered to my body. My shoes were leaking, too, and I squelched with every step as we ran toward Murphy.

From a distance, it looked like he was sleeping. It was only when you got closer that you could see the labored rise and fall of his big chest and hear the rough rasp of his breathing. When you got properly close, right next to him, you could see where he had been sick. All around. Not normal sick. It was thick, tarry and black, because of all the blood in it. And poison.

I still remember the smell, and the look in his huge brown eyes as we knelt beside him. They were so confused. And yet so grateful. Like we were going to make everything all right. But we couldn't.

For the second time that day, I learned that there are some things you can never put right.

We tried to pick him up and carry him. Hoppo knew where there was a vet's in town. But Murphy was so heavy and his mass of steaming, wet fur made him heavier. We hadn't even made it out of the park when he began to cough and retch again. We laid him back down on the wet grass.

"Maybe I could run to the vet's, fetch someone back?" I said.

Hoppo just shook his head and said in a hoarse, choked voice, "No. It's no good."

He buried his face in Murphy's thick, sodden fur, clinging to that dog like he was trying to stop him from leaving, from falling from this world to the next.

But of course no one, not even the person who loves you most in the world, can stop that. All we could do was try to comfort him, whisper softly in his floppy ears and try to wish away all the pain. Eventually, that must have been enough, because Murphy took one final hacking breath, and then no more.

Hoppo sobbed into his still body. I tried to hold back the tears but couldn't stop them streaming down my face. Later, I would think that we cried more for a dead dog that day than we ever did for Metal Mickey's brother. And that would come back to bite us, too.

Finally, we summoned up the strength to try to carry him back to Hoppo's house. It was the first time I had ever really touched anything dead. He was even heavier than before, I thought. *Dead-weight.* It took us the best part of half an hour, with a few people stopping to watch but none offering to help.

We laid him down on his bed in the kitchen.

"What will you do with him?" I asked.

"Bury him," Hoppo said, as if this was obvious.

"Yourself?"

"He's my dog."

I didn't know what to say, so I didn't say anything.

"You should get back," Hoppo said. "To the wake thing."

Part of me felt I should offer to stay and help him, but a bigger part just wanted to get away.

"Okay."

I turned.

"Eddie?"

"Yeah?"

"When I find out who did this, I'm going to kill them."

I never forgot the look in his eyes when he said that. Maybe that's why I didn't tell him about the chalk man and dog. Or about the fact that I never saw Metal Mickey come back after he ran out of the church.

2016

I don't consider myself an alcoholic. In the same way that I don't consider myself a hoarder. I am a man who enjoys a drink, and who collects things.

I don't drink every day and I do not, usually, turn up to school smelling of booze. Although it has happened. Thankfully, it did not get back to our head, but it did warrant a friendly word from a fellow teacher:

"Ed, go home, have a shower and buy some mouthwash. And in the future, stick to weekend benders."

In truth, I drink more than I should, more often than I should. Today, I feel the urge. A tightness in my throat. A dryness on my lips that no amount of licking will dispel. I don't just need a drink. I need *to* drink. A subtle tic of grammar. A huge difference of intention.

I call into the supermarket and select a couple of sturdy reds from the wine aisle. Then I pick up a bottle of good bourbon and wheel my cart to the self-checkout. I make some small talk with the woman supervising the tills and deposit the bottles in my car. I arrive back home just after six, select some old vinyls I haven't played for a while and pour my first glass of wine.

That's when the front door slams, hard enough to cause the candlesticks on the mantelpiece to shudder and my full drink to wobble precariously on the table.

"Chloe?"

I presume it must be. I locked the doors, and no one else has a key. But Chloe doesn't normally slam doors. If anything, Chloe slinks in like a cat, or some kind of supernatural mist.

I look longingly at my glass of wine and then, with a resentful sigh, I stand and walk into the kitchen, where I can now hear her noisily opening and closing the fridge, and clinking glasses. There's another sound, too. One I'm not so familiar with.

It takes me a moment, and then it sinks in. Chloe is crying.

I'm not good with crying. I don't do it much myself. Not even at my dad's funeral. I don't like the mess, the snot, the noise. No one looks attractive crying. Even worse, if a woman is crying, then she will almost certainly need comforting. I'm not good at comforting either.

I hesitate at the kitchen door. Then I hear Chloe say: "Oh, for fuck's sake, Ed. Yes, I'm crying. Either come in and deal with it, or fuck off."

I push the door open. Chloe sits at the kitchen table. A bottle of gin and a large tumbler sit in front of her. No tonic. Her hair is more disheveled than usual and black mascara streaks her cheeks.

"I won't bother asking if you're all right . . ."

"Good. I might just ram this gin bottle up your arse."

"Do you want to talk about it?"

"Not really."

"Okay." I hover by the table. "Is there anything I can do?"

"Sit down and have a drink."

While that has been my intention all along tonight, gin isn't really my drink of choice, but I sense the offer is non-negotiable. I take a glass out of the cupboard and let Chloe pour me a large measure.

She shoves it across the table, unsteadily. I'm guessing this drink is not her first, or second, or third. This is unusual. Chloe likes to go out. Chloe likes a drink. But I don't think I've ever seen her really drunk.

"So," she says, slurring slightly. "How was your day?"

"Well, I tried to report my friend missing to the police."

"And?"

"Despite the fact that he didn't return to his hotel last night, hasn't got his wallet or bank cards and isn't answering his phone, apparently he can't be officially declared missing until no one has seen him for twenty-four hours."

"No shit."

"Yes shit."

"You think something's happened to him?"

She sounds genuinely concerned.

I take a gulp of gin. "I don't know—"

"Maybe he went home."

"Maybe."

"So what are you going to do?"

"Well, I suppose I have to go back to the police station tomorrow."

She stares into her glass. "Friends, eh? More trouble than they're worth. Although not as bad as family."

"I suppose," I say cautiously.

"Oh, trust me. Friends, you can cut loose. Family, you never lose. They're always there, in the background, screwing with your mind."

She throws back the gin and pours another.

Chloe has never talked about her personal life before and I've never asked. It's like with kids. If they want to tell you something, they'll tell you. If you have to ask, you'll send them scuttling back inside their shell.

Of course, I *have* wondered. For a while, I thought her presence in my home might be something to do with a boyfriend, a bad break-up. After all, there are plenty of house-shares in Anderbury, with people closer to her age and outlook. You do not choose the big, spooky old house with the strange, single man unless you have a reason for wanting solitude and privacy.

But Chloe has never told, so I've never pushed it, scared perhaps that I might drive her away. Finding a lodger to fill my spare room is one thing. Finding a companion to fill my loneliness is quite another.

I take a second sip of gin, but the desire to drink is fading fast. There's nothing like dealing with a drunk to put you off the idea of getting wasted yourself.

"Well," I say. "Both family and friendships can be difficult . . ."

"Am I your friend, Ed?"

The question throws me. Chloe stares at me with an earnest, unfocused stare, facial muscles a little lazy, lips parted.

I swallow. "I hope so."

She smiles. "Good. Because I would never do anything to hurt you. I want you to know that."

"I know," I say, even though I don't. Not really. People can hurt you without even realizing they're doing it. Chloe hurts me a little bit every day just by existing. And that's okay.

"Good." She squeezes my hand, and I'm alarmed to see her eyes fill with tears again. She wipes at her face. "Christ, I'm such a fucking idiot."

She takes another swig of her drink, and then says, "I should tell you something . . ."

I don't like those words. Nothing good ever comes of a sentence that starts that way. Just like, "We should talk . . ."

"Chloe," I say.

But I am saved, quite literally, by the bell. Someone is at the front door. I don't get many visitors, and certainly not ones who arrive unannounced.

"Who the fuck is that?" Chloe says with her customary warmth and good cheer.

"I don't know."

I shuffle wearily to the front door and open it. Two men in gray suits stand outside. I know, even before they open their mouths, that they are police. There's just something about them. The tired faces. The bad haircuts. The cheap shoes.

"Mr. Adams?" the taller, dark-haired one asks.

"Yes?"

"I'm DI Furniss. This is Sergeant Danks. You came to the station this afternoon to file a missing person's report for a friend of yours, Mick Cooper?"

"I tried. I was told he wasn't officially missing."

"Right. We're sorry about that," the shorter, bald one says. "Could we come in?"

I want to ask why, but as they will end up coming in anyway it doesn't seem worth it. I stand aside. "Of course."

They walk past me into the hallway and I shut the door. "Just through here."

Out of habit, I take them into the kitchen. As soon as I see Chloe, I realize this might have been a mistake. She is still in her "going out" clothes. These consist of a skintight black vest decorated with skulls, a tiny Lycra miniskirt, fishnet tights and Doc Martens.

She glances up at the policemen. "Ooh, company, how nice."

"This is Chloe, my lodger. And friend."

The pair are too professional even to raise an eyebrow, but I'm sure I know what they're thinking. Older man with a pretty young thing living in his house. I'm either sleeping with her, or I am just an old lech. Sadly, it is the latter.

"Can I get you anything?" I say. "Tea, coffee?"

"Gin?" Chloe holds up the bottle.

"Afraid we're on duty, miss," Furniss says.

"Okay," I say. "Err, well, please, have a seat."

They glance at each other.

"Actually, Mr. Adams, it might be better if we spoke to you alone."

I glance at Chloe. "If you don't mind?"

"Well, *excuse* me." She grabs the bottle and the glass. "I'll be next door, if you need me."

She gives the two police officers a dark look and slinks from the room.

They sit, chairs scraping, and I perch awkwardly at the head of the table. "So can I ask what this is about, exactly? I told the duty sergeant everything I could earlier."

"I know it probably feels like you're repeating yourself, but if you could just tell us everything again, in detail?"

Danks takes out his pen.

"Well, Mickey left here yesterday evening."

"Sorry, could you go back a little further? Why was he here? I understand he lives in Oxford?"

"Well, he's an old friend and he was coming back to Anderbury and wanted to meet up."

"How old?"

"We were childhood friends."

"And you've kept in touch?"

"Not really. But sometimes it's nice to catch up."

They both nod.

"Anyway, he came round for dinner."

"And what time was this?"

"He arrived at about seven fifteen."

"He drove?"

"No, he walked. The hotel he's staying in isn't far and I suppose he thought he'd have a drink."

"How much would you say he drank?"

"Well"—I think back to the empty beer bottles in the recycling—"you know how it is. You're eating, talking . . . maybe six or seven beers."

"A fair amount, then."

"I suppose."

"So what sort of state would you say he was in when he left?"

"Well, he wasn't falling over and slurring, but he was quite drunk."

"And you let him walk back to the hotel?"

"I offered to call him a taxi, but he said the walk would help sober him up."

"Right. And what time would you say this was?"

"About ten, ten thirty. Not that late."

"And that was the last time you saw him that evening?"

"Yes."

"You handed his wallet in to the duty sergeant?"

With some bloody difficulty. She wanted me to keep hold of it, but I was insistent.

"Yes."

"How did you come to be in possession of it?"

"Mickey must have forgotten it when he left my house."

"And you didn't try to give it back to him last night?"

"I didn't realize until today. Chloe found it and called me."

"And what time was this?"

"Around lunchtime. I tried to call Mickey to let him know he'd left his wallet, but he didn't reply."

More scribbling.

"So that was when you went to the hotel to see if your friend was okay?"

"Yes. And they told me he hadn't come back last night. That's when I decided to go to the police."

More nods. Then Furniss asks, "How would you say your friend seemed last night?"

"Fine . . . erm, okay."

"He was in good spirits?"

"Well, I suppose so."

"What was the purpose of his visit?"

"Can I ask if that's relevant?"

"Well, all those years with no contact, then a visit out of the blue. It's a bit strange."

"People are strange, as Jim Morrison might say."

They look at me blankly. Not classic rock fans.

"Look," I say, "it was a social call. We talked about a lot of things—what we were both up to. Work. Nothing of any real significance. Now, can I please ask what all these questions are about? Has something happened to Mickey?"

They seem to consider my question and then Danks closes his notebook.

"A body was found today that matches the description of your friend, Mickey Cooper."

A body. Mickey. I try to force this information down. It sticks in my throat. I can't speak. It's hard to breathe.

"Are you okay, sir?"

"I . . . I don't know. It's a shock. What happened?"

"We recovered his body from the river."

"I bet he's all bloated and green and fish have eaten his eyeballs."

"Mickey drowned?"

"We're still trying to establish the exact circumstances of your friend's death."

"If he fell in the river, what is there to establish?"

Something seems to pass between them.

"Old Meadows Park is in the opposite direction to your friend's hotel?"

"Well, yes."

"So, why was he there?"

"Maybe he decided to walk a bit farther to sober up? Or maybe he went the wrong way?"

"Maybe."

They sound skeptical.

"You don't think Mickey's death was an accident?"

"On the contrary, I'm sure that's the most likely explanation. However, we do have to explore all other options."

"Like?"

"Is there anyone who might have wanted to do Mickey harm?"

I feel a pulse begin to beat at the side of my head. Anyone who would have wanted to do Mickey harm? Well, yes, I can think of at least one person, but that person is hardly in a position to go running around parks at night, pushing Mickey in the river.

"No, I can't think of anyone." In a slightly firmer voice I add, "Anderbury is a quiet town. I can't imagine anyone hurting Mickey."

They both nod. "I'm sure you're right. This is probably a very sad, unfortunate accident."

Just like his brother, I think. Sad, unfortunate and a little too much of a coincidence . . .

"We're sorry to have to bring you this news, Mr. Adams."

"It's okay. It's your job."

They push their chairs back. I stand to show them out.

"There was one other thing?"

Of course. There always is. "Yes?"

"We found an item on your friend that was a little confusing. We wondered if you might be able to shed some light on it?"

"If I can."

Furniss takes a clear plastic bag out of his pocket. He lays it on the table.

Inside the bag: a piece of paper with a stick hangman drawn on it, and a single piece of white chalk.

1986

"Oh, ye of little faith."

My dad used to say that sometimes to my mum when she didn't believe he could do something. It was an in-joke, I guess, because she would always look back at him and say, "No, me of no faith." And they would laugh.

I guess the point was that my parents weren't religious, and they were pretty open about it. I suppose that's why some people in the town viewed them with a bit of suspicion, and why a lot took the side of Reverend Martin over the clinic. Even those who supported Mum didn't want to come out and say it; it was like they would be disagreeing with God or something.

Mum grew thinner that autumn, and older, too. It had never really occurred to me until then that my parents were older than other parents (perhaps because when you're twelve, anyone over twenty is pretty ancient). Mum hadn't had me until she was thirty-six, so she was almost fifty.

Part of it was working extra hard. She seemed to come home later and later each night, leaving Dad to cook tea, which was always interesting, if not always edible. Most of it—I guessed—had to do with the protesters who still circled the clinic's entrance every day. Now about twenty of them. I had seen posters, too, in the windows of some shops in town:

CHOOSE LIFE   STOP THE MURDER
SAY NO TO LEGAL MURDER
JOIN THE ANDERBURY ANGELS

That's what the protesters called themselves, the Anderbury Angels, which I suppose was Reverend Martin's idea. They didn't look much like angels. I always thought of angels as serene and calm. The protesters were red-faced and angry, they shouted and spat. Looking back, I guess, like a lot of radicalized people, they believed they were doing the right thing, for some sort of higher purpose. So much so that they could excuse all the wrong things they did in their cause.

IT WAS OCTOBER by this point. Summer had grabbed its beach towels, buckets and spades and packed up for the season. The chimes of the ice-cream vans had already been replaced by the spit and bang of illicitly bought rockets; the scent of blossom and barbecues by the more acrid smell of bonfires.

Metal Mickey hung out with us less. He had changed since his brother died. Or maybe we just didn't know how to act with him anymore. He was colder, harder. He had always been snide and sarcastic, but now he was even more caustic. He looked different, too. He had grown (although Metal Mickey would never be tall), his features had sharpened and his braces had come off. In a way, he was no longer Metal Mickey, our friend. Suddenly, he was Mickey Cooper, Sean Cooper's brother.

If we were all a bit awkward around him, he and Hoppo seemed particularly at odds. It was the sort of building antagonism that simmered away slowly but was bound, at some point, to boil over into a full-blown fight. And it did. The day we got together to sprinkle Murphy's ashes.

Hoppo hadn't buried him after all. His mum had taken Murphy's body to the vet's to be cremated. Hoppo kept the ashes for a while, then decided he wanted to leave them in the spot where Murphy used to lie, and where he breathed his last, in the park.

We arranged to meet up at the playground at eleven on a Saturday. We sat on the roundabout, Hoppo clutching his little box of Murphy, all of us wrapped up in duffel coats and scarves. It was cold that morning. Bite-through-your-gloves and snap-at-your-face cold. That, and the fact that we were doing a pretty grim job, had all of us feeling down. When Mickey rocked up, fifteen minutes late, Hoppo leapt up.

"Where've you been?"

Mickey shrugged. "Just had stuff to do. Now there's only me at home, Mum has me doing more chores." He said it in his usual combative kind of way.

It sounds cruel, but everything he said always went back to the fact that his brother was dead. Yes, we knew it was sad and tragic and all of that, but I suppose we just wished that he would stop going on about it, every minute of every day.

I saw Hoppo sag a little and relent. "Well, you're here now," he said, in a tone that should have smoothed things over. Like Hoppo always did. But that morning Mickey was having none of it.

"Dunno what your beef is, anyway. S'only a stupid dog."

I almost felt the crackle in the air.

"Murphy was not just a dog."

"Yeah? So what could he do? Talk, do card tricks?"

He was goading Hoppo. We all knew it, Hoppo knew it, but just because you know someone is trying to make you mad doesn't mean you can stop yourself rising to it, although Hoppo did a good job.

"He was my dog and he meant a lot to me."

"Yeah, and my brother meant a lot to *me*."

Fat Gav climbed off the roundabout. "We know, okay. This is different."

"Yeah, you all give a shit about the fact that a stupid dog is dead, but no one gives a shit that my brother is dead."

We all stared at him. No one knew what to say. Because, in a way, he was right.

"See. None of you can even talk about him and yet we're here because of some stupid, dumb, flea-ridden mutt."

"Take that back," Hoppo said.

"Or what?" Mickey grinned and took a step closer to Hoppo. Hoppo was a lot taller than Mickey; stronger, too. But Mickey had this crazy light in his eyes. Just like his brother. And you can't fight crazy. Crazy always wins.

"He was a stupid, dumb, flea-ridden mutt who shat himself all the time and stank. It's not like he would have lived much longer anyway. Someone just put him out of his misery."

I saw Hoppo's fists clench, but I still don't think he would have actually hit Mickey if Mickey hadn't reached forward and knocked the box out of his hand. It hit the concrete floor of the playground and broke open, ashes flying up in a small cloud.

Mickey scuffed at them with his feet. "Stupid, dead, stinking old dog."

That's when Hoppo charged forward with a weird, strangled cry. They both fell to the ground, and for a few seconds it was nothing but flailing fists and wrestling in the gray dust that used to be Murphy.

Fat Gav stepped in to try to break the fight up. Nicky and I followed. Somehow we managed to pull them apart. Fat Gav got Mickey. I tried to hold Hoppo, but he shrugged me off.

"What is the *matter* with you?" he shouted at Mickey.

"My brother died, or did you forget?" He stared around at us. "Did you all forget?"

He wiped at his nose, which was dribbling blood.

"No," I said. "We haven't forgotten. We just want to be friends again."

"Friends. Yeah, right." He sneered at Hoppo. "You want to know who hurt your stupid dog? *I* did. So you would know how it feels to lose someone you love. Maybe you should all know how it feels."

Hoppo screamed. He wrenched himself away from me and threw his fist hard at Mickey.

I'm not quite sure what happened next. Either Mickey moved, or maybe Nicky tried to step in. Either way, I remember turning around to see Nicky on the ground, clutching at her face. Somehow, in the scrum, Hoppo's flying fist had caught her smack bang in the eye.

"You fucker!" she cried. "You stupid fucking fucker!"

I wasn't sure whether she meant Hoppo or Mickey, or whether it made any difference by that point.

Hoppo's face turned from anger to horror. "I'm sorry. I'm sorry."

Fat Gav and I ran over to try to help her. She shook us off a bit shakily. "I'm fine."

But she wasn't. Her eye was already swelling, ripe and purple. I knew, even then, that this was bad. I also felt angry. Angrier than I ever had. This was all Mickey's fault. Right then—even though I really wasn't a fighter—I wanted to smash his face in just as much as Hoppo had. But I never got the chance.

By the time we had got Nicky to her feet, Fat Gav gabbling about getting her back to his mum's and putting some frozen peas on her eye, Mickey had gone.

AS IT TURNED out, he was lying. The vet said that Murphy had probably been poisoned at least twenty-four hours before the funeral, maybe even longer. Mickey hadn't killed Murphy. It didn't really matter, though. Mickey's presence had become its own poison, contaminating everyone around him.

The peas helped Nicky's eye go down a bit, but it still looked pretty bruised when she set off home. I hoped she wouldn't get into trouble. I told myself she would probably make up some story to tell her dad and things would be fine. I was wrong.

That evening, just as my dad was making my tea, there was a banging at the front door. Mum was still at work, so Dad wiped his hands on his jeans and rolled his eyes. He walked to the door and opened it. Reverend Martin stood outside. He wore his vicar's clothes and a small black hat. He looked like someone out of a picture of the olden days. He also looked really mad. I hovered in the hallway.

"Can I help you?" my dad said, in a way that sounded like it was the last thing he wanted to do.

"Yes. You can keep your son away from my daughter."

"I'm sorry?"

"My daughter has a black eye because of your son and his little gang."

I almost blurted out that they weren't actually *my* gang. But then I also felt quite proud hearing them called that.

Dad turned. "Ed?"

I shuffled uncomfortably. My cheeks flamed. "It was an accident."

He looked back at the reverend. "If my son says it was an accident, I believe him."

The pair of them stared at each other. Then Reverend Martin smiled.

"What should I expect? The apple does not fall far from the rotten tree: 'You are of your father the devil, and the lusts of your father you will do. When he speaks a lie, he speaks of his own: for he is a liar, and the father of it.' "

"Preach all you like, Reverend," Dad said. "But we all know you don't practice it."

"Meaning?"

"Not the first black eye your daughter has sported, is it?"

"That is slander, Mr. Adams."

"Really?" Dad took a step forward. I was pleased to see Reverend Martin flinch slightly. " 'For nothing is hidden that will not be made manifest, nor is anything secret that will not be known and come to light.' " Dad smiled a nasty smile of his own. "Your church won't protect you forever, Reverend. Now get the hell off my doorstep before I call the police."

The last thing I saw was Reverend Martin's open mouth before my dad slammed the door shut in his face.

I felt my chest swell with pride. My dad had won. He had beaten him.

"Thanks, Dad. That was ace. I didn't know you knew stuff from the Bible."

"Sunday school—some bits stick in your head."

"It really was just an accident."

"I believe you, Eddie . . . but . . ."

No, I thought. No "but." Buts were never good, and this one I sensed was particularly bad. Buts were, as Fat Gav once put it, "the kick in the balls of a good day."

Dad sighed. "Look, Eddie. Maybe it would be better if you didn't see Nicky, just for a while, anyway."

"She's my friend."

"You've got other friends. Gavin, David, Mickey."

"Not Mickey."

"Oh, have you fallen out?"

I didn't reply.

Dad bent and placed his hands on my shoulders. He only did that when he was being really serious.

"I'm not saying you can't ever be friends with Nicky again but, right now, things are complicated, and Reverend Martin . . . well, he's not a very nice man."

"So?"

"Maybe it's best if you just keep your distance?"

"No!" I pulled away.

"Eddie—"

"It's not best. You don't know. You don't know anything."

Even though I knew it was childish and stupid, I turned and ran upstairs.

"Your tea's ready—"

"I don't want it."

I did. My stomach was growling, but I couldn't eat a thing. Everything was going wrong. My whole world—and when you're a kid your friends *are* your world—was being torn apart.

I pushed aside my chest of drawers and prised open the loose boards underneath. I considered the contents inside and then pulled out a small box of colored chalks. I picked up the white and, without really thinking, I started scrawling across the floorboards, again and again and again.

"Eddie."

A *tap, tap* at the door.

I froze. "Go away."

"Eddie. Look, I'm not going to stop you from seeing Nicky . . ."

I waited, chalk in hand.

". . . I'm just *asking* you, okay? For me and your mum."

Asking was worse, and Dad knew it. I closed my fist around the chalk, crumbling it to pieces in my hand.

"What do you say?"

I didn't say anything. I couldn't. It felt like all my words had lodged in my throat, choking me. Eventually, I heard my dad's heavy footsteps trudge back downstairs. I looked down at my drawings. White chalk figures, scribbled in a frenzy, over and over again. Something stirred uneasily in my stomach. Quickly, I scrubbed them out with my sleeve until the floor was just a misty white blur.

THE BRICK CAME through the window later that night. It was fortunate I was already in bed and Mum and Dad were eating a late supper in the kitchen, because if they had been in the front room, they might have been hurt by flying glass, or worse. As it was, the brick put a sizable hole in the glazing and smashed up the telly but no one was injured.

Predictably, the brick had a little message secured around it with an elastic band. Mum never told me what it said at the time. She probably thought it might have scared or upset me. Later, she confessed that the note said: "Stop killing babies, or your family will be next."

The police turned up, again. And a man came to put a wooden board over the window. Afterward, I heard Mum and Dad arguing in the living room when they thought I had gone back to bed. I crouched on the stairs, listening, feeling a little scared. Mum and Dad never argued. Yes, sometimes they snapped at each other, but not proper arguing. Not harsh, raised voices like this argument.

"We can't go on like this." Dad, sounding angry and upset.

"Like what?" Mum, tense and taut.

"You know what I mean. Bad enough you're working all hours, bad enough those idiot evangelists are intimidating women outside your clinic, but now this: threats against your own family?"

"It's just scare tactics, and you know we don't bow to scare tactics."

"This is different. It's personal."

"It's just threats. This sort of thing has happened before. Eventually, they'll get bored. They'll move on to some other godly cause. It will die down. It always does."

Even though I couldn't see him, I could picture my dad shaking his head and pacing up and down, like he did when he was upset.

"I think you're wrong, and I'm not sure I want to take that chance."

"Well, what would you have me do? Leave my job? My work? Stay at home and climb the walls while we try to scrape by on a freelance writer's salary?"

"That's not fair."

"I know. I'm sorry."

"Couldn't you go back? To Southampton? Let someone else take over Anderbury?"

"This was my project. My ba—" She seemed to catch herself. "This was my opportunity to prove myself."

"At what? Becoming a hate figure for those crazies?"

A pause.

"I am not leaving my job, or the clinic. Don't ask me."

"And what about Eddie?"

"Eddie is fine."

"Really? You know that, bearing in mind you've hardly seen him recently?"

"So you're saying he isn't fine?"

"I'm saying, with everything that's been happening—the fight at Gavin's party, the Cooper boy, David Hopkins's dog—he's had enough upset and upheaval. We always said we were going to give him security and love, and I don't want to see this hurt him, in any way."

"If I thought for one minute that any of this would hurt Eddie—"

"What? You'd quit then?" My dad's voice sounded odd. Kind of sour and bitter.

"I will do whatever it takes to protect my family, but that and continuing my work are not mutually exclusive."

"Well, let's hope not, eh?"

I heard the living-room door open and the rustle of clothing.

"Where are you going?" Mum asked.

"For a walk."

The front door slammed, loud enough to cause the banisters to tremble and a small cloud of plaster dust to fall from the landing wall above me.

Dad must have gone for a long walk, because I didn't hear him come back. I must have fallen asleep. But I did hear something else I had never heard before: Mum crying.

2016

I sit down in a pew near the rear of the church. It's empty, predictably. People have found other places of worship these days. Bars and shopping centers, TV and virtual, online worlds. Who needs the word of God when the word of some reality-TV star will do just as well?

I haven't been inside St. Thomas's myself since Sean Cooper's funeral, even though I have walked past it a lot. It's a quaint old building. Not as big or grandiose as Anderbury Cathedral, but pretty, nonetheless. I like old churches, but just to look at rather than worship inside. Today is an exception, although I am not really here to worship. I'm not really sure why I'm here.

St. Thomas stares down at me benevolently from the large stained-glass window. Patron saint of who the hell knows? For some reason, I imagine him as a cool sort of saint. Not a boring Mary or Matthew. A bit of a hipster. Even the beard is back in fashion.

I wonder if saints have to live completely blameless lives or if you can live like a sinner then just perform a few miracles and be sainted anyway? That seems to be the way with religion. Murder, rape, kill and maim, but all will be forgiven as long as you repent. Never seemed entirely fair to me. But then God, like life, is not fair.

Besides, as Mr. Christ himself pointed out, who among us is

without sin? Most people have done bad stuff at some point in their lives, stuff they wish they could take back, stuff they regret. We all make mistakes. We all have good and bad in us. Just because someone does one terrible thing, should that overshadow all the good things they've done? Or are there some things so bad that no good act can redeem them?

I think about Mr. Halloran. About his beautiful pictures, about the way he saved Waltzer Girl's life, and how—in a way—he saved my dad and me, too.

Whatever he may have done afterward, I don't believe he was a bad man. Just like Mickey wasn't a bad kid. Not really. Yes, he could be a little shit at times, and I'm not entirely sure I liked the adult he grew into either. But did anyone really hate him enough to kill him?

I stare back at St. Thomas. He isn't being a lot of help. I am not feeling any divine inspiration. I sigh. I'm probably reading too much into all of this. Mickey's death was almost certainly a tragic accident and the letter just an unpleasant coincidence. Probably just some malicious troll who discovered our addresses and wanted to cause mischief. At least, that's what I have been trying to convince myself of ever since the police visit.

The problem is, whoever sent the letters, they've succeeded. They have cracked open the box. The one I keep tightly sealed, locked and padlocked, right at the very back of my mind. And once open, Ed's box, just like Pandora's, is a bit of a bugger to close again. Worse, what lies at the bottom is not hope. But guilt.

There's a song I've listened to, something Chloe plays a lot and I have grown relatively tolerant of, by some punk/folk singer: Frank Turner.

The chorus is about no one getting remembered for the things they didn't do.

But that's not entirely true. My life has been defined by the things I didn't do. The things I didn't say. I think it's the same for a lot of people. What shapes us is not always our achievements but our omissions. Not lies; simply the truths we don't tell.

When the police showed me that letter, I should have said something. I should have gone and shown them the identical letter I had received. But I didn't. I still don't know why, just as I can't truly say why I never confessed about the things I knew or did all those years ago.

I don't even know how to feel about Mickey's death. Every time I try to picture him now all I see is young Mickey, twelve-year-old Mickey, with his mouth full of metal and his eyes full of spite. Yet he was still a friend. And now he is gone. No longer a *part* of my memories but simply a memory.

I stand and bid St. Tommy goodbye. As I turn to leave I see movement. The vicar. A plump, blond-haired woman who favors wearing Ugg boots with her vicar's smock. I've seen her around town. She seems nice enough, for a vicar.

She smiles. "Did you find what you need?"

Maybe the church *has* become more like a shopping center than I realized. Sadly, my basket remains empty.

"Not yet," I say.

MUM'S CAR IS parked outside when I get back. Shit. I remember now our conversation about Mittens, aka the Hannibal Lecter of the cat world. I shove open the door, shed my coat on the coatstand and walk into the kitchen.

Mum is sitting at the table, Mittens—thankfully—is in a cat box by her feet. Chloe stands at the counter, making coffee. She is dressed, relatively modestly for Chloe, in a baggy sweatshirt, leggings and stripy socks.

Despite this, I can still feel Mum's disapproval radiating outward like an aura. Mum doesn't like Chloe. I never expected her to. She never liked Nicky either. There are some girls mums will never like, and of course they are exactly the sort of girls you will always fall head over heels in love with.

"Ed—at last," Mum says. "Where have you been?"

"I, err, just went for a walk."

Chloe turns. "And you didn't think to tell me your mum was coming over?"

They both glare at me. As if the fact that they can't stand being in each other's company is my fault.

"Sorry," I say. "I lost track of time."

Chloe plonks a mug in front of my mum and says to me, "Make yourself some coffee. I'm going for a shower."

She exits the room and Mum looks at me. "Charming girl. Can't imagine why she hasn't got a boyfriend."

I walk over to the coffee machine. "Perhaps she's just fussy."

"That's one word for her."

Before I can retort she says, "You look terrible."

I sit down. "Thanks. I got some bad news last night."

"Oh?"

I recount as concisely as possible the events of the last thirty-six hours.

Mum sips her coffee. "How sad. And to think, that's just how his brother died."

Something I have thought about. A lot.

"Fate can be cruel sometimes," she says. "Somehow, it doesn't surprise me, though."

"It doesn't?"

"Well, Mickey always seemed like a boy who didn't have a lot of luck in life. First, his brother. Then that awful accident with Gavin."

"That was *his fault*," I say indignantly. "He was the driver. Gav's the one who's in a wheelchair because of him."

"And that's a lot of guilt to live with, to weigh you down."

I stare at her, exasperated. Mum always likes to see the opposite point of view, which is fine, when it doesn't concern you, your friends or your loyalties.

"He didn't look like he was weighed down by anything except an expensive shirt and a nice new set of veneers."

Mum ignores me, just like she used to when I was a little boy and I said something she considered unworthy of comment.

"He was going to write a book," I say.

She puts her mug down and her face grows more serious. "About what happened, when you were children?"

I nod. "He wanted me to help him."

"And what did you say?"

"I said I'd think about it."

"I see."

"There was something else—he said he knew who killed her."

She looks at me with her wide, dark eyes. Even at seventy-eight, they are still sharp and clear.

"Did you believe him?"

"I'm not sure. Maybe."

"Did he say anything else about the things that happened back then?"

"Not really. Why?"

"Just curious."

But Mum never asks a question because she's just curious. Mum never *just* does anything.

"What is it, Mum?"

She hesitates.

"Mu-um?"

She lays a cool, crinkled hand on mine. "It's nothing. I'm sorry about Mickey. I know you hadn't seen him for a long time. But you were friends, once. You must be upset."

I'm about to push her on it when the kitchen door opens and Chloe walks back in.

"Need a refill," she says, holding up her mug. "Not interrupting, am I?"

I glance at Mum.

"No," she says. "Not at all. I was just going."

BEFORE SHE DEPARTS Mum leaves several large bags which are apparently vital for Mittens's continuing harmony and well-being.

Based upon previous experience, I thought all Mittens needed for continuing harmony and well-being was an endless supply of baby birds and mice to disembowel, usually on my bed while I'm waking with a hangover, or on the kitchen table while I'm eating breakfast.

I release him from his cat box and we regard each other suspiciously before he leaps up onto Chloe's lap and stretches out with barely disguised feline smugness.

I hate cruelty to animals but, for Mittens, I could make an exception.

I leave the pair of them settled on the sofa, purring contentedly (Chloe or Mittens, I'm not quite sure). Then I walk upstairs to my study, unlock a drawer in my desk and take out the innocuous brown envelope. I stuff it into my pocket and walk back downstairs.

"Just popping to the shop," I shout, and before Chloe can give me a shopping list to rival *War and Peace* and potentially wallpaper a small room, I hurry out of the house.

It's a market day. So the streets are already lined with cars that couldn't get a space in one of the car parks in town. Soon the coaches will arrive and the narrow pavements will become jammed with tourists, peering at Google Maps and pointing iPhones at anything with a beam or a thatched roof.

I walk to the small corner shop, buy a packet of cigarettes and a lighter. Then I make my way across town to The Bull. Cheryl is serving, but Gav is not, for once, sitting at his usual table nearby.

Before I even reach the bar Cheryl looks up. "He's not here, Ed . . . and he already knows."

I FIND HIM in the playground. The old one, where we used to hang around on hot, sunny days, munching on gobstoppers and Wham bars. The one where we found the drawings that led us to her body.

He sits in his wheelchair, near the old bench. From here you can just about see the glint of the river and the crime-scene tape still fluttering around the trees where they pulled Mickey's body from the water.

The gate creaks as I push it open. The swings have resumed their traditional position, twisted around the bar at the top. There is litter on the ground, and cigarette butts, some more suspicious-looking than others. I've seen Danny Myers and his gang hanging around here in the evenings. Not in the day. No one ever comes here in the day.

Gav doesn't turn as I approach, although he must have heard the gate creak. I sit down on the bench next to him. He has a paper bag in his lap. He holds it out to me. Inside is a selection of retro sweets. Even though I don't really feel like it, I take a flying saucer.

"Three quid this cost me," he says. "From one of those posh sweet shops. Remember how we used to buy a big bag for 20p?"

"I do. That's why I've got so many fillings."

He chuckles, but it sounds forced.

"Cheryl said you know about Mickey," I say.

"Yep." He takes out a white mouse and chomps on it. "And I'm not even going to pretend I'm sorry."

I'd believe him, except I can see that his eyes are red-rimmed and his voice is a little thick. When we were kids, Fat Gav and Mickey were best friends, until it all started to fall apart. Way before the accident, although that was the final rusty nail in a rotten and splintered coffin.

"The police came to talk to me," I say. "I was the last person to see Mickey that night."

"You didn't push him in, did you?"

I don't smile, if indeed it *is* a joke. Gav looks at me and frowns. "It *was* an accident?"

"Probably."

"Probably?"

"When they pulled him out of the river they found something in his pocket."

I glance around the park. It's not busy. A solitary dog-walker ambles along the riverside path.

I take out my own letter and hand it to him. "One of these," I say.

Gav leans forward. I wait. Gav always had a pretty good poker face, even as a kid. He could tell a lie almost as smoothly as Mickey. I sense he's debating whether to tell one now.

"Look familiar?" I say.

He nods and eventually says in a weary tone, "Yeah. I got one. Hoppo, too."

"Hoppo?"

I let this sink in and, stupidly, for a moment, I feel a familiar childish resentment that they didn't tell me. Of being left out of the loop.

"Why didn't you say anything?" I ask.

"We both thought it was some kind of sick joke. What about you?"

"The same, I suppose." I pause. "Except now, Mickey's dead."

"Well, it was a good punchline then."

Gav reaches into the bag of sweets, takes out a cola bottle and stuffs it into his mouth.

I regard him for a moment. "Why do you hate Mickey so much?"

He barks out a small laugh. "You really have to ask?"

"So that's it? The accident?"

"I think that's a pretty good reason, don't you?"

He's right. Except, suddenly I'm sure he's holding something back. I reach into my pocket and pull out the unopened packet of Marlboro Lights.

Gav stares at me. "When did you start smoking again?"

"I haven't. Yet."

"Got a spare?"

"You *cannot* be serious?!"

He almost manages a smile.

I open the packet and pull out two cigarettes. "I thought you gave up, too."

"Yeah. Today seems a good day to break resolutions."

I hand the cigarette to him. Then I light mine and pass over the lighter. The first drag makes me feel a bit dizzy, a bit sick and a bit fucking fantastic.

Gav blows out smoke and says, "Fuck, these things taste like a pile of *stinking Buckaroo.*" He glances at me. "But really *great* stinking Buckaroo, my man."

We both grin.

"So," I say. "Seeing as we're breaking resolutions, want to talk about Mickey?"

He looks down, and the grin fades.

"You know about the accident?" He waves the cigarette. "Stupid question. 'Course you do."

"I know what people told me," I say. "I wasn't there."

He frowns, remembering. "No, you weren't, were you?"

"Studying, I guess."

"Well, Mickey was driving that night. Like always. You know how much he loved that little Peugeot of his."

"Tore round in it like a maniac."

"Yeah. That's why he never drank. He'd rather drive. Me. I'd rather get shitfaced."

"We were teenagers. That's what you do."

Except I didn't. Not really. Not then. Of course, I've more than made up for it since.

"I really went for it at that party. Got stupid drunk. Comatose drunk. When I started throwing up everywhere, Tina and Rich wanted me gone, so they persuaded Mickey to drive me home."

"But Mickey had been drinking, too?"

"Apparently. I don't remember seeing him have a drink but then I don't remember much about that night."

"He was over the limit when he was breathalyzed?"

He nods. "Yeah. Except he told me someone must have spiked his drink."

"When did he tell you that?"

"He came to visit me in hospital. He didn't even say sorry, just started going on about how it wasn't really his fault. Someone had put booze in his drink and if I hadn't been so out of it he wouldn't have had to drive me home anyway."

Typical Mickey. Always shifting the blame onto someone else.

"I understand why you still hate him."

"I don't."

I stare at him, cigarette poised on the way to my lips.

"I did," he says. "For a while. I wanted to blame him. But I couldn't."

"I don't understand."

"The accident isn't the reason I don't talk about Mickey, or why I never wanted to see him again."

"Then why?"

"Because it reminds me that I deserved what happened. I deserve to be in this chair. It's karma. For what I did."

Suddenly I hear Mr. Halloran's voice again:

"Karma. What you sow, you reap. You do bad things and they'll come back eventually and bite you on the backside."

"What did you do?" I ask.

"I killed his brother."

1986

As well as cleaning houses for people, Hoppo's mum also cleaned the primary school, the vicarage and the church.

That's how we found out about Reverend Martin.

Gwen Hopkins arrived at St. Thomas's as usual on Sunday morning at 6:30 a.m., to mop, dust and polish before the first service at 9:30 a.m. (I guess Sunday rest didn't apply to those doing the reverend's work.) The clocks hadn't gone back, so it was still pretty dark as she walked up to the big oak doors, took out the key she kept on a rack in her kitchen and inserted it into the lock.

All the keys to the places she cleaned hung on that rack, with the addresses of the owners on. Not very secure, or clever, especially as Hoppo's mum smoked, so she would often linger outside the back door at night and sometimes forget to lock it again.

That morning, she would later tell the police (and the newspapers), she noticed that the keys to the church were on the wrong peg. She didn't think much of it, nor the fact that the back door was unlocked, because, as she said, she was a bit forgetful, but she did usually put the keys on the right pegs. The problem was, everyone knew exactly where she kept them. A miracle, really, someone hadn't used them for stealing stuff before.

All you would have to do was sneak in, take a key and then let yourself into someone's house when you knew they were out. Maybe you'd just take a small thing they wouldn't notice, like a tiny ornament, or a pen from a drawer. Something that wasn't valuable and they would probably think they had misplaced. Maybe that's what you'd do. If you were the sort of person who likes to take things.

The first clue that something was amiss was when Gwen found the church door unlocked. But she dismissed it. Maybe the reverend was already in. Sometimes he woke early and she would find him in the church, running through his sermons. It wasn't until she let herself into the nave that she realized something was wrong. Very wrong.

The church wasn't dark enough.

Normally, the pews and the pulpit at the end of the nave were solid, black shadows. This morning they glimmered, with tracings of white.

Perhaps she hesitated. Perhaps the hairs on the back of her neck shivered a little. One of those faint trembles of fear you put down to your imagination playing tricks on you but, actually, the real trick is fooling yourself that everything is all right.

Gwen traced a faint cross over her chest then fumbled for the light switch near the door and flicked it on. The lights along the sides of the church—old, some broken, in need of refitting—buzzed and spluttered into life.

Gwen screamed. The inside of the church was covered in drawings. On the stone floor, the wooden pews and the pulpit. Everywhere she looked. Dozens and dozens of white stick figures drawn in chalk. Some dancing, some waving. Some far more profane. Stick men with stick penises. Stick women with huge breasts. Worst of all, stick hangmen, with nooses around their stick necks. It was weird, creepy. More than creepy—downright scary.

Gwen almost turned and ran. She almost dropped her cleaning bucket right then and sprinted from the church as fast as her pale white legs could carry her. If she had, it might have been too late. As it was, she hesitated. And that's when she heard a faint noise. A tiny, feeble groan.

"Hello? Is anyone here?"

Another groan, slightly louder. One she couldn't ignore. A groan of pain.

She crossed herself again—harder, deliberately—and walked down the aisle, her scalp prickling, skin pimpled with goosebumps.

She found him behind the pulpit. Curled up on the floor in a fetal position. Stripped naked, apart from his clerical collar.

The cloth had been white but was now stained red. He had been beaten violently around the head. One more blow and it would have killed him, the doctors said. As it was, he was spared death, if "spared" was the right word.

The blood wasn't just from his head, though. It was also from the wounds on his back. Carved with a knife; two huge, ragged lines spreading out from his shoulder blades and down to his buttocks. It was only after all the blood was cleaned off that people realized what they were . . .

Angel wings.

REVEREND MARTIN WAS taken to hospital and hooked up to a lot of tubes and things. There was an injury to his brain and the doctors needed to work out how bad it was to see if they needed to give him an operation.

Nicky went to stay with one of her dad's protester friends—an older lady with frizzy hair and thick glasses. She didn't stay there long, though. A day or so later a strange car pulled up outside the vicarage. A bright yellow Mini. It had a lot of stickers on: Greenpeace, a rainbow, "Fight AIDS"—all sorts of stuff.

I didn't actually see her. I heard it from Gav, who heard it from his dad, who heard it from someone in the pub. A woman climbed out of the car. A tall woman, with red hair that flowed almost to her waist, dressed in dungarees, a green army jacket and para boots.

"Like one of those Greenham Common types."

But it turned out she wasn't from Greenham Common. She was from Bournemouth and she was Nicky's mum.

Not dead, like we all thought. Very far from dead, in fact. That was just what Reverend Martin had told everyone, including Nicky. Apparently, she had left when Nicky was very little. I wasn't sure why. I didn't get how any mum could just leave. But now she was back, and Nicky would be going to live with her, because she had no other relatives and her dad was in no condition to look after her.

The doctors did their operation and said he ought to get better, perhaps even make a full recovery. But they couldn't say for sure. You could never tell with head injuries. He was able to sit up on his own in a chair. To eat and drink, go to the toilet, with a little help. But he couldn't—or wouldn't—talk, and they had no idea if he understood anything that anyone said to him.

He was taken to some home for people who weren't right in the head, to "convalesce," my mum said. The church footed the bill. Which was probably just as well, because I guess Nicky's mum couldn't have afforded it, and wouldn't have wanted to either.

As far as I know, she never took Nicky to visit him. Perhaps it was her way of getting back at him. All those years he had told Nicky she was dead and stopped her from seeing her daughter. Or maybe Nicky didn't want to go. I wouldn't have blamed her.

Only one person visited him regularly, without fail, every week, and it wasn't any of his faithful congregation, or his devoted "angels." It was my mum.

I never understood why. They had hated each other. Reverend Martin had done horrible things and said horrible things to my mum. Sometime later she would say to me, "That's the point, Eddie. The thing you have to understand is that being a good person isn't about singing hymns, or praying to some mythical god. It isn't about wearing a cross or going to church every Sunday. Being a good person is about how you treat others. A good person doesn't need a religion, because they are content within themselves that they are doing the right thing."

"And that's why you visit him?"

She smiled strangely. "Not really. I visit him because I'm sorry."

. . .

I WENT WITH her once. I don't know why. Perhaps I had nothing better to do. Perhaps it was just nice to have Mum's company for a while, because she still worked really hard and we didn't have much time together. Perhaps it was the morbid curiosity of a child.

The home was called St. Magdalene's and it was about a ten-minute drive away, on the road to Wilton. It was up this narrow lane, lined with lots of trees. It looked nice: a big old house, with a long striped lawn and pretty white tables and chairs laid out in front.

A wooden hut stood at the far end, and a couple of men in overalls—gardeners, I guess—worked busily. One strolled up and down with a large, whirring lawn mower; the other chopped up dead tree branches with an ax and chucked them into a pile, ready for a bonfire.

An old lady sat at one of the garden tables. She wore a flowered dressing gown and an elaborate hat on her head. As we drove past she raised a hand and waved: "Nice of you to come, Ferdinand."

I looked at Mum. "Is she talking to us?"

"Not really, Eddie. She's talking to her fiancé."

"Oh, is he coming to visit?"

"I doubt it. He died forty years ago."

We parked and crunched up a gravel driveway to a big doorway. Inside, it wasn't like I imagined. It was still nice, or at least they had tried to make it nice, with yellow painted walls, ornaments and pictures and stuff. But it smelled of doctors. A distinctive smell of disinfectant, pee and rotting cabbage.

It made me feel like I might throw up, even before we got to the reverend. A lady in a nurse's uniform led us down to this long room with lots of chairs and tables in it. A TV flickered in one corner. A couple of people were sitting in front of it. A really fat woman, who looked like she was half asleep, and a young man with glasses and some kind of hearing aid. Occasionally, he jumped up, waved his arms in the air and shouted: "Whip me, Mildred!" It was both funny and kind of embarrassing at the same time. The nurses didn't seem to notice at all.

Reverend Martin sat in a chair near the French doors, hands resting on his legs, face as expressionless as that of a shop-window dummy. He had been positioned so he could look out at the garden. I don't know whether he really appreciated this. He gazed out blankly, at something—or perhaps nothing—in the distance. His eyes didn't move at all, not when someone walked past, or even when the hearing-aid man shouted. I'm not sure he even blinked.

I didn't run out of the room, but I came close. Mum sat down to read to him. Some classic book by some dead author. I made an excuse to go and walk around the garden, just to get away and get some fresh air. The old lady in the big hat was still sitting out there. I tried to stay out of her view, but as I drew close she turned.

"Ferdinand isn't coming, is he?"

"I don't know," I stuttered.

Her eyes focused on me. "I know you. What's your name, boy?"

"Eddie."

"Eddie, *ma'am.*"

"Eddie, ma'am."

"You're here to visit the reverend."

"My mum is."

She nods. "Want to know a secret, Freddie?"

I thought about telling her it was Eddie, then decided against it. There was something a bit scary about the old woman, and not just because she was old, although that was part of it. As a kid, old people, with their droopy skin and scraggy hands, bristling with blue veins, are kind of monstrous.

She beckoned me with one thin, bony finger. The nail was all yellow and curled. Part of me wanted to run away. On the other hand, what kid doesn't want to know a secret? I took a small step closer.

"The reverend . . . he's got them all fooled."

"How?"

"I've seen him, at night. The devil, in disguise."

I waited. She sat back and frowned. "I know you."

"It's Eddie," I said again.

Suddenly, she pointed at me. "I know what you did, Eddie. You took something, didn't you?"

I jumped. "No, I didn't."

"Give it back. You give it back or I'll have you horsewhipped, you little vagabond."

I backed away, her cries echoing after me: "You give it back, boy. Give it back!"

I ran as fast as I could, back up the path to the house, heart thudding, face flaming. Mum was still reading to the reverend. I sat on the steps outside till she had finished.

But before that, I quickly returned the small china figurine I had taken from the communal room.

THAT WAS ALL later. Much later. After the police visit. After they arrested Dad. And after Mr. Halloran was forced to resign from the school.

Nicky had gone to live with her mum in Bournemouth. Fat Gav went round to call for Mickey once or twice—to try to make up—but both times Mickey's mum told him Mickey couldn't come out and slammed the door in his face.

"*That* was a pile of stinking Buckaroo," Fat Gav said, because later he had seen Mickey down the shops, hanging around with a couple of older kids. Rough kids who used to hang out with his brother.

I didn't really care who Mickey hung out with. I was glad he wasn't part of our gang anymore. I *did* care that Nicky had gone, more than I could admit to Hoppo and Fat Gav. It wasn't the only thing I didn't admit to them. I never told them that she came to see me one last time. On the day she left.

I was in the kitchen, doing homework at the table. Dad was hammering somewhere and Mum was vacuuming. I had the radio on, so it was a miracle I heard the doorbell at all.

I waited for a moment. Then, when it became apparent that no one else was going to answer it, I slipped from my chair, trotted into the hall and pulled the door open.

Nicky stood outside, clutching the handlebars of her bike. Her skin was pale and her red hair was dull and tangled, the skin beneath her left eye still shaded yellow and blue. She looked like one of Mr. Halloran's abstract paintings. A patchwork, pallid version of herself.

"Hi," she said, and even her voice didn't sound like her own.

"Hi," I said back. "We were going to come and see you, but . . ."

I trailed off. We weren't. We were too scared of what to say. Like with Mickey.

"That's okay," she said.

But it wasn't. We were supposed to be her friends.

"D'you want to come in?" I asked. "We've got some lemonade and biscuits."

"Can't. Mum thinks I'm packing. I sneaked out."

"You're leaving today?"

"Yeah."

My heart dropped like a deadweight. I felt something give inside.

"I'm really going to miss you," I blurted out. "We all are."

I braced myself for a biting, sarcastic reply. Instead, she suddenly stepped forward and wrapped her arms around me. So tight, it didn't really feel like a hug, more like a death grip; like I was the last raft on a dark and stormy ocean.

I let her hold on. I breathed in the smell of her knotted curls. Vanilla and chewing gum. I felt the rise and fall of her chest. The small buds of her breasts through her baggy jumper. I wished that we could stay like that forever. That she wouldn't ever tear herself away.

But she did. She turned just as suddenly and swung her leg over her bike. Then she pedaled furiously down the road, red hair flying behind her like a mass of angry flames. Not another word. No goodbye.

I watched her go and realized something else: she hadn't mentioned her dad. Not once.

. . .

THE POLICE CAME to talk to Hoppo's mum again.

"So do they know who did it yet?" Fat Gav asked Hoppo, popping a fizzy cola bottle into his mouth.

We were sitting on a bench in the school playground. The place where the five of us always used to sit, on the edge of the field near the hopscotch squares. Now there was just the three of us.

Hoppo shook his head. "I don't think so. They were asking her about the key, who knew where it was kept. They asked about the drawings in the church again, too."

That caught my attention. "The drawings. What did they ask?"

"Had she seen anything like them before? Had the reverend mentioned any other messages or threats? Did anyone have a grudge against him?"

I shifted uncomfortably. *Look out for the chalk men.*

Fat Gav looked at me. "What is it, Eddie Munster?"

I hesitated. I'm not sure why. These were my mates. My gang. I could tell them anything. I should tell them about the other chalk men.

But something stopped me.

Perhaps because Fat Gav, although he was funny and loyal and generous, was not good at keeping secrets. Perhaps because I didn't want to tell Hoppo about the drawing in the graveyard, because then I would have to explain why I didn't say anything at the time. Plus, I still remembered what he said that day. "*When I find out who did this, I'm going to kill them.*"

"Nothing," I said. "It's just, we drew chalk men, didn't we? I hope the police don't think it was us."

Fat Gav snorted. "That was just stupid shit. No one is going to think we went and bashed a vicar's head in." Then his face brightened. "I bet it was some Satanist or something. A devil-worshipper. Is your mum sure it was chalk? Not *blooooood*?" He reared up, curled his hands into claws and gave this big *Hah, hah, hah, haaaah* evil laugh.

Then the bell rang for afternoon lessons and the subject, if not closed, was put away for a little while.

. . .

WHEN I GOT back from school a strange car was parked on the drive and Dad was sitting in the kitchen with a man and woman in shapeless gray suits. They looked hard and unfriendly. Dad sat with his back to me, but from the way he was slumped in his chair I knew his face would be troubled, bushy brows drawn together in a frown.

I didn't get a chance to see much more because Mum emerged from the kitchen and pulled the door closed behind her. She ushered me down the hall.

"Who are they?" I asked.

Mum wasn't one for sugarcoating the truth. "Detectives, Eddie."

"Police? Why are they here?"

"They just need to ask your dad and me a few questions, about Reverend Martin."

I stared at her, heart already beating a little faster. "Why?"

"It's just routine. They're talking to lots of people who knew him."

"They haven't talked to Fat Gav's dad, and he knows everyone."

"Don't be cheeky, Eddie. Go and watch some television while we finish up."

Mum never suggested I watch television. Usually it was no TV until I had done my homework, so I knew something was up.

"I was going to get a drink."

"I'll bring you one."

I looked at her for a bit longer. "Nothing's wrong, is it, Mum? They don't think Dad has done anything?"

Her eyes softened. She laid her hand on my arm and gave it a gentle squeeze. "No, Eddie. Your dad has done absolutely nothing wrong. Okay? Now, off you go. I'll bring you some squash in a minute."

"Okay."

I wandered into the living room and turned on the telly. Mum never brought me a drink. But that was all right. Soon after, the policeman and woman left again. Dad went with them. And I knew that wasn't all right. Not one bit.

. . .

IT TURNED OUT Dad *had* gone for a walk the night the reverend was attacked, but he only walked as far as The Bull. Fat Gav's dad vouched for the fact he was there, drinking whiskey. (My dad didn't drink often, but when he did he never drank beer like other dads, only whiskey.) Fat Gav's dad had spoken to him, but he was busy that night and, besides, Fat Gav's dad said, "You know when a punter just wants some time on their own." Still, he had been thinking about not serving my dad any more when he left, just before closing.

Dad couldn't remember much after that, but he did remember sitting down to get some fresh air, on one of the benches in the churchyard, which was on the way back home. Someone had seen him there at around midnight. Mum told the police Dad got back about 1 a.m. The police couldn't say for sure when Reverend Martin was attacked, but they believed it was sometime between midnight and three in the morning.

They probably didn't have enough to charge Dad, but it was all they needed—what with the fight and the threats against Mum—to get him down to the police station and question him some more. Maybe they would have even kept him there, if it hadn't been for Mr. Halloran.

He walked into the police station the next day to tell them that he had seen my dad asleep on a bench in the churchyard that night. Worried about leaving him there, he had woken him and helped him to walk home, just to the gate. This was between midnight and one. It had taken them a good forty minutes (even though it was only a ten-minute walk) because Dad was in such a state.

And no, Mr. Halloran told the police, my dad did not have any blood on him, and he was not angry or violent. He was just drunk and a little emotional.

That pretty much cleared my dad. Unfortunately, it also led to questions about what Mr. Halloran was doing wandering around the churchyard at that time of night, and that's how everyone found out about Waltzer Girl.

2016

We think we want answers. But what we really want are the *right* answers. Human nature. We ask questions that we hope will give us the truth we want to hear. The problem is, you can't choose your truths. Truth has a habit of simply being the truth. The only real choice you have is whether to believe it or not.

"You stole Sean Cooper's bike?" I say to Gav.

"I knew he often left it out on the driveway at night. He thought he was such a big man no one would dare take it. So I did. Just to piss him off." He pauses. "I never thought he'd go into the river to try and get it. Never thought he'd end up drowning."

No, I think. But everyone knew how much Sean loved that bike. It must have crossed Fat Gav's mind that stealing it could only end in trouble.

"Why did you do it?" I ask.

Gav blows out a ring of smoke. "I saw what he did to you. In the playground that day."

The admission is like a punch in my guts. Thirty years ago, and my cheeks still burn with shame at the memory. The rough tarmac rubbing my knees. The stale, sweaty taste in my mouth.

"I was in the park," he says. "I saw it all happening, and I didn't do a thing. I just stood there. Then I saw Mr. Halloran run over, so I told myself it was all right. But it wasn't all right."

"There was nothing you could have done," I say. "They'd have just turned on you."

"I should still have tried. Friends are everything. Remember? That's what I always said. But when it came to it, I let you down. I let Sean get away with it. Like everyone did. These days, he'd end up in jail for something like that. Back then, we were all so scared of him." He looks at me fiercely. "He wasn't just a bully. He was a fucking psychopath."

He's right. About some of it. I'm not sure Sean Cooper was a psychopath. A sadist, certainly. Most kids are, to some extent. But maybe he would have been different when he got older. I think about what Mr. Halloran had said at the graveyard:

He never got the chance to change.

"You've gone quiet," Gav says.

I drag harder on the cigarette. The nicotine hit makes my ears hum.

"The night after Sean died, someone drew a chalk man on my driveway. A *drowning* chalk man. Like some kind of message."

"It wasn't me."

"So who, then?"

Gav grinds his cigarette out on the bench. "Who knows? Who cares? The fucking chalk men. It's all anyone remembers about that summer. More people give a shit about some stupid drawings than the people who got hurt."

It's true. But the two were irrevocably intertwined. Chicken and egg. Which came first. The chalk men or the killing?

Gav says, "You're the only person who knows, Ed."

"I won't say anything."

"I know." He sighs. "Have you ever done anything so bad you can't tell even your closest friends?"

I stub my own cigarette down to the flattened filter. "I'm sure most people have."

"You know what someone once told me? Secrets are like arseholes. We all have them. It's just that some are dirtier than others."

"Nice mental image."

"Yeah." He chuckles. "What a pile of shit."

IT'S LATE AFTERNOON before I make it back home. I let myself in, walk into the kitchen and immediately frown at the unpleasant odor of cat litter. I peer into the plastic tray. There don't appear to be any deposits. Which might be fortunate or worrying, depending on what level of evil Mittens is operating at today. I make a mental note to check my slippers before I put them on.

The bourbon sits, temptingly, on the kitchen worktop, but instead (clear head and all that) I grab a beer from the fridge and walk upstairs. I linger for a moment by Chloe's room. I can't hear anything from inside but I can feel a faint vibration through the floorboards, which probably means she has her headphones on and is listening to music. Good.

I tiptoe into my own room and close the door. Then I place my beer on the bedside table, crouch down and push aside the chest of drawers by the window. It's heavy and it scrapes across the old floorboards a little, but I'm not too worried about the noise. When Chloe listens to music she likes to listen to it at eardrum-bursting volume. A minor earthquake could pass her by unnoticed.

I take out an old screwdriver I keep in my underwear drawer and use it to prise up the floorboards. Four of them. More than when I was child. I have more to hide now.

I remove one of the two boxes wedged into the cavity, lift the lid and stare at the contents. I take out the smallest item and carefully unwrap the tissue paper. Inside is a single gold hoop earring. Not real gold; a cheap piece of costume jewelry, slightly tarnished now. I hold it in my hand for a moment, letting the metal warm in my palm. The first thing I took from her, I think. The day it all began, at the fairground.

I understand how Gav must feel. If he hadn't stolen Sean Cooper's bike, then he might still be alive. One small act of childish stupidity that resulted in a terrible tragedy. Not that Gav could have foreseen how it would end. Neither could I. But still, a strange feeling washes over me. A sense of discomfort. Not guilt, exactly. Its twin. Responsibility. For all of it.

I'm sure Chloe would tell me that this is because I'm the sort of insular, self-obsessed man who takes everything on himself and believes that the world revolves around him. That's true, to an extent. Being solitary can lead to introspection. On the other hand, maybe I haven't given enough time to introspection, or thinking about the past. I wrap the earring carefully back up and replace it in the box.

Maybe it's time to take a ride all the way back down good old memory lane. Except, this is not a sun-dappled stroll along a path of fond recollections. This particular route is dark, overgrown with tangled knots of lies and secrets, and full of hidden potholes.

And along the way, there are chalk men.

1986

"We can't choose who we fall in love with."

That's what Mr. Halloran told me.

I suppose he was right. Love isn't a choice. It's a compulsion. I know that now. But perhaps, sometimes, you *should* choose. Or, at least, choose *not* to fall in love. Fight it, take yourself away from it. If Mr. Halloran had chosen not to fall in love with Waltzer Girl, everything might have been different.

This was after he had left school for good, when I sneaked out and rode my bike across town to see him in his little cottage. A cold day. The sky iron gray and as hard and unyielding as a block of concrete. Occasionally, it would drib and drab a bit of drizzle here and there. Too despondent to even rain properly.

Mr. Halloran had been made to resign. There hadn't been an announcement. I think they just hoped he would go quietly. But of course, we all knew he was leaving, and we all knew why.

Mr. Halloran had visited Waltzer Girl in hospital as she recovered. He carried on visiting her after she came out. They would meet for coffee or at the park. I guess they must have been pretty secretive about it, because no one had seen them, or perhaps they had and didn't realize. Waltzer Girl had changed her hair. She had dyed it lighter, almost blond. I wasn't sure why. I thought her hair was pretty before. But maybe she just felt she needed to change it because she had changed. Sometimes she walked with a stick now. Sometimes with a limp. I guess if anyone *did* see them, they probably just thought that Mr. Halloran was being nice. Back then, he was still a hero.

That all turned on its head pretty fast when people found out that Waltzer Girl had been going to his cottage in the evenings and he had been sneaking around to her house when her mum was out. That was why he was making his way back past the churchyard that night.

Then the shit really hit the fan, because Waltzer Girl was only seventeen and Mr. Halloran was over thirty and a teacher. People stopped calling him a hero and started calling him a pervert and a pedo. Parents went up to the school to talk angrily to the head. Even though he hadn't officially, or legally, done anything wrong, she had no choice but to ask him to go. It was the school's reputation and the "safety" of the children.

Stories started to spread about how Mr. Halloran would drop erasers so he could look up the girls' skirts in class, or how he would hang around at PE, staring at girls' legs, or how, in the canteen once, he had touched one of the girls serving on the boob when she went to clear his table.

None of it was true, but rumors are like germs. They spread and multiply almost in a breath and, before you know it, everyone is contaminated.

I'd like to say I stuck up for Mr. Halloran and defended his name in front of the other kids. But that's not true. I was twelve, and this was school. I laughed at the jokes about him and didn't say a word when people called him names or spread another outrageous tale.

I never told them that I didn't believe them. That Mr. Halloran was good. Because he had saved Waltzer Girl's life, and saved my dad, too. I couldn't tell them about the beautiful pictures he painted, or the day he rescued me from Sean Cooper, or how he helped me understand that you should hold on to things that were special. Hold on really tight.

I guess that's why I went round to see him that day. As well as having to resign from his job, he had to leave the cottage. It was rented out by the school and the new teacher, his replacement, would be moving in.

I still felt a bit scared and awkward when I propped my bike outside and knocked on the door. It took a while for Mr. Halloran to open it. I was just wondering whether I should leave, or if he was out, even though his car was parked on the street outside, when the door swung open and Mr. Halloran was standing there.

He looked different somehow. He had always been thin, but now he looked gaunt. His skin, if humanly possible, was even paler. His hair was loose and he wore jeans and a dark T-shirt that showed off his sinewy arms, the only color in them the blue of his veins, startlingly bright through the translucent skin. That day, he really did look like some kind of strange, inhuman creature. Like the Chalk Man.

"Hi, Eddie."

"Hello, Mr. Halloran."

"What are you doing here?"

A good question, because now I was here, I actually had no idea.

"Do your mum and dad know you're here?"

"Well, no."

He gave a small frown, then he stepped outside and looked around. I didn't really get why at the time. Later, I would understand—with all the accusations flying around, the last thing he wanted was to be seen inviting a young boy into his cottage. I think he might even have been on the verge of turning me away, but then he looked at me and his voice softened: "Come on in, Eddie. Would you like a drink? Squash or milk?"

I didn't really, but it seemed rude to say no, so I said, "Erm, milk would be cool."

"Okay."

I followed Mr. Halloran into the small kitchen.

"Sit down."

I sat on one of the wobbly pine chairs. The worktops in the kitchen were stacked with boxes; most of the living room, too.

"You're leaving?" I asked, which was a stupid question, because I already knew he was.

"Yes," Mr. Halloran said, taking some milk out of the fridge and checking the date before searching the boxes for a glass. "I'm going to stay with my sister in Cornwall."

"Oh. I thought your sister was dead."

"I have another sister, an older one. She's called Kirsty."

"Oh."

Mr. Halloran brought the milk over. "Is everything okay, Eddie?"

"I, erm, I wanted to thank you, for what you did for my dad."

"I didn't do anything. I just told the truth."

"Yeah, but you didn't have to and if you hadn't . . ."

I let the sentence trail off. This was awful. More awful than I thought it would be. I didn't want to be here. I wanted to go, and yet I felt I couldn't.

Mr. Halloran sighed. "Eddie, all of this, it has nothing to do with your dad or you. I intended to leave soon anyway."

"Because of Waltzer Girl?"

"You mean Elisa?"

"Oh, yeah." I nodded. Sipped my milk. It tasted a bit off.

"We think a fresh start might be best, for both of us."

"So she's coming with you, to Cornwall?"

"Eventually. I hope."

"People are saying bad things about you."

"I know. They're not true."

"I know."

But he must have felt I needed some more convincing, because he continued: "Elisa is a very special girl, Eddie. I didn't mean for this to happen. I just wanted to help her, to be a friend."

"So why couldn't you just be her friend?"

"When you're older, you'll understand better. We can't choose who we fall in love with, who will make us happy."

But he didn't look happy. Not like people in love were supposed to. He looked sad and sort of lost.

. . .

I CYCLED HOME, feeling confused and a little lost myself. Winter was creeping in and, at barely three o'clock in the afternoon, the day was losing substance and dissolving into a dusty twilight.

Everything felt cold and bleak and hopelessly changed. Our gang had been torn apart. Nicky was living with her mum in Bournemouth. Mickey had his new, unpleasant mates. I still hung out with Hoppo and Fat Gav, but it wasn't the same. A group of three brought its own problems. I had always thought of Hoppo as my best mate, but sometimes, now, when I went round to call for him, he was already out with Fat Gav. That brought a different feeling: resentment.

Mum and Dad were different, too. Since the attack on Reverend Martin, the protests around Mum's work had died down. "Like cutting the head off the beast," Dad said. But while Mum was more relaxed, Dad seemed sharper and on edge. Maybe the whole police thing had shaken him, or maybe it was something else. He was forgetful and irritable. Sometimes I would catch him sitting in a chair, staring into space, as if he was just waiting for something but didn't know what.

That waiting feeling seemed to hang over the whole of Anderbury. Everything seemed somehow on hold. The police had still not charged anyone with the attack on Reverend Martin, so perhaps suspicion was part of it: looking, wondering if someone you knew could be capable of such a thing.

The leaves curled and crinkled and eventually lost their fragile grip on the trees. A feeling of withering and dying seemed to pervade everything. Nothing felt fresh or colorful or innocent anymore. Like the whole town had been temporarily suspended in its own dusty time capsule.

Of course, as it turned out, we *were* waiting. And when the girl's pale hand beckoned from a careless fall of crumpled leaves, it felt as though the whole town let out a long, stagnant breath. Because it had happened. The worst had finally come.

2016

I wake early the next morning. Or rather, I finally give up on sleep after hours of tossing and turning, broken only by half-remembered dreams.

In one of them Mr. Halloran is riding the Waltzers with Waltzer Girl. I'm pretty sure it's Waltzer Girl, because of her clothes, even though she is missing her head. It rests on Mr. Halloran's lap and it screams every time the fairground worker, who I realize is Sean Cooper, spins them round and round.

"Scream if you want to go faster, Shitfaces. I said, SCREAM!"

I haul myself from bed, shaken and distinctly unrested. Then I throw on some clothes and pad downstairs. I presume Chloe is still asleep, so I kill time, making coffee, reading and smoking two cigarettes outside the back door. Then, when the clock slips past nine and the hour seems just about respectable, I pick up the phone and call Hoppo.

His mum answers.

"Hello, Mrs. Hopkins. Is David there?"

"Who is this?"

Her voice is tremulous and frail. A marked contrast to my own mum's clipped, precise tones. Hoppo's mum has dementia. Like my dad, except Dad's Alzheimer's started earlier and progressed faster.

It's the reason why Hoppo still lives in the same house where he grew up. To care for his mum. We sometimes joke that the pair of us, two grown men, have never left home. It's a slightly bitter joke.

"It's Ed Adams, Mrs. Hopkins," I say now.

"Who?"

"Eddie Adams. David's friend."

"He's not here."

"Oh, d'you know when he'll be back?"

A long pause. Then sharper. "We don't want any of it. We've already got double glazing."

She slams the phone down. I stare at it for a moment. I know I shouldn't take too much notice of what Gwen says. My dad would often lose track of conversations and come out with completely random things.

I call Hoppo's mobile. It goes to voicemail. It always does. If it wasn't for the fact that he runs a business, I would swear he never even turns the damn thing on.

I swig the remains of my fourth coffee then walk into the hallway. It's a cool day for mid-August and the wind is sharp. I look around for my long overcoat. It's usually hanging on the coat stand near the door. I haven't worn it for a while, due to the clement weather. However, now I need it, it doesn't appear to be here.

I frown. I don't like misplacing things. It was the start of my dad's decline, and every time I lose my keys I have a minor panic attack. First losing the objects, then losing the names for the objects.

I still remember Dad staring blankly at the front door one morning, mouth working silently, brows furrowed in a deep frown. And then, suddenly, he clapped his hands together like a child, grinned and pointed at the door handle.

"The door *hanger.* The door *hanger.*" He turned to me. "I thought I'd forgotten it."

He was so happy, so pleased, I couldn't contradict him. I just smiled. "Great, Dad. Really great."

I check the coat stand again. Maybe I left the coat upstairs. But no, why would I have worn my coat upstairs? Still, I trudge up and look around my room. Back of my bedside chair? Nope. Slung on the hook behind the door? Nope. Wardrobe? I sort through the clothes on hangers . . . and then I spot something bundled into a corner, right at the bottom.

I bend down and pull it out. My coat. I stare at it. Creased, crumpled, a bit damp. I try to think back to the last time I saw it. The night Mickey came round. I remember hanging his expensive sports jacket on the peg next to it. And afterward? I can't remember wearing it after then.

Or maybe I did. Maybe I slipped it on later that night, strolled out into the cool, slightly damp night air and . . . *and what?* Pushed Mickey into the river? *Ridiculous.* I think I would remember pushing my old friend into the river in the middle of the night.

Really, Ed? Because you don't remember coming downstairs and drawing chalk men all over the fireplace, do you? You'd had a lot to drink. You have no idea what else you might have done that night.

I silence the niggling little voice. I had no reason to hurt Mickey. He was giving me a great opportunity. And if Mickey did know who really killed Waltzer Girl—if he could exonerate Mr. Halloran—I'd be pleased about that, wouldn't I?

So what is the coat doing stuffed into the bottom of your wardrobe, Ed?

I look back down at it, run my fingers over the coarse wool. And then I spot something else. On the cuff of one of the sleeves. Several dull, rusty-red splodges. My throat constricts.

Blood.

BEING AN ADULT is only an illusion. When it comes down to it I'm not sure any of us ever really grow up. We simply grow taller and hairier. Sometimes, I still feel amazed that I am allowed to drive a car, or that I have not been found out for drinking in the pub.

Beneath the veneer of adulthood, beneath the layers of experience we accrue as the years march stoically onward, we are all still children, with scraped knees and snotty noses, who need our parents . . . and our friends.

Hoppo's van is parked outside. As I round the corner, I see Hoppo himself, climbing off his old bike, two carrier bags full of sticks and bark hung over the handlebars, a bulging rucksack on his back. My mind flashes back to sunny summer days when we'd often come back from the woods together, Hoppo laden down with bits of wood and kindling for his mum.

Despite everything, I can't help a small smile as he swings his leg off the bike and props it against the curb.

"Ed, what are you doing here?"

"I tried calling, but your mobile was off."

"Oh yeah. Just over at the woods. Not a great signal."

I nod. "Old habits die hard."

He grins. "Mum's memory might be going, but she would still never forgive me if we actually paid for firewood."

Then the smile fades, perhaps as he sees my face. "What's wrong?"

"Have you heard about Mickey?"

"What's he done now?"

I open my mouth, my tongue flounders around and, eventually, my brain shoves it in the direction of the most obvious words: "He's dead."

"Dead?"

Funny how people always repeat that word, even though they know they've heard it correctly. A kind of denial by delay.

After a moment Hoppo asks, "How? What happened?"

"He drowned. In the river."

"Jesus. Like his brother."

"Not exactly. Look, can I come in?"

"Yeah, sure."

Hoppo heaves his bike up the short pathway. I follow. He unlocks the door. We walk down a dark, narrow hallway. I haven't visited Hoppo's house since we were kids and, even then, we didn't go inside much, because of the mess. We played in the back garden occasionally, but never for long because the garden was small, not much more than a yard. Often there was dog poo that hadn't been picked up, some fresh, some white.

The house smells of sweat, stale food and disinfectant. To my right, through the open living-room door, I see the same worn floral sofa, the white lace covers a grubby nicotine yellow. In one corner, the TV. In another, a commode and a walking frame.

Hoppo's mum sits in a high-backed chair, slightly to one side of the sofa, staring blankly at some daytime quiz show. Gwen Hopkins was always tiny, but illness and age seem to have shrunk her further. She looks lost within a long flowered dress and a green cardigan. Her wrists poke out of the sleeves like tiny husks of shriveled, dried meat.

"Mum?" Hoppo says gently. "Ed's here. You remember Eddie Adams?"

"Hello, Mrs. Hopkins," I say, in the slightly raised voice people always adopt with the elderly and the ill.

She turns slowly, eyes struggling to focus, or perhaps it's her mind struggling to gain a grip. Then she smiles, revealing even, creamy-white dentures. "I remember you, Eddie. You had a brother. Sean?"

"Actually, Mum," Hoppo steps in, "that was Mickey. Mickey had a brother called Sean."

She frowns then smiles again. "Oh, of course. *Mickey.* How is he?"

Hoppo says quickly, "He's fine, Mum. Really well."

"Good, good. Could you get me some tea, David, dear?"

"Of course, Mum." He glances at me. "I'll just go and put the kettle on."

I stand in the doorway and smile at Gwen awkwardly. There's a bit of a smell in the room. I'm not sure the commode has been emptied recently.

"He's a good boy," Gwen says.

"Yes."

She frowns. "Who are you?"

"Ed. Eddie. David's friend."

"Oh, yes. Where's David?"

"Just in the kitchen."

"Are you sure? I thought he took the dog for a walk."

"The dog?"

"Murphy."

"Right. No, I don't think he took Murphy for a walk."

She waves a knotted, veined hand at me. "You're right. Murphy's dead. I meant Buddy."

Buddy was the dog Hoppo had after Murphy. Now also dead.

"Oh. Of course."

I nod. She nods back. We nod at each other. We would have looked good in the back of a car.

She leans toward me over the arm of her chair. "I remember you, Eddie," she says. "Your mother killed babies."

My breath snags in my throat. Gwen continues to nod and smile, but there is something different about it; a sour twist at the corner of her lips, a sudden clarity in the faded blue eyes.

"Don't worry. I won't tell them." She leans forward, taps her nose and gives a slow, trembling wink. "I can keep a secret."

"Here we go." Hoppo reemerges, carrying a cup of tea. "Everything okay?"

I glance at Gwen, but the clarity is fading, eyes clouding once more with confusion.

"Fine," I say. "We were just chatting."

"Right, Mum. Tea." He sets the cup on the table. "Remember, it's hot. Blow on it first."

"Thank you, Gordy."

"Gordy?" I look at Hoppo.

"My dad," he whispers.

"Oh."

My own dad didn't used to get people confused. But sometimes he would resort to calling me "son," as if I wouldn't notice that he had forgotten my name again.

Gwen settles back in her chair, staring at the TV, lost once more in her own world, or maybe some other world. Thin, I think, that fabric between realities. Maybe minds aren't lost. Maybe they just slip through and find a different place to wander.

Hoppo offers me a brief, bleak smile. "Why don't we go into the kitchen?"

"Sure," I say.

If he'd suggested swimming with sharks I would have agreed, just to get out of that hot, stinking living room.

The kitchen isn't much better. Dirty plates are piled in the sink. The worktops overflow with stacks of envelopes, old magazines, discount packs of juice and cola. The table has been hastily cleared, but I can still see the remnants of some old radio, or maybe the inner workings of an engine. I'm not a "hands on" man, whereas Hoppo was always good with his hands—putting things together and taking them apart again.

I sit on one of the old wooden chairs. It creaks and gives a little.

"Tea? Coffee?" Hoppo offers.

"Err, coffee, thanks."

Hoppo goes to the kettle, which is at least brand new, and grabs a couple of mugs from the draining board.

He pours in some coffee straight from the jar, then turns to face me.

"So. What happened?"

Once again, I recount the events of the last three days. Hoppo listens quietly. His face doesn't change until I come to the last thing.

"Gav says you got a letter, too?" I say.

He nods and adds boiling water to the coffee. "Yeah, a couple of weeks back."

He walks to the fridge, gets out some milk, sniffs it and then adds a splash to both coffees. "I just thought it was some kind of sick joke."

He brings the drinks over to the table and sits down opposite me.

"The police think it was an accident, though—Mickey's death?"

I had been a little vague over this, but now I say, "At the moment."

"You think that will change?"

"They found that letter."

"That doesn't necessarily mean anything."

"No?"

"What? You think someone is going to start picking us off, one by one, like something out of a book?"

Actually, I hadn't thought of it quite like that, but now he's said it, it seems all too plausible. And it makes me think of something else. Did Nicky get a letter, too?

"I'm joking," he says. "You said yourself, Mickey was drunk. It was dark; there are no lights along that stretch of the path. He probably just fell in. Drunk people fall into rivers all the time."

He's right, *but*. There's always a "but." A nagging, annoying fellow, tying Boy Scout knots in your gut.

"Is there something else?"

"When Mickey came round that night, we were talking, and he said . . . he knew who really killed Elisa."

"Bullshit."

"Well, that's what I thought, but what if he was telling the truth?"

Hoppo takes another sip of coffee. "So you think the 'real' killer pushed Mickey in the river?"

I shake my head. "I don't know."

"Look, Mickey was always good at stirring things up. Seems like he's even doing it now he's dead." He pauses. "Besides, you're the only person he told about this theory, right?"

"I think so."

"So how would the 'real' killer know Mickey was on to them?"

"Well—"

"Unless it was you."

I stare at him.

Dull, rusty-red splodges. Blood.

"Joking," he says.

"Of course."

I sip my coffee. *Of course.*

ON MY WAY back home from Hoppo's I take out my phone and call Chloe. I still feel that things aren't quite right between us. Like something is hanging without resolution. It bothers me. Aside from Hoppo and Gav, she's about the only real friend I have.

She answers on the third ring. "Hiya."

"Hi. It's me."

"Right."

"Contain your enthusiasm."

"I'm trying."

"'Sorry about my mum yesterday."

"'S'okay. Your mum. Your house."

"Well, I'm sorry anyway. What are you doing for lunch?"

"I'm at work."

"Oh. I thought you were off today."

"Someone's ill."

"Right. Well—"

"Look, apology accepted, Ed. I have to go. Customer."

"Okay. Well, I'll see you later."

"Maybe."

She ends the call. I stare at the phone for a moment. Chloe never makes anything easy. I pause and light a cigarette, thinking about picking up a sandwich on the way home. Then I reconsider. Chloe might be at work, but she must still have a lunch break. I decide I won't be put off so easily. I turn around and head back into town.

I've never actually visited Chloe at work before. I have to confess that an "alternative rock/Goth" clothing store is not exactly my usual habitat. I suppose I was a little scared of embarrassing her, and myself.

I'm not even sure exactly where it is. I wander through town, dodging tourists and elderly shoppers and eventually discover it, up a side street, sandwiched between a secondhand store and a shop selling silver jewelry and wind chimes. I look up at the sign: Gear (the marijuana symbol suggesting more than just clothing). Feeling about a century old, I push open the door.

The shop is dimly lit and loud. Something that could be music—or could just as easily be someone being pulled limb from limb—screams from speakers above my head and immediately makes my eardrums ache.

A few skinny teens lurk around the clothing—staff members or customers, I'm not sure. What I *am* sure of is that Chloe is not here. I frown. A slight young lady with scarlet hair on one side, a shaved skull on the other and an abundance of silver in her face stands behind the till. As she turns, I see that the T-shirt draped over her skinny frame bears the statement: "Pierced. Penetrated. Mutilated." Nice.

I walk up to the till. Pierced Girl looks up and smiles. "Hi. Can I help you?"

"Erm, actually, I was looking for someone else."

"Shame."

I laugh, a little nervously. "Err, she works here. A friend. Chloe Jackson."

She frowns. "Chloe Jackson?"

"Yes, thin. Dark hair. Wears a lot of black."

She continues to stare at me, and I realize that could describe pretty much everyone in here.

"Sorry. It doesn't ring a bell. You're sure she works here?"

I was, but now I'm beginning to doubt myself. Perhaps I've got the wrong shop.

"Is there another shop like this in Anderbury?"

She considers. "Not really."

"Right."

Perhaps seeing the look on my face and taking pity on the poor, confused middle-aged man, she says, "Look. I've only been here a couple of weeks. Let me ask Mark. He's the manager."

"Thanks," I say, even though that doesn't really answer

anything. Chloe said she was at work *today*, and, as far as I am aware, she has been coming to work here for the last nine months.

I wait, staring at a row of watches with leering red skulls on their faces and a rack of birthday cards with greetings like "Fuck Birthdays" and "Happy Birthday, you cunt" printed on them.

After a few minutes a lanky youth with a shaved head and an enormous, bushy beard ambles up.

"Hey. I'm Mark, the manager."

"Hi."

"You're looking for Chloe?"

I feel a small measure of relief. He knows her.

"Yes. I thought she worked here."

"She did, but not recently."

"Oh? Well, when did she leave?"

"Must have been about a month ago."

"Right. I see." Although I really don't. "And we're definitely talking about the same Chloe?"

"Thin, black hair, often wears it in pigtails?"

"Sounds like her."

He eyes me cautiously. "You say she's a friend?"

"I thought she was."

"To be honest with you, I had to let her go."

"How do you mean?"

"She had an attitude. She was rude to a few customers."

Again, sounds like Chloe.

"I thought that was expected in a shop like this?"

He grins. "Insouciance, not insults. Anyway, then she had this outright screaming match with a woman who came in. I had to step in. Thought it was going to come to blows. After that, I sacked her."

"I see."

I let all of this slowly digest, like salmonella. I'm aware that they are both looking at me.

"Sorry," I say. "It seems I've been given some misinformation." A polite way of saying I have been lied to, by someone I thought I knew. "Thanks for your help." I walk toward the door, and then I have my Columbo moment. I turn. "The woman Chloe got into an argument with—what did she look like?"

"Slim, attractive for an older woman. Long red hair."

I freeze, every nerve ending standing to attention.

"Red hair?"

"Yeah. Flaming red. Actually, she was pretty hot."

"I don't suppose you caught her name?"

"I wrote it down—she didn't really want me to, but I had to, in case she filed a complaint or something."

"I don't suppose you still have the bit of paper? I mean, I know it's asking a lot. But . . . it's really important."

"Well, I always like to help a customer." He frowns, tugs at his beard and looks me up and down. "You *are* a customer, aren't you? Only I don't see a bag . . ."

Of course. Nothing comes for free. I sigh, walk back and pick up the nearest black sweatshirt decorated with leering skulls. I hold it out to Pierced Girl.

"I'll take this."

She smiles, opens a drawer and pulls out a crumpled slip of paper. She hands it over to me. I can just make out the spidery scrawl:

"Nicola Martin."

Nicky.

1986

"You gotta have a dream. If you don't have a dream, how you gonna have a dream come true?"

Oddly, I always think of that song when I think of the day we found her. I know a lot of songs from old musicals, perhaps because that was what they always seemed to be playing in the care home when we visited Dad. This was after Mum had eventually admitted defeat in looking after him at home.

I've seen a lot of horror, but it is still my dad's terrifying decline with Alzheimer's, before he could even collect his pension, that haunts my days and wakes me in a cold sweat. There is violent, sudden and bloody death, and there is something far worse. I know, if I had to, which I would choose.

I was twenty-seven when I watched my dad die. I was twelve years, eleven months and eight days old when I saw my first dead body.

In a strange way, I had been expecting it. Ever since the attack on Reverend Martin. Perhaps ever since Sean Cooper's accident and the very first chalk man.

And also, because I had had a dream.

I was in the woods. Deep in the woods. Trees rose up like gnarly old giants, stretching creaking limbs toward the sky. A pale moon peeked blearily between their bent and twisted fingers.

I stood in a small clearing, surrounded by piles of rotting brown leaves. The damp night air settled on my skin and sank deep into my bones. I was wearing only my pajamas, trainers and a hoodie. I shivered and zipped the hoodie right up. The metal of the zipper rested, icy cold, against my chin.

Real. Too real.

There was something else. A smell. Sickly sweet, yet sour. It invaded my nostrils and clogged up my throat. One time we had stumbled over this dead badger in the woods. It had gone all rotten and was heaving with maggots. This was the same smell.

I knew right away. It had been almost three months since the accident. A long time underground. A long time to lie in a hard, shiny coffin while wriggly brown worms slid over your softening flesh and started to burrow their way inside.

I turned. Sean Cooper, or what was left of him, smiled at me, his lips cracked and flaking around long white stalks of teeth protruding from black rotting gums.

"Hey, Shitface."

Where his eyes used to be there were now just dark, empty caverns. Except, they weren't quite empty. Inside, I could see things moving. Shiny black things, busily skittering around inside the soft flesh of his sockets.

"What am I doing here?"

"You tell me, Shitface."

"I don't know. I don't know why I'm here. I don't know why *you're* here."

"That's easy, Shitface. I'm Death—your first, up-close experience. Seems like I'm on your mind a lot."

"I don't want to think about you. I want you to go away."

"Tough shit. But don't worry—you'll have other crap to have nightmares about soon."

"What?"

"What do you think?"

I looked around. The trunks of the trees were covered in drawings. White chalk men. They were moving. They shifted and shimmied over the bark, like they were dancing some weird, horrible jig. Their stick limbs flailed and waved. They had no faces but, somehow, I knew they were grinning. And not in a good way.

My skin shriveled on my bones. "Who drew them?"

"Who do you think, Shitface?"

"I don't know!"

"Oh, you know, Shitface. You just don't know yet."

He winked, somehow managing this without eyes or lids, and then he was gone. Not in a cloud of dust this time but a sudden fall of leaves that drifted to the ground and immediately began to curl and die.

I looked back up. The chalk men had gone. The woods had gone. I was in my bedroom, my body trembling with fear and cold, my hands tingling and numb. I shoved them deep into my pockets. And that was when I realized.

My pockets were full of chalk.

OUR GANG HADN'T all got together since the fight. Nicky had left, obviously, and Mickey had his new mates now. If he saw Fat Gav, Hoppo and me, he would usually just ignore us. Sometimes we would hear his gang snigger as we walked past and someone murmur, "Faggots" or "Benders" or something else insulting.

That morning, as I walked into the playground, I barely even recognized him. His hair had grown and lightened. He was starting, spookily, to look a lot like his brother. I was pretty sure he was even wearing some of Sean's clothes.

In fact, for one horrible moment, I thought it *was* his brother, sitting on the roundabout, waiting for me.

Hey, Shitface. Wanna suck my cock?

And this time I was certain—well, almost certain—that this was not a dream. It was daylight, for a start. Ghosts didn't exist in daylight, or zombies. They only existed in that sleepy hollow between midnight and dawn, crumbling to dust at the sun's first rays. Or so, at the age of twelve, I still believed.

Then Mickey smiled, and it was just him. He slid off the roundabout where he had been perched, chewing gum, and sauntered over.

"Hey, Eddie Munster. So you got the message?"

I had. Drawn in blue on the driveway when I came downstairs. The symbol we used when we wanted to meet in the playground, and three exclamation marks. One meant it was pretty urgent. Two meant you had to get there right away. Three meant that it was a matter of life or death.

"What did you want to meet for? What's so urgent?"

He frowned. "Me? I didn't leave the message."

"You left me a message. In blue."

He shook his head. "*No.* I got a message from Hoppo. Green."

We stared at each other.

"Whoah. The prodigal son returns!" Fat Gav strode into the playground. "What gives?"

"Did someone leave you a message to come here?" I asked him.

"Yeah. You did, Penis-breath."

We were partway through explaining when Hoppo arrived. "So who told *you* to come?" Fat Gav asked.

Hoppo looked at him oddly. "You. What's going on?"

"Someone wanted to get us all here together," I said.

"Why?"

You know, Shitface. You just don't know it yet.

"I think someone is going to be hurt, or they have been already."

"Fuck off," Metal Mickey snorted.

I looked around. Another message. There would be one, I was sure. I started to circle the playground. The rest of them watched me like I was mad. And then I pointed. Beneath the baby swings. A drawing, in white chalk. But this one was different. This figure had long hair and wore a dress. Not a chalk *man*, a girl, and drawn next to her several white chalk trees.

I still remember that moment clearly. The crispness of the white chalk on the black tarmac. The faint squeak of the rusty old baby swing and the biting chill of the early-morning air.

"What's that shit?" Metal Mickey asked, walking over. Hoppo and Fat Gav followed. They all peered down at the drawing.

"We need to go to the woods," I said.

"You *cannot* be serious!" Fat Gav exclaimed, but it came out a bit halfheartedly.

"I'm not going to the woods," Metal Mickey said. "It'll take ages, and for what?"

"I'll go," Hoppo said and, even though I knew he was probably only saying it to piss Mickey off, I felt glad of his support.

Fat Gav rolled his eyes, then shrugged. "Okay. I'm in."

Metal Mickey stood mutinously to one side, hands jammed in his pockets.

I looked at the other two. "C'mon."

We walked back across the playground and picked up our bikes.

"Wait." Metal Mickey strolled over. He glared at us. "This had better not be a fucking joke."

"No joke," I said, and he nodded.

We wheeled our bikes out of the playground. I glanced back at the swings. I'm not sure if any of the others had noticed, but there was something different about the chalk figure of the girl. She was broken. The lines of her body weren't constant. Arms. Legs. Head. They weren't joined.

IN A STRANGE way—the way that, when something awful happens, you have this overwhelming desire to just laugh until you can't stop—the ride to the woods that morning was the most exhilarating, the most enjoyable, it had ever been.

We didn't go to the woods much in winter, except for Hoppo, who cycled out sometimes to collect wood. Today, the sun was shining and the icy wind snapped at our faces and tugged at our hair. My skin felt fresh and tingly. My limbs felt like they could cycle faster than ever. Nothing could stop us. I wanted that cycle ride to go on and on but, of course, it couldn't. Far too quickly, the dark mass of the woods drew into view.

"Now what?" Metal Mickey asked, slightly breathless.

We climbed off our bikes. I stared around. And then I spotted it. Drawn on the wooden fence near the stile. A single white chalk arm with a finger pointing straight ahead.

"Onward and over, then," Fat Gav said, hefting his bike over the stile.

He had a look in his eyes that reflected how I felt. A heightened awareness, a kind of almost hysterical excitement. I'm not sure if any of them knew exactly what they were looking for. Or perhaps they did and just didn't want to say it out loud.

Every kid wants to find a dead body. About the only thing a twelve-year-old boy wants to find more is a spaceship, buried treasure or a porn mag. We wanted to find something bad that day. And we did. I'm just not sure anyone realized how bad it would be.

Fat Gav led the way, which I remember feeling miffed about. This was supposed to be *my* adventure. *My* thing. But Fat Gav had always been our leader so, in another way, it felt right. The gang was back together again. Almost.

We seemed to go a long way into the woods before we saw it. Another stick hand on the trunk of a tree.

"This way," Fat Gav said, panting a bit.

"Yeah, we can see that," Metal Mickey said.

Hoppo and I just looked at each other and grinned. It felt more like it used to be. The stupid squabbling. Metal Mickey making snide comments.

We plowed on, off the rough pathway and farther into the heart of the woods. Occasionally, there would be a sudden rush of noise and a group of starlings or crows would take flight from the trees. Once or twice I thought I saw rustling in the undergrowth. Maybe a rabbit, or sometimes you saw foxes here.

"Stop," Fat Gav ordered, and we all ground to a halt.

He pointed at another tree, directly in front of us. On the tree trunk not a stick arm this time but another stick girl. Beneath it was a massive pile of leaves. We all looked at each other. And then back down at the pile of leaves. Something was sticking out of the top.

"Holy fuck!" Fat Gav said.

Fingers.

HER NAILS WERE short and clean and painted a pretty pastel pink. Not chipped or broken or anything. The police would say that she hadn't struggled. Or perhaps she had had no chance. Her skin was paler than I remembered, the summer tan faded to a more wintry hue. She wore a small silver ring with a green stone in the center on her middle finger. I knew, the first moment I saw it, that the arm belonged to Waltzer Girl.

Hoppo bent down first. He was always the least squeamish. I had once seen him put an injured bird out of its misery with a rock. He brushed away more leaves.

"Oh, shit," Metal Mickey whispered.

The jagged end of bone was very white. I noticed it more than the blood. That had dried to a dull, rusty tone, almost blending in with the leaves that still partially covered the arm. Just the arm. Severed at the shoulder.

Fat Gav sat down suddenly and heavily on the ground. "It's an arm," he muttered. "It's a fucking arm."

"Well spotted, Sherlock," Metal Mickey said, but even his practiced sneer sounded a little shaky.

Fat Gav looked at me hopefully. "Maybe it's a joke? Maybe it's not real?"

"It's real," I said.

"What do we do?"

"We call the police," Hoppo said.

"Yeah, yeah," Fat Gav muttered. "I mean, maybe she's still alive—"

"She's not alive, you fat moron," Metal Mickey said. "She's dead, just like Sean."

"You don't know that."

"We do," I said, and pointed to another tree, with another chalk finger drawn on it. "There are more directions . . . to the rest of her."

"We need to get the police," Hoppo said again.

"He's right," Metal Mickey said. "C'mon. We should go."

Nods of agreement. We all started to move. Then Fat Gav said, "Shouldn't someone stay . . . in case . . ."

"What? In case the arm gets up and runs away?" Metal Mickey said.

"No. I don't know. Just to make sure something doesn't happen to it."

We all looked at each other. He was right. Someone should stay guard. But no one wanted to. No one wanted to stay in the quiet hollow of the woods with a dismembered arm, listening to the rustling of the undergrowth, jumping at every flight of birds, wondering . . .

"I'll do it," I said.

After the others left I sat beside her. Tentatively, I reached out and touched her fingers. Because that's what she looked like she was doing. Reaching out her hand, pleading for someone to hold it. I expected her hand to be stiff and cold. But actually, it still felt soft and almost warm.

"I'm sorry," I said. "I'm so sorry."

I'm not quite sure how long I remained in the woods. Probably no longer than half an hour. When the gang eventually returned, with two local policemen to start with, my legs had gone completely numb and I think I must have fallen into some strange half-trance.

But I was still able to assure the police that no one had disturbed the arm. That it was exactly as we found it. And that was almost true.

The only difference was a slightly paler circle around her middle finger where a ring had been.

THEY FOUND THE rest of her under separate piles of leaves around the woods. Well, almost all of her. I guess that's why it took them a while to work out who she was. Of course, I already knew. But no one ever asked. They asked lots of other questions. *What were we doing in the woods? How did we find the body?* When we told them about the chalk drawings on the trees, they were pretty interested in *that*, but when I tried to tell them about the other chalk figures, the messages, I'm not sure they quite got it.

That's the thing with adults. Sometimes it doesn't matter what you say; they only hear what they want to hear.

As far as the police were concerned, we were just kids playing in the woods who followed the chalk directions and stumbled over a body. It wasn't quite how it had happened, but I guess it was close enough. I suppose that's how myths and stuff grow. The past is told and retold, and things get a bit twisted and smudged and, eventually, the new story becomes fact.

Everyone at school wanted to talk to us, naturally. It was a bit like after the fair, except this time people were even more interested, because she was dead. And in bits.

We had an assembly and a policeman came to tell us how we must be extra careful and not talk to any strangers. Of course, now there were lots of strangers around the town. People with cameras and microphones standing talking in the street or by the woods. We weren't allowed to go back there. Tape had been strung up all around the trees and policemen stood guard.

Fat Gav and Metal Mickey took great delight in filling in the gory details and making even more up. Hoppo and I let them do most of the talking. I mean, it was exciting and everything. But I felt a bit guilty, too. It didn't seem right, taking so much pleasure from a dead girl. And it seemed really unfair that Waltzer Girl should survive the day at the fair and have her leg saved, only for it to be cut off again. That really was a pile of stinking Buckaroo.

I felt bad for Mr. Halloran, too. He had seemed so sad the last time I saw him, and that was when Waltzer Girl was alive and they were going away to live together. Now she was dead and wouldn't be going anywhere, except the same, dark, cold place as Sean Cooper.

I tried to say this to Mum and Dad over dinner one night.

"I feel bad for Mr. Halloran."

"Mr. Halloran? Why?" Dad asked.

"Because he saved her, and now she's dead, and it was all for nothing."

Mum sighed. "You and Mr. Halloran still did a brave thing that day. It wasn't for nothing. You must never think that, whatever people say."

"What are people saying?"

Mum and dad exchanged "adult" looks, the sort that adults seem to think, because you're a kid, somehow, magically, you can't see.

"Eddie," Mum said. "We know you're fond of Mr. Halloran. But sometimes we don't know people as well as we think we do. In fact, Mr. Halloran hasn't been here long. None of us really knows him at all."

I stared at them. "Do people think he killed her?"

"We didn't say that, Eddie."

They didn't have to. I was twelve, not stupid.

I felt my throat tighten. "He wouldn't have killed her. He loved her. They were going to go away together. He said."

Mum frowned. "When did he say that, Eddie?"

I had talked myself into a corner. "When I went to see him."

"You went to see him? When was this?"

I shrugged. "A couple of weeks ago."

"At his house?"

"Yeah."

My dad put his knife down with a clatter. "Eddie. You must never go round there again, do you understand?"

"But he's a friend."

"Not anymore, Eddie. Right now, we don't know what he is. You mustn't see him anymore."

"Why?"

"Because we say so, Eddie," Mum said sharply.

My mum *never* said that. She used to say that you can't tell a child something and expect them to do it without a reason. But she had a look on her face right now that I had never seen before. Not when the parcel arrived. Not when the brick came through our window.

Not even when the bad things happened to Reverend Martin. She looked scared.

"Now, promise me?"

I dropped my eyes and muttered, "I promise."

Dad rested a large, heavy hand on my shoulder. "Good boy."

"Can I get down now, go to my room for a bit?"

"Of course."

I slid from my seat and padded upstairs. On my way, I uncrossed my fingers.

2016

Answers. To a question I hadn't even asked. Hadn't even considered asking. Was Chloe all she seemed? Had she been lying to me?

I had to let her go. She had an argument with a customer. Nicky.

I rifle through my kitchen drawers, scrabbling through old takeaway menus, tradesmen's cards and supermarket flyers, trying to piece together the bits of my scrambled mind, trying to think of a rational explanation.

I mean, maybe Chloe got another job and just didn't bother telling me. Maybe she was embarrassed about being sacked—although that doesn't sound like Chloe. Maybe the argument with Nicky was completely coincidental. Maybe it wasn't even the Nicky I know (or knew). It could be some other slim, attractive older woman with flaming red hair called Nicola Martin. Yeah, right. I'm grasping, but it's *possible.*

Several times, I almost call her. But I don't. Not yet. First, I need to make another call.

I slam the drawer shut and head upstairs. Not to my bedroom, but to my collection room. I stare around at the stacked boxes, mentally dismissing some straightaway.

After Nicky left she sent a postcard to all of us with her new address. I wrote a few times but never had a reply.

I take down three boxes from one of the upper shelves and start working through them. The first box yields no results, nor the second. Feeling disheartened, I open the third.

When Dad died, I got another postcard. Just one word. *Sorry. N.* And this time, a phone number. I never called it.

My eyes alight on a creased card with a picture of Bournemouth pier on the front. I snatch it up and turn it over. Bingo. I take out my phone.

It rings and rings. It might not even be the right number anymore. She's probably changed phones. This is—

"Hello?"

"Nicky, it's Ed."

"*Ed?*"

"Eddie Adams—"

"No, no. I know who you are. I'm just surprised, that's all. It's been a while."

It has. But I can still tell when she is lying. She's not surprised. She's worried.

"I know."

"How are you?"

Good question. Many answers. I settle on the easiest.

"I've been better. Look, I know this is a bit out of the blue, but could we talk?"

"I thought we were."

"In person."

"What about?"

"Chloe."

Silence. For so long I wonder if she has hung up on me.

Then she says, "I finish work at three."

THE TRAIN TO Bournemouth gets in at three thirty. I spend the journey pretending to read, occasionally turning the pages of the latest Harlan Coben. After the train pulls in, I shuffle out of the station and join the throng of people heading down toward the seafront. I cross at the pedestrian lights and meander through Bournemouth Gardens.

Despite it barely being twenty miles away, I rarely visit Bournemouth. I'm not really a seaside kind of person. Even as a child, I was slightly scared of the charging waves and hated the feeling of the squishy, gritty sand between my toes; a feeling compounded when I once saw someone bury their half-eaten sandwiches in the sand. From then on, I steadfastly refused to set foot on the beach without my flip-flops or trainers on.

Today, not the warmest of late-summer days, there are still a reasonable number of people wandering around the gardens and playing on the crazy golf (one thing I did enjoy as a child).

I reach the promenade, skirt the now empty site where the once monstrous IMAX cinema slowly decayed after years of disuse, walk past the amusement arcade then turn right toward the seafront cafés.

I sit outside one, nursing a lukewarm cappuccino and smoking. Only one other table is occupied, by a young couple. A woman with short, bleached-blond hair and a companion with dreadlocks and multiple piercings. I feel—and no doubt look—very old and very straight.

I take out my book but, again, I can't concentrate. I glance at my watch. Almost quarter past four. I take another cigarette out of the packet—my third in half an hour—and hunch over to light it. When I look up, Nicky is standing in front of me.

"Disgusting habit." She pulls out a chair and sits down. "Got a spare one?"

I push the packet and lighter across the table, grateful my hand doesn't shake. She slips a cigarette out and lights it, giving me a chance to study her. She looks older. Obviously. Time has etched lines onto her forehead and around the corners of her eyes. The red hair is straighter and streaked with blond. She is still slim, dressed in jeans and a checked shirt. Beneath the careful makeup, I can just see a faint sheen of freckles. The girl beneath the woman.

She looks up. "Yeah. I've aged. So have you."

I am suddenly very aware of how I must look to her. A stringy, disheveled man in a musty jacket, crumpled shirt and half-knotted tie. My hair is awry and I'm wearing my glasses to read. I'm amazed she recognizes me at all.

"Thanks," I say. "Glad we've got the pleasantries out of the way."

She stares at me with her vivid green eyes. "You know the weird thing?"

Many answers. "What's that?"

"I wasn't surprised when you called. In fact, I think I was expecting it."

"I wasn't sure I even had the right number."

A black-clad waiter with a hipster beard he doesn't look old enough to grow and one of those trendy, gravity-defying quiffs saunters over.

"Double espresso," Nicky orders.

He gives the barest inclination that he has heard her and ambles away again.

"So?" she says, turning back to me. "Who's going to go first?"

I realize I have no idea where to start. I look into my coffee for inspiration. None is forthcoming. I decide to go with the obvious. "So, you stayed in Bournemouth?"

"I moved away for work, for a while. I came back."

"Right. What do you do?"

"Nothing exciting. Just clerical stuff."

"Great."

"Not really. It's actually pretty boring."

"Oh."

"You?"

"Teaching. I'm a teacher now."

"In Anderbury?"

"Yes."

"Good for you."

The waiter returns with her coffee. She thanks him. I sip my cappuccino. The movements seem deliberate and exaggerated. We're both stalling.

"So, how's your mum?" I ask.

"She died. Breast cancer. Five years ago."

"I'm sorry."

"Don't be. We didn't get on so well. I left home when I was eighteen. I hadn't seen her much since."

I stare at her. I always thought Nicky had had the happy ending. Getting away from her dad. Her mum coming back. I guess, in real life, there are no happy endings, just messy, complicated ones.

She blows out smoke. "D'you still see the others?"

I nod. "Yeah. Hoppo's a plumber now. Gav took over The Bull." I hesitate. "Did you know about the accident?"

"I heard."

"How?"

"Ruth used to write to me. It's how I found out about your dad."

Ruth? A distant memory stirs. Then I place it. Frizzy-haired friend of Reverend Martin. The woman who took Nicky in after the attack.

"But she kept going on about visiting my dad," she continues. "After a while, I stopped reading her letters. Then I changed address and didn't let her know." She sips her coffee. "He's still alive, you know."

"I know."

"Ah, yes." She nods. "Your mum. The Good Samaritan. Ironic, no?"

I offer a small smile. "You never visited once?"

"Nope. I'll visit him when he's dead."

"Never thought about moving back to Anderbury?"

"Too many bad memories. And I wasn't even around for the worst of it."

No, I think. She wasn't. But she was still part of it.

She leans forward to stub out her cigarette.

"So, we've done the small talk. Shall we cut to the chase? Why are you asking about Chloe?"

"How do you know her?"

She studies me for a moment, and then she says, "You first?"

"She's my lodger."

Her eyes widen. "Shit."

"Reassuring."

"Sorry, but . . . well, it's just—" She shakes her head. "I can't believe she would do that."

I stare at her, confused. "Do what?"

She reaches over and takes another cigarette from the packet without asking. Her shirt sleeve slips back, revealing a small tattoo on her wrist. Angel wings. She notices me noticing.

"In memory of my dad. A tribute."

"But he's still alive."

"I don't call that living."

And I don't call that tattoo a tribute. It's something else. Something I'm not sure I'm entirely comfortable with.

"Anyway," she continues, lighting the cigarette and taking a deep drag, "I didn't know her until just over a year ago. That's when she found me."

"Found you? Who is she?"

"My sister."

"YOU REMEMBER HANNAH Thomas?"

It takes me a moment. Then it clicks. Waltzer Girl's blond protester friend. The policeman's daughter. And, of course . . .

"She was the girl Sean Cooper raped," I say. "And got pregnant."

"Except he didn't," Nicky says. "That was a lie. Sean Cooper didn't rape Hannah Thomas. And he wasn't the father of her baby."

"So who was?" I stare at her, confused.

She looks back at me like I'm an idiot. "C'mon, Ed. Think about it."

I think about it. And realization dawns. "Your dad? *Your dad* got her pregnant?"

"Don't look so shocked. Those protesters were like Dad's own little harem. Groupies. They worshipped him like a rock star. And Dad? Well, let's just say the flesh is weak."

I try to process this. "So why did Hannah lie and say it was Sean Cooper?"

"Because Dad told her to. Because *her* dad couldn't kill a kid who was already dead."

"How did you find out?"

"I heard them arguing about it one night. They thought I was asleep. Just like they thought I was asleep when they were fucking."

I think back to the evening I saw Hannah Thomas in the living room with Mum.

"She came to see Mum," I said. "She was really upset. Mum was comforting her." I smile thinly. "Funny how principles go out the window when it's *your* unwanted baby and *your* life."

"Actually, she wanted to keep the baby. Dad wanted her to get rid of it."

I stare at her incredulously. "He wanted her to have an *abortion*? After everything he did?"

Nicky raises an eyebrow. "Funny how your godly beliefs go out the window when it's *your* bastard kid and *your* reputation at stake."

I shake my head. "Fucker."

"Yeah. Pretty much."

My brain scrambles around again, trying to think this all through.

"So she had the baby? I don't remember."

"The whole family moved away. Her dad got a transfer or something."

And then Reverend Martin got attacked, so he certainly wasn't in any position to keep in touch.

Nicky taps cigarette ash into the ashtray, which is starting to look like a government health warning.

"Fast-forward almost thirty years," she says. "And Chloe turns up on my doorstep. I still don't know exactly how she tracked me down.

"She said she was Hannah's daughter, my half-sister. I didn't believe her at first. Told her to go away. But she gave me her phone number. I didn't intend to call it, but I don't know, I suppose I was curious . . .

"We met for lunch. She brought photos, told me stuff that convinced me she *was* who she said she was. I found myself liking her. Maybe she reminded me a bit of myself when I was younger."

Maybe that's why I liked her, too, I think.

"She told me her mum had died—cancer," she continues. "She didn't have a great relationship with her stepdad. Again, I sympathized.

"We met up a few more times. Then, one day, she said she had to leave her flat and was having problems finding somewhere. I told her she could stop at mine for a bit, if it would help."

"So what happened?"

"Nothing. For three months she was the perfect lodger—almost too perfect."

"And then?"

"I came home one evening. Chloe must have gone out. She'd left her bedroom door ajar . . . and her laptop was open on her desk."

"You snooped in her room."

"*My* room and . . . I don't know, I was just—"

"Invading her privacy?"

"Well, I'm glad I did. I found she had been writing about me. About the chalk men. About all of us. Like she was doing research."

"For what?"

"Who knows?"

"Did she explain?"

"I didn't give her the chance. I made sure she packed her bags that night. She said she was planning to move out anyway. Had a new job in Anderbury."

She stubs out the second cigarette and takes a large gulp of coffee. I notice her hand shakes just a little.

"How long ago was that?"

"About nine or ten months ago?"

So, about the time she turned up on my doorstep, thanking me for giving her the room at short notice.

The wind gusts along the promenade. I shiver and pull up the collar of my jacket. Just the wind. That's all.

"If you hadn't seen her in months, what was the argument at the shop all about?"

"You know about that?"

"It's how I found out she knew you." I frown. "How did *you* find out where she worked?"

"There aren't many places in Anderbury that would employ Chloe."

True.

"And I went to see her because I had a letter—"

My heart falters. "The hangman and the chalk?"

She stares at me. "How did you know?"

"I got one, too, and Gav, Hoppo . . . and Mickey."

Nicky frowns. "So she sent one to all of us?"

"*She?* You think Chloe sent those letters?"

"Of course," she snaps.

"Well, did she admit it?"

"No. But who else could it be?"

There's a pause. I think about the Chloe I know. The sassy, funny, bright person I have become rather more than accustomed to having around. None of it makes sense.

"I don't know," I say. "But I'd rather not jump to conclusions."

She shrugs. "Fine. Your funeral."

Talking of which. I wait as she sips her coffee and then I say, more gently, "Have you heard about Mickey?"

"What about him?"

Ed Adams—bringer of joy and happy news.

"He's dead."

"*Christ.* What happened?"

"He fell in the river, drowned."

She just stares at me. "The river in Anderbury?"

"Yes."

"What was he doing in Anderbury?"

"He came to see me. He was thinking about writing a book about the chalk men. Wanted me to help. We had a fair bit to drink, he insisted on walking back to his hotel . . . but he didn't make it."

"Fuck."

"Yeah."

"But it was an accident?"

I hesitate.

"Ed?"

"Look, this is going to sound crazy, but before he left that night Mickey told me he knew who really killed Elisa."

She snorts. "And you believed him?"

"What if he was telling the truth?"

"Well, that would be a first."

"But *if* he was, maybe his death wasn't an accident."

"So? Who cares?"

For a moment, I'm taken aback. I wonder if she was always so hard. A stick of rock with "BITE ME" stamped all the way through.

"You don't mean that."

"Yes. I do. Mickey spent his life making enemies. He wasn't anyone's friend. You were, once. That's why I came to meet you. But now I'm done."

She pushes her chair back. "Take my advice—go home, kick Chloe out and just . . . get on with your life."

I should listen to her. I should let her go. I should finish my drink and catch my train. But then my life is one long wreck of "should haves," crashing into each other in a big tangled mess of regrets.

"Nicky. Wait."

"*What?*"

"What about your dad? Don't you want to know who was responsible?"

"Ed, just leave it."

"Why?"

"Because I *know* who's responsible."

For the second time, I'm wrong-footed. "You know? How?"

"Because she told me."

THE TRAIN BACK to Anderbury is delayed. I try to dismiss it as an unfortunate coincidence and find I can't. I pace the concourse, cursing the fact I decided to take the train rather than drive (and also stay and drink a bottle of wine rather than catch an earlier train). I glare intermittently at the Departures board. Delayed. It might just as well read: "Determined to screw with you, Ed."

I arrive back just after nine, hot, crumpled and numb down one side from being crushed against the window by a man who looked as if he played rugby for the Titans (the gods, not the team).

By the time I get a bus back from the station and walk up to the house I'm feeling tired, edgy and regrettably sober. I push open the gate and walk up the driveway. The house is in darkness. Chloe must have decided to go out. Maybe for the best. I'm not sure I'm ready for the conversation we need to have just yet.

The first cold finger of unease tickles the back of my neck when I reach the front door and find it's unlocked. Chloe can be frustratingly flippant but she is not usually irresponsible or forgetful.

I hover for a moment, like an unwelcome salesman on my own front step, and then I push the door open.

"Hello?"

The only reply is the breathless silence of the house and a faint humming from the kitchen. I turn the hallway light on and stand there, clutching my redundant keys.

"Chloe?"

I walk into the kitchen, flick on the light and stare around.

The back door is ajar, and a cool draft washes over me. The countertops are littered with the remnants of dinner preparation: a pizza on the side. Some salad in a bowl. A half-drunk glass of wine on the table. The humming noise I can hear is the oven.

I bend down and turn it off. The silence immediately seems

louder. The only sound I can hear now is the blood thumping in my ears.

"Chloe?"

I take a step forward. My foot skids on something on the floor. I look down. My heart goes into arrest. The roaring in my ears increases. Red. Dark red. Blood. A tenuous trail of it leads to the open back door. I walk forward, heart still jitterbugging in my chest. At the back door, I hesitate. It's almost dark. I retrace my steps, grab a torch from the junk drawer and step outside.

"Chloe? Are you out here?"

I walk cautiously around to the back of the house and shine the torch out onto the overgrown wilderness that extends to a small copse of trees. Some of the long grass has been trampled down. Someone has traipsed across the garden recently.

I follow the rough path. Weeds and nettles snag at my trousers. The torchlight picks out something in the grass. Something red and pink and brown. I bend down and my stomach flips like a Russian gymnast.

"Shit."

A rat. An eviscerated rat. Its stomach has been ripped open and its intestines spill out like a jumbled mass of tiny, uncooked sausages.

Something rustles to my right. I jump up and spin around. A pair of green discs gleam at me from the long grass. Mittens leaps forward with a guttural hiss.

I stumble backward, a scream lodged in my throat. "Fuck."

Mittens eyes me with amusement—*"Scare ya much, Eddie, boy?"*—then casually slinks forward, picks up the remains of the rat between his sharp white teeth, and saunters off with it into the night.

I allow myself a brief burst of hysterical laughter. "Fucking *fuck.*"

A rat. *That* was the blood. Just a rat and the fucking *fucker* of a cat. Relief floods through me. And then a little voice whispers in my ear:

"But the cat and the rat don't explain the open back door, do they, Eddie? Or the unfinished dinner preparation? What's that all about?"

I turn back to the house.

"Chloe!" I shout.

And then I break into a run. I charge up the stairs and reach her door. I knock once then shove it open, part of me hoping to see a disheveled head shoot up from her bed. But her bed is empty. The room is empty. Impulsively, I pull open her wardrobe. Empty hangers rattle. I yank out the drawers of her chest. Empty. Empty. Empty.

Chloe has gone.

1986

I thought it might be a while before I got a chance to sneak out. As it was, I only had to wait a couple of days, until the weekend.

Mum got a call and had to rush to the clinic. Dad was supposed to be watching me, but he had a deadline to meet and had locked himself in his study. I saw the note Mum left him: "Make Eddie breakfast. Cereal or toast. NO crisps or chocolate! Love, Marianne."

I don't think Dad even read it. He seemed more distracted than ever. When I went to the cupboard I found that he had put the milk on a shelf inside and the coffee in the fridge. I shook my head, got a bowl out, emptied in a few Rice Krispies and a splash of milk, then left them on the draining board with a spoon resting in the bowl.

I grabbed a packet of crisps and ate them quickly in the living room while I watched *Saturday Superstore.* Then I left the TV on and tiptoed back upstairs to my bedroom. I slid my chest of drawers to one side, pulled out the shoebox and lifted off the lid.

The ring nestled inside. It was still a little dirty with muck from the woods, but I didn't want to clean it. It wouldn't be hers anymore then; it wouldn't be special. That was important. If you wanted to hold on to something, you had to hold on to every part of it. To remember its time and place.

But there was someone else who needed it more. Someone who

loved her, who didn't have anything to remember her by. I mean, he had the paintings. But they weren't part of her, they hadn't touched her skin or rested against her as she slowly cooled on the woodland floor.

I rewrapped the ring in some loo roll and tucked it carefully in my pocket. I don't think I knew exactly what I intended to do at that point. In my head, I imagined I would go and see Mr. Halloran, tell him how sorry I was, give him the ring, and he would be really grateful, and I would have repaid him for all the things he had done for me. I *think* that's what I wanted, anyway.

I heard movement from next door: a cough, the squeak of Dad's chair and the rattle and hum of the printer. I slid the chest of drawers back into place and crept down the staircase. I grabbed my thick winter coat and scarf and, just in case Dad came down and was worried, I scribbled a quick note: "Gone round to Hoppo's. Didn't want to disturb you. Eddie."

I wasn't normally a disobedient kid. But I was stubborn, obsessive even. Once I had an idea, I wouldn't be shaken from it. I can't say I had a moment of doubt or trepidation as I wheeled my bike out of the garage and set off down the road in the direction of Mr. Halloran's cottage.

Mr. Halloran should have already left for Cornwall. But the police had asked him not to go because of the investigation. I didn't know it at the time, but they were very close to deciding whether they had enough evidence to charge him with Waltzer Girl's murder.

Actually, they had very little real evidence. Most of it was circumstantial and hearsay. Everyone wanted him to be guilty because that would be nice, neat and understandable. He was an outsider and, not only that, a strange-looking outsider, one who had already proved himself to be a pervert by corrupting a young girl.

Their theory was that Waltzer Girl had wanted to end the relationship and Mr. Halloran must have flipped and killed her when she told him. This was partially backed up by Waltzer Girl's mum, who told the police that her daughter had come home in tears the previous day after an argument with Mr. Halloran. Mr. Halloran agreed they had argued but denied they had split up. He even admitted they were supposed to meet in the woods that night (with all the scandal and rumors, they had taken to meeting there in secret) but, after the argument, he hadn't gone. I'm not altogether sure what the real truth was, and no one could confirm or deny either story, apart from a girl who would never speak again, except in a place where her voice was all muffled with dirt and worms.

It was quiet for a Saturday morning, but then it was one of those mornings where the day itself doesn't seem to want to get out of bed, like a sulky teenager, reluctant to throw off the covers of night and pull back the curtains of dawn. At ten o'clock it was still murky and gray, only the odd passing car offering sporadic illumination along my route. Most of the houses were in darkness. Even though it wasn't long till Christmas, hardly anyone had any decorations up. I guess nobody felt much like celebrating. Dad hadn't bought a tree yet and I had barely thought about my birthday.

The cottage stood out like a white ghost, the edges slightly blurred in the misty light. Mr. Halloran's car was parked outside. I stopped a short distance away and looked around. The cottage sat on its own, at the end of Amory's Lane, a small street with only a few other cottages on it. No one seemed to be about. Still, instead of leaving my bike propped outside Mr. Halloran's, I left it tucked into a hedgerow across the road, where it couldn't easily be seen. Then I crossed quickly and trotted up the pathway.

The curtains were open but there were no lights on inside. I raised a hand, knocked on the door and waited. No sound of movement. I tried again. Still silence. Well, not exactly silence. I thought I could hear something. I debated. Maybe he didn't want to see anyone. Maybe I should just go home. I almost did. But something—I'm still not quite sure what—seemed to nudge me and say: *Just try the door.*

I placed my hand on the door handle and twisted it. The door opened. I stared at the beckoning sliver of darkness.

"Hello? Mr. Halloran?"

No reply. I took a deep breath and stepped inside.

"Hello?"

I looked around. Boxes were still piled everywhere, but there was a new addition to the small living room. Bottles. Wine, beer and a couple of chunkier ones that said "Jim Beam." I frowned. I supposed all adults drank sometimes. But this was a lot of bottles.

From upstairs I could hear the sound of taps running. That was the faint noise I had heard before. I felt relieved. Mr. Halloran was running a bath. That's why he hadn't heard me at the door.

Of course, it left me in a bit of an awkward position. I couldn't really shout upstairs. He might be naked or something. Also, he would know I had let myself into his house, uninvited. But I didn't want to go back outside and wait either, in case someone saw me.

I debated with myself and then made a decision. I crept into the kitchen, slipped the ring out of my pocket and placed it right in the middle of the table, where it wouldn't be missed.

I should have left a note, but I couldn't see any paper or a pen. I glanced upstairs. There was an odd patch on the ceiling. Darker than the rest. It crossed my mind, briefly, that this was somehow not right, along with the continuously running water. Then a car suddenly backfired out in the street. I jumped, the intrusion of noise reminding me I was in someone else's house, and also about Mum and Dad's warning. Dad might have finished working now, and what if Mum had come home? I'd left a note but there was always the chance Mum might be suspicious and call Hoppo's mum to check.

Heart pounding, I scuttled out of the cottage and pulled the door closed behind me. Then I raced across the street and grabbed my bike. I cycled back home, as fast as I could, propped my bike by the back door, shed my coat and scarf and threw myself onto the sofa in the living room. Dad came downstairs about twenty minutes later and popped his head in.

"All right, Eddie? Been out?"

"Went to call for Hoppo, but he wasn't there."

"You should have let me know."

"I left a note. I didn't want to disturb you."

He smiled. "You're a good boy. How about we make some cookies for when Mum comes home?"

"Okay."

I liked baking with Dad. Some boys thought cooking was girly, but it wasn't when Dad did it. He didn't really follow any recipes, and he put odd things in. They either tasted great or a bit weird, but it was always an adventure finding out.

We were just taking the raisin, Marmite and peanut butter cookies out of the oven when Mum came back an hour or so later.

"We're in here!" Dad called.

Mum walked in. Straightaway I knew something was wrong.

"Everything okay at the clinic?" Dad asked.

"What? Yes. All sorted. Fine." But she didn't look like everything was fine. She looked worried and upset.

"What's wrong, Mum?" I asked.

She glanced at Dad and me and, finally, she said, "I drove past Mr. Halloran's on the way home."

I felt myself tense. Had she seen me? Surely not. I'd been home for ages. Or perhaps someone else had seen me and told her, or perhaps she just knew, because she was my mum and she had a sixth sense about me doing stuff that was wrong.

But, actually, it wasn't any of that.

"There were police outside . . . and an ambulance."

"An ambulance?" Dad said. "Why?"

She said in a quiet voice, "They were bringing a body out, on a stretcher."

SUICIDE. THE POLICE had arrived to arrest Mr. Halloran but instead they found him upstairs in an overflowing bath which was already causing the ceiling below to blister and sag. The water dripping from the ceiling onto the kitchen table was a pale pink. It was darker red in the bath, where Mr. Halloran lay, deep cuts all the way up his arms, from wrist to elbow. Lengthways. Not a cry for help. A scream of goodbye.

They found the ring. Still crusted with the dirt from the woodland floor. That decided it for the police. It was the firm bit of evidence they needed. Mr. Halloran had killed Waltzer Girl, and then himself.

I never confessed. I should have, I know. But I was twelve, and scared, and I'm not sure anyone would have believed me anyway. Mum would have thought I was trying to help Mr. Halloran, and the fact was, no one could help him, or Waltzer Girl, now. What good would telling the truth do?

There were no more messages. No more chalk men. No more terrible accidents or awful murders. I think the worst thing that happened in Anderbury over the next few years was some gypsies stealing the lead from the church roof. Oh, and when Mickey crashed his car into a tree, almost killing himself and Gav of course.

That's not to say people instantly forgot. The murder, and all the other stuff that happened, gave Anderbury a grim notoriety. The local newspapers wallowed in it for weeks.

"They'll be giving free chalks with the weekend editions soon," I heard Mum mutter one evening.

Fat Gav told me that his dad had thought about changing the name of the pub to The Chalk Man but his mum had talked him out of it.

"Too soon," she said.

For a while afterward, you'd see groups of strangers in town. They wore anoraks and sensible shoes and came with cameras and notebooks. They filed into the church and traipsed through the woods.

"Rubberneckers," my dad called them.

I had to ask him what that meant.

"People who like to look at something terrible, or visit the place where something terrible happened. Also known as morbid death hounds."

I think I preferred the second description better. *Death hounds.* That's what the people looked like, with their lank hair, droopy faces and the way they always seemed to have their noses pressed to windows or bent close to the ground, clicking away with their cameras.

Sometimes you would hear them ask questions, too: *Where was the cottage where the Chalk Man lived? Did anyone know him personally? Had anyone got any of his drawings?*

They never asked about Waltzer Girl. No one did. Her mum gave one interview to the newspapers. She talked about how Elisa had loved music, how she had wanted to be a nurse to help people who got hurt, like her, and how brave she had been after the accident. But it was only a small article. It was almost like people *wanted* to forget her. Like remembering she was a real person who died spoiled the story.

Eventually, even the death hounds drifted back to their kennels. Other terrible events took their turn on the front pages. Occasionally, the murder was mentioned in a magazine article, or rehashed on some true-crime program on TV.

There were loose ends, yes. Odd things that didn't quite make sense. Everyone assumed that Mr. Halloran had attacked Reverend Martin and drawn the pictures in the church, but no one could explain why. They never found the ax he used to chop up the body . . .

And, of course, they never found Waltzer Girl's head.

Still, I suppose, although none of us could ever agree on the beginning, we all believed that the day Mr. Halloran died was the day it ended.

2016

My dad's funeral was, in a way, several years too late. The man I knew had died a long time before. What remained was an empty husk. All the things that made him who he was—his compassion, humor, warmth, even his bloody weather forecasts—had gone. His memories, too. And perhaps that was the worst. For who are we if not the sum of our experiences, the things that we gather and collect in life? Once you strip those away we become just a mass of flesh, bone and blood vessels.

If there is such a thing as a soul—and I am yet to be convinced—then my dad's had departed way before pneumonia eventually took him in a sterile, white hospital bed, moaning and delirious; a shrunken, skeletal version of the tall, vital father I had known all my life. I didn't recognize that shell of a human being. I'm ashamed to say that when they told me he had gone it was not grief I felt first but relief.

The funeral was small and held at the crematorium. Just my mum and me, a few friends from the magazines Dad wrote for, Hoppo and his mum, Fat Gav and his family. I didn't mind. I don't think you can judge the worth of a person by how many people turn up when they're dead. Most people have too many friends. And I use the term "friends" loosely. Online "friends" are not real friends. Real friends are something different. Real friends are there, no matter what. Real friends are people you love and hate in equal measure but who are as much a part of you as yourself.

After the service we all went back to our house. Mum had made sandwiches and snacks but, mostly, people just drank. Even though Dad had been looked after in the care home for over a year before his death, and even though the house was more full of people than it had ever been, I don't think it ever felt emptier than it did that day.

Mum and I visit the crematorium together every year on the anniversary of his death. Mum may go more often. There are always fresh flowers by the small plaque that bears his name and a line or two in the Book of Remembrance.

I find her there today, sitting on one of the benches in the garden. The sunshine is sporadic. Gray clouds scuttle restlessly across the sky, hurried along by an impatient breeze. Mum is dressed in blue jeans and a smart red jacket.

"Hello."

"Hi, Mum."

I sit down next to her. The familiar small round glasses sit on her nose and glint in the light as she turns toward me.

"You look tired, Ed."

"Yeah. Been a long week. Sorry you had to cut your holiday short."

She waves a hand. "I didn't have to. I chose to. Besides, once you've seen one lake you've seen them all."

"Thanks for coming back, anyway."

"Well, it was probably enough time with Mittens, for both of you."

I smile. It takes an effort.

"So are you going to tell me what's wrong?" She looks at me just like she used to when I was a kid. The way that makes me feel like she can see right to the heart of my lies.

"Chloe has gone."

"Gone?"

"Packed up, left, disappeared."

"Without a word?"

"Yes."

And I don't expect any. Actually, that's a lie. For the first couple of days, I half expected, half hoped that she would get in touch. She would stroll in casually, make herself a coffee and gaze at me with one ironically raised eyebrow while she gave a laconic and plausible explanation which would make me feel small, foolish and paranoid.

But she didn't. Now, almost a week later, whichever way I try to look at it, I really can't think of any explanation, except the obvious one. She's a devious young woman who played me.

"Well, I was never a fan of the girl," Mum says. "But that doesn't sound like her."

"Guess I'm not a very good judge of character."

"Don't blame yourself, Ed. Some people are very good liars."

Yes, I think. They are.

"D'you remember Hannah Thomas, Mum?"

She frowns. "Yes, but I don't—"

"*Chloe* is Hannah Thomas's daughter."

Behind the glasses her eyes widen a little, but she holds on to her composure. "I see. And she told you that, did she?"

"No. Nicky did."

"You've spoken to Nicky?"

"I went to see her."

"How is she?"

"Probably about the same as when you went to see her five years ago . . . and told her what really happened to her dad."

There is a much longer silence. Mum looks down. Her hands are gnarled and stippled with blue veins. Our hands always give us away, I think. Our age. Our nerves. Mum's hands could do wonderful things. They could tease knots out of my tangled hair, gently stroke my cheek, bathe and plaster a scraped knee. Those hands could do other things, too. Things some people might find less palatable.

Eventually, she says, "Gerry persuaded me to go. I told him

everything. And it felt good, to confess. He made me see that I owed it to Nicky to let her know the truth."

"And what is the truth?"

She smiles sadly. "I've always told you: never have regrets. You make a decision, and you make it for the right reason at the time. Even if it proves to be the wrong decision later, you live with it."

"Don't look back."

"Yes. But that's easier said than done."

I wait. She sighs.

"Hannah Thomas was a vulnerable young girl. Easily led. Always looking for someone to follow. To worship. Sadly, she found him."

"Reverend Martin?"

She nods. "She came to see me one evening—"

"I remember."

"You do?"

"I saw her in the living room with you."

"She should have made an appointment at the clinic. I should have insisted, but she was so upset, poor girl, she didn't know who to talk to, so I let her come in, made her a cup of tea—"

"Even though she was one of the protesters?"

"I'm a doctor. Doctors don't get to judge. She was pregnant. Four months. She was scared to tell her father. And she was only just sixteen."

"She wanted to keep the baby?"

"She didn't know what she wanted. She was just a little girl."

"So what did you tell her?"

"I told her what I told all the women who came to the clinic. I talked her through all her options. And, of course, I asked if the baby's father would want to help."

"What did she say?"

"At first, she wouldn't say who it was, but then it all came pouring out. How she and the reverend were in love but the church wanted to stop them seeing each other." She shakes her head. "I gave her the best advice I could and she went away a little calmer. But I admit, I was upset, conflicted. And then, that day, at the funeral, when her father burst in and accused Sean Cooper of raping her—"

"You knew the truth?"

"Yes. But what could I do? I couldn't breach Hannah's confidence."

"But you told Dad?"

She nods. "He already knew she had come to see me. That evening, I told him everything. He wanted to go to the police, to the church, to expose Reverend Martin, but I persuaded him to keep quiet."

"He couldn't, though, could he?"

"No. When the brick came through our window he was so angry. We argued—"

"I heard you. Dad went out and got drunk . . ."

I know the rest, but I let Mum finish.

"Hannah's father and some of his cronies were in the pub that night. Your dad, well, he'd had a lot to drink, he was angry . . ."

"He told them that Reverend Martin was the father of Hannah's baby?"

Mum nods again. "You have to understand, he couldn't have foreseen what would happen. What they would do to Reverend Martin that night. Break in, drag him to the church, beat him like they did."

"I know," I say. "I understand."

Just like Gav couldn't have foreseen what would happen when he stole Sean's bike. Just like I couldn't have foreseen what would happen when I left Mr. Halloran the ring.

"Why didn't you say anything afterward, Mum? Why didn't Dad say something?"

"Andy Thomas was a police officer. And we couldn't prove anything."

"So that was it? You let them get away with it?"

She takes a while to reply. "It wasn't just that. Andy Thomas and his friends were drunk, out for blood that night. I've no doubt they were the ones who beat Reverend Martin to a pulp . . ."

"But?"

"Those horrible chalk drawings and the cuts on his back? I still find it hard to believe they were the ones who did that."

Angel wings. My mind flashes to the small tattoo on Nicky's wrist. "*In memory of my dad.*"

And something else she said, just before she left, when I asked her about the drawings:

"*My dad loved that church. Only thing he did love. Those drawings. Violating his precious sanctuary. Forget the beating. That's what would have killed him.*"

A coldness sweeps over me. A cool waft of icy gossamer.

"It must have been them," I say. "Who else could it have been?"

"I suppose." She sighs. "I did the wrong thing, Ed. Telling your dad. Not speaking up about who really attacked the reverend."

"That's why you visit him, every week? You feel responsible?"

Mum nods. "He might not have been a good man, but everyone deserves some forgiveness."

"Not from Nicky. She said she'll visit him when he's dead."

Mum frowns. "That's odd."

"One word for it," I say.

"No, I mean, it's odd because she *has* been visiting him."

"Sorry?"

"According to the nurses, she's come every day for the last month."

YOUR WORLD SHRINKS as you grow older. You become Gulliver in your very own Lilliput. I remember St. Magdalene's nursing home as being a grand old building. An imposing mansion at the end of a long, winding driveway, surrounded by acres of neatly striped green lawns.

Today, the driveway is shorter, the lawn outside no bigger than a large suburban garden, slightly overgrown and patchy. No sign of a gardener to tend it and keep things trim. The old hut leans lopsidedly, the door hanging open, revealing a few bits of neglected equipment and some old overalls hanging on hooks. Farther down the lawn, where I encountered the old lady in the fancy hat, the same set of wrought-iron garden furniture squats on rusted legs, abandoned to birds' mess and the elements.

The house itself is smaller, the white walls in need of re-rendering, the old wooden windows in dire need of replacing. It looks—similar to some of its inhabitants, I suppose—like a once grand dame, now fading in her twilight years.

I press the buzzer on the front door. There's a pause, a crackle and then an impatient female voice says, "Yes?"

"Edward Adams, here to visit Reverend Martin."

"Okay."

The door buzzes and I push it open. Inside, the home isn't that different to the way I remember it. The walls are still yellow, or maybe more mustard. I'm pretty sure the same pictures are hanging on them, and it smells the same. Fragrance à la Institution. Detergent, pee and stale food.

In one corner of the hallway is an empty reception desk. A computer displays a jittery screensaver and a light blinks on the phone. The visitors' book lies open. I walk forward and glance around. Then I run my finger down the page, scanning names and dates . . .

There aren't all that many in here. Either the residents have no family or, as Chloe might have said, they have cut them loose, left them to sink slowly into the muddy swamps of their own minds.

I spot Nicky's name right away. She visited last week. So, why did she lie?

"Can I help you?"

I jump. The visitors' book falls shut. A stout, hard-faced woman with hair pulled back into a bun and alarming false nails regards me with raised eyebrows. At least, I think they're raised. They could just be painted on.

"Hello," I say. "I was . . . err . . . just about to sign in."

"You were, were you?"

Nurses have the same look as mums. The one that says: *Don't bullshit me, boy. I know exactly what you were doing.*

"Sorry, the book was open at the wrong page and . . ."

She snorts dismissively, walks over and flicks the book open to today's page. She jabs at it with one glittery purple talon. "Name. Person you're visiting. Friend or relative."

"Okay."

I pick up a biro, write my name and "Reverend Martin." After a moment's hesitation, I tick "friend."

The nurse watches me. "You been here before?" she asks.

"Erm, my mother usually visits."

She looks at me more intently. "*Adams.* Of course. Marianne."

Her features soften. "She's a good woman. Comes and reads to him every week, all these years." She frowns suddenly. "She's okay, isn't she?"

"Yes. Well, she has a cold. That's why I'm here."

She nods. "The reverend is in his room at the moment. I was just going to go and get him out for afternoon tea, but if you'd like to?"

I wouldn't. Actually, now I'm here, the thought of seeing him, being close to him, fills me with revulsion, but I don't have much choice.

"Of course."

"Straight down the corridor. The reverend's room is the fourth one on your right."

"Great. Thanks."

I set off slowly, dragging my feet. I didn't come for this. I came to find out if Nicky had visited her dad. I'm not sure why. It just felt important. Now I'm here, well, I don't really know *why* I'm here, except for having to carry on with the charade.

I reach the reverend's room. The door is shut. I almost turn around and walk straight back down the corridor. But something—morbid curiosity, maybe—stops me. I raise my hand and knock. I'm not really expecting a reply, but it seems polite. After a moment, I push the door open.

If the rest of the home has tried—and failed—to appear more

than just a hospital for people whose minds are ill beyond repair, then the reverend's room has stubbornly resisted such homely touches.

It is bare and austere. No pictures adorn the walls, no flowers stand in vases. There are no books or ornaments or mementos. Just a cross hung on the wall above the neatly made bed and a Bible on the table beside it. The double window—single glazed, a rickety-looking lock, not exactly up to health-and-safety standards—looks out over more untended lawn, which stretches all the way to the edge of the woods. A good view, I suppose, if you are of any mind to appreciate it, which I doubt very much the reverend is.

The man himself, or what remains of him, sits in a wheelchair in front of a small television in one corner of the room. A remote has been placed on the arm of his chair. But the TV screen remains blank.

I wonder if he is asleep, but then I see that his eyes are wide open, staring blankly, like before. The effect is just as disconcerting. His mouth is moving very slightly, giving the impression that he is having some kind of internal monologue with someone only he can see or hear. God, perhaps.

I force myself to walk into the room, then hover for a moment uncertainly. It feels like an intrusion, despite the fact that I'm sure the reverend is barely aware of my presence. Eventually, I perch awkwardly on the end of the bed next to him.

"Hello, Reverend Martin."

No response. But then, what did I expect?

"You probably don't remember me? Eddie Adams. My mum is the one who comes to visit you every week, despite . . . well, despite everything."

Silence. Except the low, wheezy rasp of his breathing. Not even a clock tick-tocking. Nothing to mark the passing of the hours. But then, in here, perhaps that's the last thing you want. To be reminded of the slow dragging of time. I look down, away from the reverend's staring eyes. Despite the fact that I'm an adult, they still make me feel a little spooked and uncomfortable.

"I was just a kid when you saw me last. Twelve. A friend of Nicky's. You remember *her*? Your daughter?" I pause. "Stupid question. I'm sure you do. Somewhere. Inside."

I pause again. I hadn't intended to say anything, but now I'm here, I find I actually want to talk.

"My dad. He had some problems with his mind. Not like yours. His problem was that everything was just seeping out. Like a leak. He couldn't hold on to anything: his memories, his words—himself, eventually. I suppose you're the opposite. It's all locked in. Somewhere. Deep down. But still there."

Either that or it's just erased, destroyed, gone forever. But I don't believe that. Our thoughts, our memories, they have to go somewhere. Dad's might have seeped away from him, but Mum and I tried to mop up what we could. To remember for him. To keep the most precious times safe, in our own minds.

Except, as I get older, I'm finding them harder to retrieve. Events, things someone said, what they wore, or how they looked, are becoming more indistinct. The past is fading, like an old photograph, and as hard as I try, there's nothing I can do to stop it.

I look back at the reverend, and almost shoot off the side of the bed, onto the floor.

He is looking straight back at me, gray eyes clear and hard.

His lips move and a faint whisper escapes. "Confess."

My scalp crawls. "*What?*"

His hand suddenly grabs my arm. For a man who has spent the last thirty years unable to go to the toilet unaided, his grip is surprisingly strong.

"Confess."

"Confess what? I didn't—"

Before I can say anything else a knock at the door sends me spinning back the other way. The reverend releases my arm.

A nurse pokes her head in. A different one from before. Thin and blond, with a kind face.

"Hello." She smiles. "Just wanted to check we were all okay in here?" The smile falters. "Everything *is* okay, isn't it?"

I try to compose myself. The last thing I want is someone hitting the panic alarm and finding myself being escorted from the premises.

"Yes. Fine. We were just . . . well, *I* was just talking."

The nurse smiles. "I always tell people: you must talk to the residents. It's good for them. It might not seem like they're listening, but they understand more than you think."

I force a smile. "I know what you mean. My dad had Alzheimer's. Often he would respond to things you thought he hadn't taken in at all."

She nods sympathetically. "There's so much we don't understand about mental illness. But there are still people inside there. Whatever might have happened to this"—she taps her head—"the heart remains the same."

I glance back at the reverend. His eyes have resumed their fixed stare. *Confess.*

"Maybe you're right."

"We're having tea in the communal room," she says more brightly. "Would you like to bring the reverend through?"

"Yes. Of course."

Anything to get out of here. I take hold of the wheelchair and push him through the door. We walk along the corridor.

"I've not seen you visiting before?" the nurse says.

"No. My mum usually comes."

"Oh, Marianne?"

"Yes."

"Is she okay?"

"She has a cold."

"Oh dear. Well, I hope she feels better soon."

She pushes open the door to the communal room—the room where Mum and I visited before—and I wheel the reverend inside. I decide to take a punt.

"Mum said his daughter has been visiting."

The nurse looks thoughtful. "Actually, yes, I have seen a young woman with him recently. Thin, black hair?"

"No," I start to say. "Nicky is . . ."

And then I pause.

I mentally slap my forehead. *Of course.* Nicky hasn't been here, whatever a smart young woman wrote in the visitors' book. But the reverend has another daughter. *Chloe.* Chloe has been coming to see her dad.

"Sorry," I backtrack. "Yes, that would be her."

The nurse nods. "I didn't know she was family. Anyway, I just need to go and serve the tea."

"Okay. Sure."

She walks away. And a few things click into place. Where Chloe has been going when she hasn't been at work. The visit last week. The same day, she returned drunk, in tears, making those odd comments about family.

But why? More research? Revisiting her past? What is she up to?

I wheel the reverend in and position him so he can see the television, which is playing an old *Diagnosis: Murder.* Christ, if you hadn't lost your mind before you came here, watching Dick Van Dyke and his family hamming it up every day would probably send you over the edge.

Then something else catches my eye. Past the television and the lolling residents in high-backed chairs a frail figure sits just outside the French doors. She's wrapped in a thick fur coat, a purple turban perched precariously on her head, wisps of white hair poking out from underneath.

Garden Lady. The one who told me a secret. But that was almost thirty years ago. I can't believe she's still alive. I suppose it's possible she was only in her sixties back then. But that would still put her in her nineties now.

Curious, I walk forward and push open the doors. The air is cool but the sun lends a faint sheen of warmth.

"Hello?"

Garden Lady turns. Her eyes are milky and hazed by cataracts. "Ferdinand?"

"No, my name is Ed. I came here once before, a long time ago, with my mother."

She leans forward and squints at me. Her eyes disappear into a concertina of brown wrinkles, like crinkled old parchment.

"I remember you. The boy. The thief."

I feel like I should deny it, but what's the point?

"That's right," I say.

"Did you put it back?"

"I did."

"Good boy."

"May I sit down?" I gesture to the only other seat out here.

She hesitates and then nods. "But only for a moment. Soon Ferdinand will be here."

"Of course."

I lower myself into the seat.

"You came to see him," she says.

"Ferdinand?"

"No." She shakes her head dismissively. "The reverend."

I glance back to where he sits, slumped in his chair. *Confess.*

"Yes. You said before—he's got them all fooled. What did you mean?"

"Legs."

"Sorry?"

She leans forward and clasps my thigh in one bony white claw. I flinch. I'm not someone who enjoys uninvited touching at the best of times. Today is definitely not the best of times.

"I like a man with good legs," she says. "Ferdinand. He has good legs. *Strong* legs."

"I see." I don't, but it seems easier to agree. "What's that got to do with the reverend?"

"The reverend?" Her face clouds again. Recognition fading. I can almost see her mind shifting, from present back to past. She lets go of my leg and glares at me. "Who are you? What are you doing in Ferdinand's seat?"

"I'm sorry." I stand up. My left leg smarts a little from her grip.

"Go and fetch Ferdinand. He's late."

"I will. It was . . . nice . . . meeting you again."

She waves a hand dismissively. I walk back through the French doors. The same nurse who saw me in stands nearby, wiping someone's mouth. She glances up.

"Didn't realize you knew Penny?" she says.

"I met her when I came with my mum, years ago. I'm surprised she's still here."

"Ninety-eight now and going strong."

Strong legs.

"And still waiting for Ferdinand?"

"Oh, yes."

"I suppose that's true love. Waiting for her fiancé for all these years."

"Well, it would be." The nurse straightens and offers me another bright smile. "Except, apparently, her late fiancé was actually called Alfred."

I WALK BRISKLY back home. I could have driven to St. Magdalene's, but it's only thirty minutes on foot from town and I wanted to clear my head. Although, to be honest, not much clearing is going on. Words and phrases keep floating around my mind, like confetti in a snow globe.

Confess. Strong legs. Her late fiancé was actually called Alfred.

There's something in there. Almost visible through the flurries. But I can't seem to clear my swirling thoughts to see it.

I pull up the collar of my coat. The sun has slipped away, gray clouds settling in its place. Twilight is already lurking, a dark shadow behind daylight's shoulder.

There's a foreign feeling about the familiar surroundings and landmarks. As if I am a stranger in my own world. As if, all the time, I have been looking at things the wrong way. Not looking *properly.* Everything seems sharper, harder. I could almost imagine if I reached out to touch a leaf on a tree that it might slice right through my fingers.

I skirt past what was once the edge of the woods but is now a sprawling housing estate. I find myself glancing constantly behind me, twitching at every gust of wind. The only people I see are a man walking a reluctant-looking Labrador and a young mum pushing a buggy toward the bus stop.

But that's not quite true. Once or twice I think I see someone or *something* else lurking in the encroaching shadows behind me: a flash of ivory skin, the brim of a black hat, and a pale glimmer of white hair, lingering for a shimmer of a second in the corner of my eye.

I make it home, feeling tense and breathless, bathed in sweat despite the cool temperatures. I place a sticky hand on the door handle. I still need to call a locksmith to change the locks. But first, I really want a drink. Strike that. I *need* a drink. Several. I walk into the hall, and then I pause. I thought I heard a noise, but it could just be the wind or the house settling. And yet . . . I look around . . . something is wrong. Something about the house is different. There's a smell. A vague aroma of vanilla. Feminine. Out of place. And the kitchen door. It's ajar. Didn't I close it before I left?

I call out: "Chloe?"

Resounding silence. Of course. Stupid. Just my nerves, strung tighter than a Stradivarius. I chuck my keys on the table. And then I almost hit the ceiling as a sardonic voice drawls from the kitchen:

"About time."

2016

Her hair is loose, worn down to her shoulders. She has bleached it blond. It doesn't suit her. She wears jeans, Converse and an old Foo Fighters sweatshirt. Her face is free from the usual heavy black eye makeup. She doesn't look like Chloe. Not my Chloe. But then, I suppose she never was.

"New look?" I say.

"Just fancied a change."

"I think I preferred the old you."

"I know. I'm sorry."

"Don't be."

"I never meant to hurt you."

"I'm not hurt. I'm pissed off."

"Ed—"

"Save it. Give me one good reason why I shouldn't call the police right now."

"Because I haven't done anything wrong."

"Stalking. Threatening letters. How about murder?"

"*Murder?*"

"You followed Mickey out to the river that night and pushed him in."

"*Christ*, Ed." She shakes her head. "Why would I kill Mickey?"

"You tell me."

"Is this the part where I admit everything, like in a bad whodunnit?"

"I thought that was why you came back."

She cocks an eyebrow. "Actually, I left a bottle of gin in the fridge."

"Help yourself."

She walks over and takes out the bottle of Bombay Sapphire. "Want one?"

"Silly question."

She pours two hefty measures, sits back down opposite me and raises her glass. "Cheers."

"What are we drinking to?"

"Confessions?"

Confess.

I take a deep swig and remember that I don't really like gin, but right now a bottle of meths would hit the spot.

"Okay. You start. Why did you come here, to live with me?"

"Maybe I've got a thing for older men."

"Once, that would have made an old man very happy."

"Now?"

"I'd just like the truth."

"Fine. Just over a year ago your mate, Mickey, got in touch with me."

"*Mickey*?" It's not the answer I was expecting. "Why? And how did he even find you?"

"He didn't. He found my mum."

"I thought your mum was dead."

"No. That's just what I told Nicky."

"Another lie. What a shock."

"She might as well be dead. She wasn't exactly a great mum. I spent half my teens in and out of care."

"I thought she found God."

"Yeah, well, after him she found booze, weed and any bloke who would buy her a vodka and Coke."

"I'm sorry."

"Don't be. Anyway, it didn't take much for her to tell Mickey who my real dad was. And by much, I reckon about half a bottle of Smirnoff."

"And then Mickey found *you*?"

"Yep."

"Did *you* know about your dad?"

She nods. "Mum told me years ago, when she was drunk. I didn't care. He was just a sperm donor, an accident of biology. But I guess Mickey's visit piqued my interest. Plus, he made me a proposition. If I helped him out with research for a book he was writing, he'd cut me into some of the cash."

I feel a depressing sense of déjà vu.

"Sounds familiar."

"Yeah. But unlike you, I insisted on an upfront payment."

I smile ruefully. "Of course you did."

"Look, I don't feel great about it, but I told myself I was also doing it for me—finding out about my family, my past."

"And the money couldn't hurt. Right?"

Her face tightens. "What d'you want me to say, Ed?"

I want her *not* to say any of this. I want this all to be some horrible nightmare. But reality is always harder and crueler.

"So, basically, Mickey paid you to snoop on Nicky and me. Why?"

"He said you might open up more. And it would make good background."

Background. I guess that's what we always were to Mickey. Not friends. Just fucking background.

"Then Nicky found out what you were doing and kicked you out?"

"Pretty much."

Except, she'd already been planning to move out. She already had a job in Anderbury.

"And I just happened to have a vacant spare room. Perfect timing."

Too perfect, of course. I had wondered why the young man who was about to move in (a rather nervy medical student) suddenly changed his mind and wanted his deposit back. But now I can hazard a guess.

"What happened to my other lodger?" I ask her.

She fingers the rim of her glass. "He might have gone for a few drinks with a young woman who told him that you were a terrible lech with a thing for student doctors and he should lock his bedroom door at night."

"How very Uncle Monty."

"Actually, I did you a favor. He was a bit of a twat."

I shake my head. There is no fool like an old fool, except perhaps a middle-aged fool. I reach for the gin and pour a tumbler full. Then I swig half of it down in one go.

"What about the letters?"

"I didn't send them."

"Then who?"

Before she can reply, I answer my own question. "It was Mickey, wasn't it?"

"Bingo. You win our star prize."

Of course. Stirring up the past. Putting the frighteners on us. It had Mickey written all over it. But I suppose, eventually, the joke had been on him.

"You didn't hurt him?"

"Of course I didn't. Jesus, Ed. Do you really think I'd kill someone?" A pause. "But you're right. I did follow him that night."

Something suddenly clicks in the back of my mind.

"You took my coat?"

"It was cold. I just grabbed it on my way out."

"Why?"

"Well, it looked better on me—"

"I mean, *why* did you follow him?"

"I know you probably won't believe me, but I was tired of lying. I overheard some of the spiel he was feeding you. I felt angry. So I went after him. To tell him I'd had enough."

"What happened?"

"He laughed at me. Accused me of being your little fuck bunny and said he couldn't wait to add that into the book, for color."

Good old Mickey.

"I slapped him," she continues. "Across the face. Maybe harder than I meant. I bloodied his nose. He swore at me and stumbled off . . ."

"Toward the river?"

"I don't know. I didn't hang around. But I didn't push him."

"And my coat?" I ask.

"It was dirty, it had Mickey's blood on it. I couldn't hang it back on the coat stand, so I just stuffed it in the bottom of your wardrobe."

"Thanks."

"I didn't think you'd miss it, and I thought I'd just get it cleaned, when stuff had died down."

"So far, so convincing."

"I'm not here to convince you, Ed. Believe what you want."

But I do believe her. Of course, that still leaves the question of what happened to Mickey afterward wide open.

"Why did you leave?" I ask.

"A friend from the shop saw you come in, heard you were looking for me. They gave me a call. I figured if you found out about Nicky, you'd find out I'd been lying. I couldn't face you, not right away."

I look down into my drink. "So you were just going to run away?"

"I came back."

"For the gin."

"Not just the gin." She reaches for my hand. Her fingernails are black, the polish chipped. "It wasn't all lies, Ed. You *are* my friend. That night when I got drunk, I just wanted to tell you the truth, about everything."

I would like to pull my hand away. But actually, I don't have that much pride. I let her pale, cool fingers rest on mine for a moment before she slides them away and reaches into her pocket.

"Look. I know I can't put everything right, but I thought this might help."

She places a small black notebook on the table.

"What's that?"

"Mickey's notebook."

"How did you get it?"

"I stole it from his coat pocket when he was visiting that night."

"You're not really convincing me of your honesty."

"I never said I was honest. I said it wasn't all lies."

"What's in it?"

She shrugs. "I haven't read much. It didn't make a lot of sense to me, but it might to you."

I flick through a few pages. Mickey's scrawl is hardly more legible than mine. It's not even written in coherent sentences. More like notes, thoughts, names (my own among them). I close it again. It could be something or nothing, but I'd rather look at it later, alone.

"Thanks," I say.

"You're welcome."

There's one more thing I need to know: "Why did you visit your dad? Was that for Mickey and his book, too?"

She glances at me, surprised. "Been doing some research yourself?"

"A little."

"Well, it wasn't anything to do with Mickey. It was for me. Pointless, of course. He hasn't got a fucking clue who I am. Maybe for the best, eh?"

She stands and picks up a rucksack from the floor. A tent is tied on top.

"Mickey's money not stretch to five star?"

"Wouldn't even stretch to a Travelodge." She eyes me coldly. "I'm using it to pay for a college course next year, if you must know."

She hefts the rucksack over her back. Under its bulky weight she looks thin and fragile.

Despite everything, I say, "You'll be okay, won't you?"

"Night or two camping in the woods doesn't hurt."

"*The woods.* You're not serious? Can't you find a hostel or something?"

She gives me a look. "It's fine. I've done it before."

"But it's not safe."

"You mean because of the Big Bad Wolf, or the wicked witch and her gingerbread house?"

"Fine. Mock me."

"That's my job." She walks toward the door. "See you, Ed."

I should have said something. *In your dreams. Not if I see you first. You never know.* Anything. Something fitting to end our relationship.

But I don't. And the moment is gone, falling down the great abyss to join all the other lost moments; the should-haves and could-haves and if-onlys that comprise the big black hole at the heart of my life.

The front door slams. I upend my glass and discover it's empty. Ditto the gin bottle. I stand and grab a bottle of bourbon instead and pour a large measure. Then I sit down and flip open the notebook again. I only mean to scan through it briefly. But four more large measures later and I'm still reading. To be fair, Chloe is right: much of it doesn't make sense. Random thoughts, streams of consciousness, plenty of nonsensical bile; plus, Mickey's spelling was even worse than his handwriting. But still, I keep coming back to one page, right near the end:

Who wanted to kill Elisa?
The Chalk Man? No one.
Who wanted to hurt Reverend Martin?
Everyone!! Suspects: Ed's dad, ~~Ed's mum~~. ~~Nicky~~. Hannah Thomas? Pregnant with Martin's baby. Hannah's father? Hannah?
Hannah—Reverend Martin. Elisa—Mr. Halloran. Link?
No one wanted to hurt Elisa—important.

HAIR.

Something is itching at the back of my brain, but I can't quite reach it to have a good scratch. Eventually, I close the notebook and push it away. It's late and I'm drunk. No one ever found any answers at the bottom of a bottle. Not the point, of course. The point of reaching the bottom of the bottle is generally to forget the questions.

I turn off the light, and start to stagger upstairs. Then I reconsider and stumble back into the kitchen. I pick up Mickey's notebook and take it with me. I use the bathroom, chuck the notebook onto the bedside table and collapse into bed. I'm hoping that the bourbon will cause me to pass out before sleep envelops me. It's an important distinction. Alcohol slumber is different. It's straight unconsciousness, on the rocks. With true sleep, you drift and you dream. And sometimes . . . you wake.

MY EYES SHOOT open. No gradual rising up through the layers of sleep. My heart is pounding, my body is coated in a slick sheen of sweat and my eyeballs feel like they are on stalks. Something has woken me. No. Correction. Something has *wrenched* me into wakefulness.

I stare around the room. Empty, except no room is ever really empty, not in the darkness. Shadows lurk in the corners and pool on the floor, slumbering, sometimes shifting. But that's not what has woken me. It's the feeling that someone, just seconds ago, was sitting on my bed.

I sit up. The bedroom door is wide open. I know I shut it when I came to bed. The hallway beyond is illuminated by a pale shaft of moonlight from the landing window. A full moon tonight, I think. Appropriate. I swing my legs out of bed, even as the tiny, rational part of my brain, the one that still exists even in a dream state, is telling me that this is a bad idea, *really* bad, one of my worst. I need to wake up. Right now. But I can't. Not from this dream. Some dreams, like some things in life, have to run their course. And even if I did wake up, the dream would come back. These types of dreams always do, until you follow them right down to the rotten core and cut out the festering roots.

I slip my feet into my slippers and pull on my dressing gown. I tie it tightly around my waist and walk out onto the landing. I look down. There's dirt on the floor and something else. Leaves.

I move more quickly, down the creaking stairs, through the hallway and into the kitchen. The back door hangs open. A wraith of cold air caresses my bare ankles while the darkness outside beckons with icy fingers. Through the gap I can smell not the freshness of night air but a different scent: dank, fetid decay. I move a hand instinctively to cover my nose and mouth. As I do, I look down. On the dark, tiled floor of the kitchen, a chalk man—one stick arm pointing to the door. Of course. A chalk man to lead the way. Just like before.

I still wait, just a moment more, and then, with one final regretful glance at the familiar comforts of the kitchen behind me, I step out of the back door.

I'm not standing on the driveway. The dream has jumped, in the way that dreams do, to another place. The woods. Shadows rustle and murmur around me, the trees groan and creak, branches shifting this way and that, spindly sleepers plagued by night terrors.

I have a torch in my hand that I don't remember picking up. I point it around and catch movement in the undergrowth ahead. I walk forward, trying to ignore the frenetic beating of my heart, concentrating on my feet snapping and crunching on the uneven ground. I'm not sure how far I walk. It seems a long time but is probably seconds. I feel I must be getting near. But near to what?

I stop. Suddenly, the woods have thinned. I'm standing in a small clearing. One I recognize. It's the same one from all those years ago.

I shine the torch around. It's empty, except for several small piles of leaves. Not crisp, orange-and-brown leaves like before. These are already dead and curling, rotten and gray. And they are moving, I realize with fresh horror. Every small pile shifting restlessly.

"*Eddieeee! Eddieeee!*"

No longer Sean Cooper's voice, or even Mr. Halloran's. I have different company tonight. Female company.

The first pile of leaves bursts open and a pale hand claws at the air like a nocturnal animal waking from hibernation. I stifle a cry. From another pile, a foot emerges and hops out, pink painted toes flexing. A leg shuffles forward on a bloody stump and, finally, the largest pile of leaves erupts and a slim, toned torso rolls out and starts to push itself across the ground like some hideous human caterpillar.

But there is still a piece missing. I stare around as the hand scuttles, on its fingertips, over to the farthest pile of leaves. It disappears underneath and then, almost majestically, she rises from the rotting mound, hair falling over her half-ruined face, carried aloft on the back of her own severed hand.

But he cut off her arm, my mind whimpers, as though that is the important detail in this tableaux of the grotesque.

My bladder, heavy with bourbon, gracelessly lets go and warm urine flows down my pajama leg. I barely notice. All I can see is her head scuttling across the woodland floor toward me, face still shrouded by a curtain of silky hair. I stagger backward, my feet catch on a tree root and I fall hard on to my backside.

Her fingers clutch at my ankle. I want to scream, but my vocal cords are shot, paralyzed. The hand/head hybrid moves delicately up my leg, skimming my wet crotch, and rests momentarily on my stomach. I have gone beyond fear. Beyond revulsion. Possibly several steps beyond sanity.

"*Edddieee,*" she whispers. "*Eddieee.*"

Her hand crawls up my chest. She starts to raise her head. I hold my breath, waiting for those accusing eyes to fall upon me.

Confess, I think. *Confess.*

"I'm sorry. I'm so sorry."

Her fingers stroke my chin and caress my lips. And then I notice something. Her fingernails. They're painted black. That's not right. That's not . . .

She flicks back her hair, newly blonded, tinged red with blood from her severed neck.

And I understand my mistake.

I WAKE IN a thrashing tangle of bedclothes on the floor at the side of the bed. My coccyx feels bruised. I lie there, panting, letting reality flood my senses. Except, it's not quite working. The closeness of the dream is still upon me. I can still see her face. Still feel her fingers touching my lips. I reach into my hair and disentangle a piece of twig. I look down at my feet. The cuffs of my pajamas and the soles of my slippers are covered in dirt and crushed leaves. I can smell the acrid stench of urine. I swallow.

There's something else, and I need to grasp it quickly before it scuttles away again like the hideous head spider from my dream.

I force myself to get up and scramble across the bed. I turn on the bedside lamp and pick up Mickey's notebook from the table. I flick hurriedly through it until I reach the final page. I stare at Mickey's scribbled notes and something suddenly blooms with absurd clarity in my mind. I can almost hear the *ping* of the lightbulb illuminating.

It's like when you stare at one of those optical-illusion pictures and, hard as you try, all you can see are a series of dots or squiggly lines. Then you move, just a fraction, and suddenly you can see the hidden picture. Clear as anything. And once you've seen it, you wonder how on earth you could have *not* seen it. It's so blindingly, crazily obvious.

I had been looking at this all wrong. Everyone had been looking at it all wrong. Perhaps because they never had the final piece of the jigsaw. Perhaps because all the pictures of Elisa, in the papers, in the news reports, showed her *before* the accident. *That* image, *that* picture, became Elisa, the girl in the woods.

But it wasn't the real picture. It wasn't the girl whose beauty had been so cruelly snatched away. It wasn't the girl Mr. Halloran and I had tried to save.

Most importantly, it wasn't the Elisa who had so recently decided that a change was in order. Who had dyed her hair. Who, from a distance, didn't even look like Elisa anymore.

"No one wanted to hurt Elisa—important. HAIR."

1986–90

When I was about nine or ten, I was a big fan of *Doctor Who.* By the time I was twelve, it had gone really lame and crap. In fact, in my earnest twelve-year-old opinion, it all started to go downhill when Peter Davison regenerated into Colin Baker, who was never as cool, with his stupid multicolored jacket and spotty cravat.

Anyway, up until then I had loved every episode, especially the ones with Daleks and the ones where they let the ending hang. A "cliffhanger," it was called.

The thing was, the "cliffhanger" was always better than the solution you waited eagerly for all week. The first episode would usually leave the Doctor in massive danger, surrounded by a horde of Daleks about to exterminate him, or on a spaceship about to blow up, or faced with some huge monster that there was absolutely no escape from.

But he always did, and it usually involved what Fat Gav would call "a huge, steaming cop-out." A secret escape hatch, or a sudden rescue by UNIT, or something incredible the Doctor could do yet again with his sonic screwdriver. Although I would still love watching the second part, I always felt a bit let down. Like I had somehow been cheated.

In real life, you don't get cheats. You don't get to escape the terrible fate because your sonic screwdriver worked on the same frequency as the Cybermen's self-destruct button. It didn't work like that.

And yet, for a while, after I heard that Mr. Halloran had died, I wanted a cheat. I wanted Mr. Halloran to somehow not be dead. To turn up and say to everyone: *Actually, I'm still alive. I didn't do it and this is what really happened . . .*

I suppose it felt, even though we had an ending, that it wasn't the *right* one. It wasn't a *good* one. It was an anticlimax. It felt like there should be something more. And there were things that niggled at me. "Plot holes," I guess you would call them, if you were talking about *Doctor Who.* Things the writers hoped you wouldn't notice, but you did. Even at twelve years old. In fact, *especially* at twelve years old. You're pretty hot on not being cheated when you're twelve.

I mean, afterward, everyone just said Mr. Halloran was crazy, as if that explained everything. But even if you were crazy, or a six-foot-tall lizard in *Doctor Who,* you still had a reason for doing things.

When I said this to the others, to Fat Gav and Hoppo (because, despite the whole finding-the-body thing together, it didn't actually bring us any closer to Mickey, and we still didn't hang out much afterward), Fat Gav would just give me a look of exasperation, twirl his finger at the side of his head and say, "He did it because he was whacko, my man. Round the bend and back again. Looney tunes. A nutjob. A fully paid-up member of the Crazy Brigade."

Hoppo didn't say much, except once, when Fat Gav had gone off on one and it was getting close to an argument. Then, he just added quietly: "Maybe he had his reasons. It's just we don't understand them, because we're not him."

I suppose, beneath it all, there was still a sense of guilt; for my part in things, especially for the stupid, crappy ring.

If I hadn't left it that day, would everyone still have believed Mr. Halloran was guilty? I mean, they probably would, because of the fact that he killed himself. But maybe, without the ring, they wouldn't have been so quick to pin Elisa's murder on him. Maybe they wouldn't have closed the case so quickly. Maybe they would have carried on looking for more evidence. For the murder weapon. For her head.

I could never give myself a satisfactory answer to those questions, those doubts. And so, eventually, I put them away. With childish things. Except I'm not sure we ever really put those away.

TIME MOVED ON, and the events of that summer began to dim in our memories. We turned fourteen, fifteen, sixteen. Exams, hormones and girls took over our thoughts.

And I had other things on my mind by that point. Dad had started to get ill. Life began to form the routine I would become miserably familiar with for several more years. Studying, then working, by day. Dealing with Dad's increasingly degenerative mind and Mum's helpless frustration by evening. That became my norm.

Fat Gav started seeing a pretty, slightly plump girl called Cheryl. He also started to lose weight. Gradually, at first. He started eating less and riding his bike around more. He joined a running club and, although he treated it all like some big joke to start with, soon he was running farther and faster and the weight continued to slip off. It was like he was shedding his old self. And I guess he did. Along with the weight, he lost the more outlandish behavior, the constant stream of gags. Instead came a new seriousness. A steelier edge. He joked less and studied more and, when he wasn't studying, he was with Cheryl. Like Mickey before him, he began to drift away. That left two: Hoppo and me.

I had a couple of not-too-serious girlfriends. And a few unobtainable crushes, including one on a rather severe-looking English teacher with dark hair and quite incredible green eyes. Miss Barford.

Hoppo—well, Hoppo never really seemed bothered about girls at all, until he met this one girl called Lucy (the one who would eventually cheat on him with Mickey and cause the fight at the party I didn't go to).

Hoppo fell, and fell really hard. As a kid, I never quite got it. I mean, she was pretty enough, but nothing special. Kind of mousy, even. Straight brown hair, glasses. She dressed a bit weird, too. Long tassled skirts and big boots, tie-dyed T-shirts and all that hippie shit. Not exactly cool.

It was only later that I realized who she reminded me of: Hoppo's mum.

Anyway, they seemed to get along and be pretty well matched. They liked the same things, although, in relationships, I guess we all bend a little and pretend to like stuff we don't to please the other person.

Friends do the same. I wasn't that keen on Lucy but I pretended to like her to please Hoppo. At that point I was seeing a girl in the year below called Angie. She had shaggy permed hair and a pretty decent body. I wasn't in love, but I fancied her and she was easy (not in that way, although, to be fair, she wasn't difficult either). She was easy to be with: undemanding, relaxed. With everything else going on with Dad, I needed that.

We went on a few double dates with Hoppo and Lucy. I can't say Lucy and Angie had much in common but Angie was the kind of affable girl who made an effort with people. Which was good, because it meant I didn't have to.

We went to the cinema, out to the pub and then, one weekend, Hoppo suggested something different.

"Let's go to the fair."

We were in the pub at the time. Not The Bull. No way would Fat Gav's dad have let us order pints of snakebite there. This was The Wheatsheaf, across town, where the landlord didn't know us and, to be honest, wouldn't have cared that we were only sixteen in any case.

It was June, so we were sitting outside in the beer garden, which was basically a small yard out the back furnished with a few rickety wooden tables and benches.

Lucy and Angie both reacted enthusiastically. I remained silent. I hadn't been back to the fair since the day of the terrible accident. I wouldn't say I had been actively avoiding fairs or amusement parks, I just hadn't felt that inclined to visit one.

But that was a lie. I was scared. I had bottled a trip to Thorpe Park the previous summer, claiming a stomach upset, which had been kind of true. My stomach churned every time I thought about going on a ride of any kind. All I could see was Waltzer Girl, lying on the ground with her leg hanging off and her lovely face reduced to gristle and bone.

"Ed?" Angie said, squeezing my leg. "What do you say? Fancy the fair tomorrow?" She whispered in my ear, a little drunkenly, "I'll let you finger me on the Ghost Train."

Tantalizing as the idea was (so far, I had only fingered Angie in the rather unexciting surroundings of my room), I still had to force a smile.

"Yeah. Sounds great."

It didn't, but I didn't want to look chicken, not in front of Angie and, for some reason, not in front of Lucy, who was giving me an odd look. A look I didn't like, as if she knew I was lying.

IT WAS HOT, the day of the fair. Just like before. And Angie was good to her word. But still, even that didn't give me all the pleasure I thought it would, although I did have a little difficulty walking when I exited the Ghost Train. It soon deflated when I saw where we had come out. Right opposite the Waltzers.

Somehow, I must have missed them before. Perhaps because they had been obscured by the crowds, or maybe because my mind was on other things, like Angie's tiny Lycra miniskirt and what waited, temptingly, a couple of inches beneath it.

Now I stood, frozen, staring at the swirling, twirling carriages. Bon Jovi blared from speakers somewhere. Girls screamed in delight as the fairground workers spun the carriages round and round.

"Scream if you want to go faster."

"Hey." Hoppo emerged by my side and then saw where I was looking. "You okay?"

I nodded, not wanting to seem like a wuss in front of the girls. "Fine, yeah."

"Shall we go on the Waltzers next?" Lucy said, linking her arm through Hoppo's.

She said it innocently enough, but to this day I'm sure there was something else behind it. A disingenuity. A slyness. She knew. And she was enjoying taunting me.

"I thought we were going on the Round Up," I said.

"We can do that after. C'mon, Eddie. It'll be fun."

I also hated that she called me Eddie. Eddie was a kid's name. At sixteen, I liked to be called Ed.

"I just think the Waltzers are lame." I shrugged. "But if you want to go on a crap ride, fine by me."

She smiled. "What d'you say, Angie?"

I knew what Angie would say. So did Lucy.

"If that's what everyone else wants to do? I'm easy."

And just for a moment I wished she wasn't. I wished she had an opinion, a backbone. Because another word for "easy" is "pushover."

"Great." Lucy grinned. "Let's go."

We walked up to the Waltzers and joined the small queue at the side. My heart was racing. My hands felt clammy. I thought I might throw up, and I hadn't even got on the ride, wasn't yet enduring the vomit-inducing spins.

The previous riders clambered off. I helped Angie up, trying to seem gentlemanly by letting her go first. I put my foot on the wobbly wooden platform, and then I paused. Something had caught my eye or, rather, something had fleetingly registered in the corner of it. Just enough to make me turn.

A tall, skinny figure stood by the Ghost Train. Dressed all in black. Tight black jeans, baggy shirt and a wide-brimmed black cowboy hat. His back was to me, watching the Ghost Train, but I could see long, white-blond hair trailing down his back.

"*You still with me, Eddie?*"

Crazy. Impossible. It couldn't be Mr. Halloran. Couldn't be. He was dead. Gone. Buried. But then, so was Sean Cooper.

"Ed?" Angie looked down at me quizzically. "You okay?"

"I . . ."

I looked back toward the Ghost Train. The figure had moved. I saw a black shadow disappear around the corner.

"Sorry, I have to go check on something."

I hopped down from the Waltzers.

"*Ed?* You can't just run off!"

Angie glared at me; it was as close as she'd ever got to being really pissed off. It left me in no doubt that our encounter in the Ghost Train might well be the last I could enjoy for a while but, right then, it didn't matter. I had to go. I had to *know.*

"Sorry," I mumbled again.

I jogged back across the fairground. I rounded the corner of the Ghost Train just as the figure disappeared behind the candyfloss and balloon stalls. I picked up my pace, bumping into a few people en route and causing them to tut and swear at me. I didn't care.

I'm not sure if I believed that the apparition I was following was real, but I was no stranger to ghosts. Even as a teenager I still checked outside my bedroom window at night in case Sean lurked below. I still worried that every bad smell might signal the touch of a decaying hand upon my face.

I hurried past the Dodgems and the Orbiter, once such a big draw, and now, with the advent of roller coasters and even bigger-thrill rides, kind of tame. I was making ground. And then the figure stopped. I paused, too, lurking behind a hot-dog stall. I watched as they reached into their pocket and pulled out a packet of cigarettes.

That's when I realized my mistake. The hands. Not fine-fingered and pale but coarse and dark brown with long, jagged nails. The figure turned. I stared at the haggard face. Lines so deep it looked like they had been carved with a blade; eyes blue stones buried within the scars. A yellow beard trailed down his chin, almost to his chest. Not Mr. Halloran, not even a young man, but an old man; a gyppo.

His voice was gravel in a rusty bucket. "What you starin' at, sonny?"

"Nothing. I . . . I'm sorry."

I turned and scurried away as fast as dignity—the remaining shreds of it—would allow. When I was far enough away to be out of sight, I paused, trying to breathe, trying to rein in the waves of nausea that threatened to swallow me. Then I shook my head and, instead of vomit, laughter spewed from my mouth. Not Mr. Halloran, not the Chalk Man, but an old fairground hand, probably with a bald crown beneath that cowboy hat.

Crazy, crazy, crazy. Like the fucking dwarf in *Don't Look Now,* a film we had illicitly watched at Fat Gav's a couple of years ago, and only because we had heard that Donald Sutherland and Julie Christie really "did it" on camera. (Actually, it was really disappointing, because you didn't see enough of Julie Christie, and you saw far too much of Sutherland's skinny white arse.)

"Ed. What's going on?"

I looked up to see Hoppo running toward me, followed by the girls. They must have all got off the Waltzers. Lucy looked pretty annoyed about it.

I tried to stop laughing, to appear sane.

"I thought I saw him. Mr. Halloran. The Chalk Man."

"*What?* Are you joking?"

I shook my head. "But it wasn't him."

"Well, of course not," Hoppo said, frowning. "He's dead."

"I know," I said. "I just . . ."

I looked up at their worried, puzzled faces, and nodded slowly. "I know. I was wrong. Stupid."

"C'mon," Hoppo said, still looking concerned. "Let's go get a drink."

I looked at Angie. She offered me a faint smile and held out her hand. I was forgiven. Too easily. As ever.

Still, I grasped it. Gratefully. And then she asked, "Who's the Chalk Man?"

WE BROKE UP not long after that. I guess we didn't have that much in common. Didn't really know each other that well after all. Or perhaps I was already a young man with history and baggage, and it would have to be a special person who could share the burden. Maybe that's why I have remained resolutely single for so long. I still haven't found that person. Not yet. Maybe never.

After the fair, I kissed Angie goodbye and walked wearily back home in the still-smoldering late-afternoon heat. The streets were strangely deserted, residents seeking shelter in the shade of beer gardens and back lawns; even the traffic on the roads was sporadic, no one wanting to swelter for too long in a big metal can.

I rounded the corner of our street, still feeling a little out of sorts from the incident at the fair. I suppose I felt a little stupid, too. I had been so easily spooked, so easily convinced it could be him. Idiot. Of course it wasn't. Couldn't be. Just another cheat.

I sighed, trudged up the driveway and pushed open the front door. Dad sat in his favorite armchair in the living room, staring blankly at the TV. Mum stood in the kitchen, making dinner. She was red-eyed, as though she had been crying. Mum didn't cry. Not easily. I guess I took after her on that front.

"What's wrong?" I asked.

She wiped her eyes but didn't bother telling me it was nothing. Mum didn't lie either. Or so I thought. Back then.

"Your dad," she said.

As if it could have been anything else. Sometimes—and I still find it shameful to admit it—I really hated Dad for being ill. For the things it made him do and say. For the vacant, lost look in his eyes. For how his illness affected Mum and me. As a teenager, you just want, more than anything, to be normal, and nothing about our life with Dad was normal.

"What's he done now?" I asked, barely managing to hide my contempt.

"He forgot me," Mum said, and I could see fresh tears welling. "I took him his lunch and, just for a moment, he looked at me like I was a stranger."

"Oh, *Mum.*"

I drew her to me and hugged her as hard as I could, like I could squeeze out all the pain, even as a small part of me wondered if, sometimes, forgetting was the kindness.

Remembering—perhaps that was the killer.

2016

"Never assume," my dad once told me. "To assume makes an 'ass' out of 'u' and 'me.' "

When I stared at him blankly, he went on, "See this chair? You believe it will still be here, where it is now, in the morning?"

"Yes."

"Then you assume."

"I suppose."

Dad picked up the chair and stood it on the table. "The only way to be sure this chair is going to stay in the exact same spot is to glue it to the floor."

"But that's a cheat?"

His voice got more serious. "People will always cheat, Eddie. And lie. That's why it's important to question everything. Always look beyond the obvious."

I nodded. "Okay."

The kitchen door opened and Mum walked in. She looked at the chair, and then at Dad and me, and shook her head.

"I'm not sure I want to know."

NEVER ASSUME. QUESTION *everything. Always look beyond the obvious.*

We assume things because it's easier, lazier. It stops us thinking too hard—usually about stuff that makes us feel uncomfortable. But not thinking can lead to misunderstandings and, in some cases, tragedies.

Like Fat Gav's reckless prank, which ended in a death. Just because he was a kid who didn't really think of the consequences. And Mum, who didn't think that telling Dad about Hannah Thomas could do that much harm, who assumed her husband would keep her confidence. And then there was the young boy who stole a small silver ring, and tried to give it back because he thought he was doing the right thing, and was, of course, so very, very wrong.

Assuming can trip us up in other ways, too. It can stop us seeing people for who they really are and make us lose sight of the people we know. I assumed it was Nicky who visited her father at St. Magdalene's, but it was Chloe. I assumed I was chasing Mr. Halloran at the fair, but it was just an old fairground hand. Even Penny the Garden Lady had led everyone up a winding path of assumptions. Everyone believed she was waiting for her dead fiancé, Ferdinand. But Ferdinand wasn't her fiancé. That was poor old Alfred. All those years, she had been waiting for her lover.

Not a case of undying love but of infidelity and mistaken identity.

FIRST THING THE next morning, I make some phone calls. Well, actually, *first thing* I make several cups of extremely strong coffee, smoke half a dozen cigarettes and *then* I make some phone calls. First to Gav and Hoppo, then to Nicky. Predictably, she doesn't answer. I leave her a garbled message, which I fully expect her to delete without listening to. Finally, I call Chloe.

"I'm not sure, Ed."

"I need you to do this."

"I haven't spoken to him in years. We're not exactly close."

"Good time to reconnect."

She sighs. "You're wrong about this."

"Maybe. Maybe not. But—as if I need to point it out—you owe me."

"Fine. I just don't get why this is so important. Why now? It was thirty years ago, for fuck's sake. Why not just leave it be?"

"I can't."

"This isn't about Mickey, is it? Because you certainly don't owe *him* anything."

"No." I think about Mr. Halloran and what I stole. "Maybe I owe someone else, and it's about time I repaid that debt."

THE ELMS IS a small retirement estate just outside Bournemouth. There are dozens of such estates dotted around the south coast. In fact, the south coast is pretty much one massive retirement estate, although some areas are a little more exclusive than others.

It's fair to say that The Elms is one of the less desirable developments. The cul-de-sac of small square bungalows is tired and a little shabby. The gardens are still neatly kept but the paintwork is flaking and peeling, the cladding weather-worn. The cars outside tell their own story, too. Small, shiny cars—all cleaned religiously every Sunday, I'm willing to bet—but all several years old. It's not a bad place to retire to. On the other hand, it's not much to show for forty years' hard graft.

Sometimes, I think that everything we strive to achieve in life is ultimately pointless. You work hard so you can buy a nice, big house for your family and drive around in the latest 4x4 Countryside Destroyer. Then the kids grow up and move out, so you trade down to a smaller, eco-friendly model (maybe with just enough room for a dog in the back). Then you retire and the big, family home is a prison of shut doors and rooms gathering dust, and the garden that was so great for family barbecues is far too much work and the kids have their own family barbecues these days, anyway. So, the house gets smaller, too. And maybe, sooner than you ever expected, there's just you to look after. And you tell yourself that it's good you moved when you did, because smaller rooms are harder to fill with loneliness. If you're lucky, you'll make your own exit before you are reduced, once again, to living in a single room, sleeping in a bed with bars, unable to wipe your own bottom.

Armed with such cheery thoughts, I ease my car into the small space outside number twenty-three. I walk up the short pathway and ring the doorbell. I wait a few seconds. I'm about to ring the bell again when I see the faint outline of a figure approaching through the frosted glass, and then hear the rattle of chains and the door being unlocked. Security conscious, I think. But then, that's hardly surprising, considering his former profession.

"Edward Adams?"

"Yes."

He holds out his hand. After a moment's hesitation, I shake it.

The last time I saw PC Thomas up close was when he was standing on the doorstep of my own home, thirty years ago. He is still thin, but not as tall as I remember. Obviously, I'm quite a bit taller myself, but it's true that age does diminish a man. The dark hair is now mostly gray and mostly gone. The square face is less rugged, more haggard. He still looks a bit like a giant piece of Lego, but slightly melted.

"Thanks for agreeing to see me," I say.

"I have to admit, I wasn't sure . . . but I suppose Chloe piqued my curiosity." He moves away from the door. "Come on in."

I walk into a small, narrow hallway. It smells faintly of stale food and strongly of air freshener. Really heavy on the air freshener.

"Living room's ahead on your left."

I walk forward and push open a door into a surprisingly large lounge with sagging beige sofas and floral curtains. The choice of the former lady of the house, I imagine.

According to Chloe, her grandfather moved back down south a few years ago, when he retired. A couple of years after that, his wife died. I wonder if that was when he stopped whitewashing the walls and weeding the garden.

Thomas gestures for me to sit in the less worn of the two sofas. "Drink?"

"Err, no, thanks. I just had a coffee." A lie, but I don't want to make this visit a social occasion, not with what I want to discuss.

"Okay." He stands for a moment, a little lost.

He doesn't get many visitors, I think. He doesn't know how to act with someone else in his home. A bit like me.

Finally, he sits, stiffly, hands resting on his knees. "So, the Elisa Rendell case. Long time ago now. You were one of the kids who found her?"

"Yes."

"And now you have a theory about who really killed her?"

"I do."

"You think the police got it wrong?"

"I think we all did."

He rubs his chin. "The circumstantial evidence was convincing. But that's all it was. Circumstantial. If Halloran hadn't topped himself, I'm not sure there would have been enough to bring a case. The only solid evidence was the ring."

I feel my cheeks flush. Even now. The ring. The damn ring.

"But there was no murder weapon, no blood evidence." A pause. "And, of course, we never found her head." He looks at me more sharply, and it's like thirty years have been stripped away. Like a light has been reignited behind his eyes.

"So what's your theory?" he asks, leaning forward.

"Could I ask you some questions first?"

"I suppose, but bear in mind I wasn't that closely involved in the case. I was just a lowly PC."

"Not about the case. About your daughter and Reverend Martin."

He stiffens. "I don't understand what that has to do with anything."

Everything, I think.

"Just humor me."

"I could just ask you to leave."

"You could."

I wait. Bluff called. I can tell he wants to throw me out, but I'm hoping curiosity and the old instincts of a copper will get the better of him.

"Okay," he says. "I'll humor you. But this is for Chloe."

I nod. "I understand."

"No. You don't. She's all I've got left."

"What about Hannah?"

"I lost my daughter a long time ago. And today was the first time I've heard from my granddaughter in over two years. If talking to you means I get to see her again, then I'll do it. You understand *that*?"

"You want me to persuade her to visit you?"

"She obviously listens to you."

Not really, but she does still owe me.

"I'll do what I can."

"Fine. That's all I can ask." He sits back. "What do you want to know?"

"How did you feel about Reverend Martin?"

He snorts. "I would have thought that was pretty bloody obvious."

"And what about Hannah?"

"She was my daughter. I loved her. I still do."

"And when she got pregnant?"

"I was disappointed. Any father would be. Angry, too. I suppose that's why she lied to me about the father."

"Sean Cooper."

"Yeah. She shouldn't have done that. I felt bad afterward, saying what I did about the boy. But at the time, if he hadn't been dead, I would have killed him."

"Like you tried to kill the reverend?"

"He got what was coming to him." He smiles thinly. "I suppose I have your dad to thank for that."

"I suppose you do."

He sighs. "Hannah, she wasn't perfect. Just a normal teenager. We had the usual disagreements, about makeup, the shortness of her skirts. When Hannah got in with Martin's religious crowd, I was pleased. I thought it would be good for her." A sour chuckle. "How wrong could I be? He ruined her. We were close before. But afterward all we did was argue."

"Did you argue the day Elisa was murdered?"

He nods. "One of the worst."

"Why?"

"Because she had gone to visit him, at St. Magdalene's. To tell him she was going to keep his baby. That she would wait for him."

"She was in love with him."

"She was a child. She didn't know what love was." He shakes his head. "Got any children, Ed?"

"No."

"Wise man. Kids, from the moment they're born, they fill your heart with love . . . and terror. Especially little girls. You want to protect them from everything. And when you can't, you feel like you've failed as a father. You've saved yourself a lot of pain by not having children."

I shift a little in my chair. Even though the room is not especially warm, I feel hot, suffocated. I try to get the conversation back on track.

"So, you were saying, Hannah went to visit Reverend Martin that day, the day Elisa was killed?"

He gathers himself. "Yes. We had a terrible argument. She ran out. Didn't come back for dinner. That's why I was out that night. Looking for her."

"You were near the woods?"

"I thought she might have gone there. I know it's where they used to meet sometimes." He frowns. "All of this was reported at the time."

"Mr. Halloran and Elisa used to meet in the woods, too."

"It's where a lot of kids met to do stuff they shouldn't. Kids . . . and perverts."

He spits out the last word. I look down. "I used to idolize Mr. Halloran," I say. "But, I suppose, he was just another older man with a thing for young girls, just like the reverend."

"No." Thomas shakes his head. "Halloran was nothing like the reverend. I'm not condoning what he did, but it wasn't the same. The reverend was a hypocrite, a liar, spouting the word of God when, really, he was using it to prey on those young girls. He changed Hannah. He pretended to be filling her with love, but all along he was filling her heart with poison, and, when that wasn't enough, he filled her belly with his bastard child."

The blue eyes blaze. Creamy spittle nestles at the corners of his lips. People say there's nothing stronger than love. They're right. That's why the worst atrocities are always committed in its name.

"Is that why you did it?" I ask quietly.

"Did what?"

"You went into the woods, and you saw her, didn't you? Just standing there, like she used to when she was waiting to meet him? Is that when you cracked? Did you grab her, choke her, before she even had a chance to turn? Perhaps you couldn't bear to look at her, and when you did, *when you realized your mistake*, it was too late.

"So you came back later, you chopped her up. I don't know why exactly. To hide the body? Or perhaps simply to confuse things—"

"What the *hell* are you talking about?"

"You killed Elisa, because you thought she was Hannah. They were the same build, Elisa had even dyed her hair blond. Easy mistake to make, in the dark, when you're emotional, angry. You thought Elisa was your daughter, who had been poisoned, corrupted and was carrying the reverend's bastard child—"

"*No!* I loved Hannah. I wanted her to keep the baby. *Yes,* I thought she should have it adopted, but I would never have hurt her. Never—"

He stands abruptly. "I shouldn't have agreed to see you. I thought you might genuinely know something, but *this*? *This* is when I ask you to leave."

I stare up at him. If I'm expecting to see guilt or fear on his face, I'm wrong. All I see is anger and pain. A lot of pain. I feel sick. I feel like a shit. Most of all, I feel that I have got this terribly, terribly wrong.

"I'm sorry. I—"

His look withers me down to my bone. "Sorry for accusing me of wanting to kill my own daughter? I'm not sure that quite covers it, *Mr.* Adams."

"No . . . no, I suppose not." I get up and walk toward the door. Then I hear him say:

"Wait."

I turn. He walks toward me.

"I should probably punch you for what you just said . . ."

I sense a "but." At least, I'm hoping for one.

"But mistaken identity? It's an interesting theory."

"And wrong."

"Maybe not entirely wrong. Just the wrong person."

"What are you saying?"

"Aside from Halloran, no one had any motive to hurt Elisa. But Hannah? Well, Reverend Martin had a lot of supporters back then. If any of them knew about their relationship, about the baby, one of them might just have been jealous enough—*crazy* enough—to kill for him."

I consider this. "But you have no idea where any of them are now?"

He shakes his head. "No."

"Right."

Thomas rubs at his chin. He seems to be debating something with himself. Finally, he says: "That night, when I was looking for Hannah near the woods, I saw someone. It was dark, and from a distance, but he was dressed in overalls, like a workman, and he had a limp."

"I don't remember hearing anything about another suspect."

"It was never followed up."

"Why?"

"Why bother, when we already had the culprit, and, handily, a dead one, who would save the expense of a trial? Besides, it wasn't really much of a description to go on."

He's right. It isn't a lot of help. "Thanks, anyway."

"Thirty years is a long time. You know, you might never get the answers you're looking for . . ."

"I know."

"Or worse. You get the answers, and they're not the ones you want."

"I know that, too."

By the time I climb back into the car, I'm shaking. I wind the window down and take out my cigarettes. I light one greedily. I had put my mobile on silent when I went into the bungalow. I pull it out now and find I have a missed call. Two, actually. I'm never that popular.

I call voicemail and listen to the two garbled messages, one from Hoppo and one from Gav. Both saying the same thing:

"Ed, it's about Mickey. They know who killed him."

2016

They are sitting at their usual table, although, unusually, Gav has a pint of ale in front of him instead of Diet Coke.

I've barely settled with my own pint when he slaps the newspaper down on the table in front of me. I stare at the headline.

YOUTHS ARRESTED OVER RIVERSIDE ATTACK

Two fifteen-year-old youths are being questioned over the fatal attack on former local resident Mickey Cooper (42). The pair were apprehended after an attempted mugging on the same stretch of riverside path two nights ago. Police are "keeping an open mind" as to whether the incidents are connected.

I scan the rest of the story. I hadn't heard about the mugging, but then, I've had other things on my mind. I frown.

"Something wrong?" Gav asks.

"It doesn't actually say these youths attacked Mickey," I point out. "In fact, it's all just conjecture."

He shrugs. "So? It makes sense. A mugging gone wrong. Nothing to do with his book, or the chalk men. Just a couple of little thugs out to score a quick buck."

"I suppose. Do they know who the kids are?"

"I heard one of them is from your school. Danny Myers?"

Danny Myers. I should feel surprised, but I'm not. It seems that nothing much can surprise me about human nature anymore. Still . . .

"You don't look convinced," Hoppo says.

"About Danny mugging someone? I can see him doing something stupid to impress his mates. But killing Mickey . . ."

I'm not convinced. It's too pat. Too easy. Too much like making an " 'ass' of 'u' and 'me.' " And there's something else, niggling at the back of my mind.

The same stretch of riverside path.

I shake my head. "I'm sure Gav's right. It's probably the most likely explanation."

"Kids today, eh?" Hoppo says.

"Yeah," I say slowly. "Who knows what they're capable of."

There's a pause. It lengthens. We sip our pints.

Eventually, I say, "Mickey would be really pissed off at being called a 'former local resident.' He'd have expected 'high-flying ad exec' at the very least."

"Yeah. Well, 'local' is probably not the worst thing he's been called," Gav says. And then his face grows hard. "I still can't believe he paid Chloe to spy on you. *And* sent us those letters."

"I think he just wanted to spice up his book," I say. "The letters were his way of creating a plot device."

"Well, Mickey was always good at making stuff up," Hoppo says.

"And stirring shit up," Gav adds. "Let's just hope that's an end to it now."

Hoppo raises his pint. "I'll drink to that."

I reach for my drink, but I must be a little distracted. My hand knocks the pint, sending it toppling over. I manage to grab the glass to stop it shattering on the floor, but ale slops out, over the side of the table, onto Gav's lap.

Gav waves a hand. "Don't worry about it." He brushes at his jeans, wiping off the spilled beer. I'm struck again by the contrast between his strong hands and the thin, wasted muscles of his legs.

Strong legs.

The words leap into my mind, unbidden.

He's got them all fooled.

I stand, so quickly I almost send the rest of the drinks flying.

It's where they used to meet sometimes.

Gav grabs his pint. "What the hell?"

"I was right," I say.

"About what?"

I stare at them. "I was *wrong*, but I was right. I mean, it's crazy. Hard to believe but . . . it makes sense. Fuck. It all makes sense."

The devil, in disguise. Confess.

"Ed, what are you talking about?" Hoppo asks.

"I know who killed Waltzer Girl. Elisa. I know what happened to her."

"What?"

"An act of God."

"I TOLD YOU on the phone, Mr. Adams. It is past visiting hours."

"And I told you I need to see him. It's important."

The nurse—the same stout, stern one who greeted me before—stares at the three of us. (Hoppo and Fat Gav insisted on coming along, too. The old gang. On one final adventure.)

"A matter of life or death, I suppose?"

"Yes."

"And it can't wait till morning?"

"No."

"The reverend isn't going anywhere anytime soon."

"I wouldn't be so sure about that."

She gives me an odd look. And I realize. She knows. They all know, and no one has ever said anything.

"I suppose it doesn't look so good, does it?" I say. "When residents get out? When you find them wandering. Better perhaps that you keep things like that quiet. Especially if you want the Church to keep on giving you funding?"

Her eyes narrow. "*You* come with me. You two"—she snaps her fingers at Hoppo and Gav—"wait here." She gives me another hard look. "Five minutes, Mr. Adams."

I follow her down the corridor. Harsh, fluorescent strip lights glare down. In daytime, the place just about gets away with pretending it is more than a hospital. Not at night. Because there is no night in an institution. There is always light, and always noise. Moans and groans, the creak of doors, the squeak of soft-soled shoes on linoleum.

We reach the reverend's door. Nurse Congeniality gives me one final warning look and holds up five fingers before she knocks.

"Reverend Martin? I have a visitor for you."

For one insane moment I expect the door to swing open and that he will be standing there, smiling coldly at me.

"*Confess.*"

But, of course, the only reply is silence. The nurse gives me a smug look and gently eases the door open.

"Reverend?"

I catch the doubt in her voice just as I catch a cool blast of air.

I don't wait. I push past her. The room is empty, the window hanging wide open, curtains flapping in the evening breeze. I turn back to the nurse.

"You don't have safety locks on your windows?"

"It never seemed necessary . . ." she stumbles.

"Yeah, even though he's gone walkies before?"

She stares steadily back at me. "He only walks when he is upset."

"And I suppose he was upset today."

"Actually, yes. He had a visitor. It left him agitated. But he never goes far."

I run to the window and peer out. Twilight is bringing its shades down fast but I can just make out the black mass of the woods. Not far to walk at all. And from here, across the grounds, who would have seen him?

"He can't come to any harm," she continues. "Usually he finds his way back on his own."

I spin round. "You said he had a visitor. Who?"

"His daughter."

Chloe. She came to say goodbye. A cloud of dread descends.

Night or two camping in the woods doesn't hurt.

"I need to sound the alarm," the nurse says.

"*No.* You need to call the police. *Now.*"

I sling my leg over the windowsill.

"Where do you think you're going?"

"Into the woods."

THEY ARE SMALLER than when we were children. This is not adult perception. The woods really have been cut back, bit by bit, by the housing estate that grew faster than the old oaks and sycamores beside it. Tonight, however, the woods seem huge again, massive. Full of darkness, danger and forbidden things.

This time, I lead the way, feet snapping and crunching on dead leaves and twigs, a torch lent to me (reluctantly) by Nurse Congeniality, picking out the route ahead. Once or twice the beam catches the glowing eyes of some animal before it scuttles away again, into the cover of blackness. There are night creatures and day creatures, I think. Despite my insomnia and sleepwalking, I am not a night creature, not really.

"You okay?" Hoppo whispers behind me, making me jump.

He insisted on coming with me. Gav is waiting back at the home, to make sure they really do call the police.

"Yeah," I whisper back. "Just thinking back to when we were kids in the woods."

"Yeah," Hoppo whispers back. "Me, too."

I wonder why we are whispering. There's no one to hear us. No one but the night creatures. Maybe I was wrong. Maybe he isn't here. Maybe Chloe listened to me and booked into a hostel somewhere. Maybe . . .

The scream rises from the woods like an echoing banshee. The trees seem to shiver and a cloud of flapping black wings rises high into the night sky.

I look at Hoppo, and we both break into a run, the torch light bobbing jaggedly in front of us. We dodge branches and leap tangled weeds . . . and emerge into a small clearing, just like before. Just like my dream.

I stop, and Hoppo lumbers into the back of me. I shine the torch around. On the ground in front of us is a small one-person tent, partially collapsed. In front of it, a rucksack and a pile of clothes. She's not here. I feel a momentary relief . . . and then I swing the torch back round. The pile of clothes. Too big. Too bulky. Not clothes. A body.

No! I run forward and fall to my knees. "Chloe."

I pull back the hoodie. Her face is pale, there are red marks around her neck, but she's breathing. Shallow, faint, but breathing. Not dead. Not yet.

We must have got here just in time, and as much as I wanted to see him, to confront him, that will have to wait. For now, making sure Chloe is okay is more important. I look over at Hoppo, who hovers uncertainly at the edge of the clearing.

"We need to call an ambulance."

He nods, pulls out his phone, and frowns. "Hardly any signal." Still he raises it to his ear . . .

. . . and suddenly it's gone. Not just his phone, but his ear. Where it used to be, there's now a gaping bloody hole. I see a flash of silver, a spurt of dark, red blood, and then his arm drops to his waist, tethered by a few ropy bits of muscle.

I hear a scream. Not Hoppo's. He stares at me mutely then simply crumples to the ground with a guttural groan. The scream is mine.

The reverend steps over Hoppo's prone body. An ax hangs from one hand, shiny and wet with blood. He's wearing gardener's overalls on top of his pajamas.

He was dressed in overalls, like a workman, and he had a limp.

One leg drags now as he stumbles unsteadily toward me. His breathing is ragged, his face gaunt and waxy. He looks like a dead man walking, except for his eyes. They're very much alive, and blazing with a light I have only encountered once before. With Sean Cooper. Illuminated by madness.

I struggle to my feet. Every nerve ending is telling me to run. But how can I leave Chloe and Hoppo? More to the point, how long does Hoppo have till he bleeds to death? Distantly, I think I can hear sirens. Maybe my imagination. On the other hand, if I can keep him talking . . .

"So you're going to kill us all? Isn't murder a sin, Reverend?"

"'The soul who sins shall die. The righteousness of the righteous shall be upon himself, and the wickedness of the wicked shall be upon himself.'"

I stand my ground even as I feel my legs weaken, watching droplets of Hoppo's blood drip from that shiny blade. "Is that why you wanted to kill Hannah? Because she was a sinner?"

"'For on account of a harlot, one is reduced to a loaf of bread. And an adulteress hunts for the precious life. Can a man take fire in his bosom and his clothes not be burned?'"

He moves closer, lame leg raking up dead leaves, ax still swinging. It's like trying to hold a conversation with a biblical Terminator. Still, I try, desperately now, voice cracking.

"She was carrying your baby. She loved you. Didn't that mean anything?"

"'If your hand causes you to sin, cut it off. It is better for you to enter life crippled than with two hands to go to hell, to the unquenchable fire. And if your foot causes you to sin, cut it off. It is better for you to enter life lame than with two feet to be thrown into hell.'"

"But you didn't cut off your own hand. And you didn't kill Hannah. You killed Elisa."

He pauses. I see the momentary uncertainty and seize on it.

"You got it wrong, Reverend. You murdered the wrong girl. An innocent girl. But you know that, don't you? And let's face it, you know, deep down, Hannah was innocent, too. You're the sinner, Reverend. You're a liar, a hypocrite and a murderer."

He roars and lurches toward me. At the last minute I duck and plow into his stomach with my shoulder. I feel a satisfying *oomph* as the breath leaves him and he stumbles backward, then a painful clump as the wooden handle of the ax strikes the side of my head, hard. The reverend crashes to the ground. Carried by my own momentum, I fall heavily on top of him.

I try to push myself up, to reach for the ax, but my head is throbbing, my vision spinning. It's just beyond my fingertips. I overstretch and slip to one side. The reverend rolls his weight onto me. He wraps his hands around my neck. I hit him in the face, trying to shake him off, but my limbs feel weak, the blows have no impact. We grapple back and forth. A concussed man battling the walking dead. His fingers squeeze tighter. I try desperately to prise them apart. My chest feels like it's going to explode, my eyeballs are hot coals bursting from their sockets. My vision is shrinking, like someone is slowly drawing the curtains.

This is not how it's supposed to end, my oxygen-deprived brain gasps. This is not my grand finale. This is a cheat, a swizz. This is . . . and suddenly there's a dull thud and his grip slackens. I can breathe. I drag his hands from my neck. My vision clears. The reverend stares back at me, wide-eyed with shock. He opens his mouth.

"*Confess . . .*"

The final word dribbles out, along with a trickle of dark red blood. His eyes continue to stare at me, but the light has been extinguished. Now they're just orbs of gristle and fluid; whatever was once behind them has finally departed.

I struggle out from underneath him. The ax is sticking out of his back. I stare up. Nicky stands over her father's body, her face and clothes spattered with blood, hands gloved in red. She looks at me, like she's only just noticed I'm there.

"I'm so sorry. I didn't know." She sinks down beside her father, tears on her cheeks mingling with blood. "I should have come sooner. I should have come sooner."

2016

There are questions. Lots of questions. I can just about manage the hows, wheres and whats, but as for the whys, I don't have all the answers. Not even close.

Apparently, Nicky drove over after she got my message. When I wasn't home, she tried the pub. Cheryl told her where we'd gone and the nurses told her the rest. Nicky, being Nicky, came after us. I'm glad—*more* than glad—she did.

Chloe decided to visit her father one last time. A mistake. As was mentioning that she was camping in the woods. And dyeing her hair blond. I think that's what did it. The sudden similarity to Hannah. An awakening in his mind.

Talking of the good reverend's mind, the medics are still arguing about that one. Was the consciousness, the walking (and killing), a temporary aberration from his near-catatonic state or was it the other way around? The invalid act was just that: an act. All along, he understood everything.

Now he is dead, we will never know. Although I'm sure someone will make their name, and probably a bit of cash, by writing a paper on it, or maybe a book. Mickey must be spitting in his grave.

The theory—mostly mine—is that the reverend killed Elisa, thinking she was Hannah, the whore carrying his bastard child and, in his deranged mind, ruining his reputation. Why did he chop her up? Well, the only explanation I have is the one he quoted at me in the woods:

"'If your hand causes you to sin, cut it off. It is better for you to enter life crippled than with two hands to go to hell, to the unquenchable fire.'"

I think chopping her up was his way of making sure she would still enter heaven. Maybe after he realized his mistake. Maybe just because. Who really knows? God might be the reverend's judge, but it would have been nice to see him in a courtroom, facing the prosecution and the unforgiving faces of a jury.

The police are talking about reopening the Elisa Rendell case. These days, they have better forensics, DNA, all that cool stuff you see on TV, that could prove beyond doubt that the reverend was responsible for her murder. I'm not holding my breath. After the night in the woods, and the memory of the reverend's hands around my neck, I doubt I will ever do that again.

Hoppo makes an almost full recovery. The doctors reattach his ear, not perfectly, but then he always wears his hair a little long. His arm, they're doing their best with, but nerves are tricky things. He has been told he may regain partial movement, he may not. It's still too early to tell. Fat Gav consoled him with the fact that he can now park wherever the hell he wants (and he still has one good wanking arm).

For a few weeks the press make themselves an annoying and unwelcome presence around the town and at my front door. I do not want to talk, but Fat Gav gives them an interview. In it, he mentions his pub several times. I have noticed, when I go in there, that business is booming. So at least one good thing has come out of this.

My life begins to resume something of a routine, except for a few things. I tell the school that I will not be returning after the autumn half-term, and I call an estate agent.

A dapper young man with an expensive haircut and a cheap suit comes to the house and looks around. I bite my tongue and try to contain my feelings of intrusion as he peers into cupboards, stamps on floorboards, mmm's and ahh's and tells me that prices have risen considerably in the last few years and, despite the fact that the house needs "some updating," still quotes a valuation that makes my eyebrows rise slightly.

The FOR SALE board goes up a few days later.

The day after that, I put on my best dark suit, smooth down my hair and carefully knot a somber gray tie around my neck. I'm just about to leave when someone knocks on the front door. I tut—*timing*—then hurry across the hall and yank it open.

Nicky stands on the doorstep. She looks me up and down. "Very smart."

"Thank you." I glance at her bright green coat. "I take it you're not coming?"

"No. I only came back today to talk to my solicitor."

Despite the fact that she saved three lives, Nicky could still be prosecuted for the manslaughter of her father.

"You can't stay a little longer?"

She shakes her head. "Tell the others I'm sorry, but—"

"I'm sure they'll understand."

"Thanks." She holds out a hand. "And I just wanted to say—goodbye, Ed."

I stare at her hand. And then, just like she did all those years ago, I step forward and wrap my arms around her. She tenses for a moment, and then hugs me back. I breathe her in. Not vanilla and chewing gum but musk and cigarettes. Not clinging on but letting go.

Eventually, we pull away from each other. Something glints around her neck.

I frown. "You're wearing your old necklace?"

She glances down. "Yes. I always kept it." She fingers the small silver crucifix. "That probably seems strange, keeping something so tied up with bad memories?"

I shake my head. "Not really. Some things you just can't let go of."

She smiles. "Take care."

"And you."

I watch her walk back down the driveway and disappear around the corner. Holding on, I think. Letting go. Sometimes, they're one and the same.

Then I grab my overcoat, check the small hip flask is still in the pocket and head out of the door.

THE OCTOBER AIR is chill. It snaps and nips at my cheeks. I climb into my car gratefully and turn the heater up to full. It has just about started to get vaguely lukewarm by the time I reach the crematorium.

I hate funerals. Who doesn't, except undertakers? But some are worse than others. The young, those taken suddenly and violently, babies. No one should ever have to see a doll-sized coffin making its descent into darkness.

Others simply feel inevitable. Obviously, Gwen's death was still a shock. But, like my dad, when you have said goodbye to your mind, the body at some point will inevitably follow.

There are not many mourners. A lot of people knew Gwen, but she didn't have many friends. Mum is here, Gav and Cheryl, a few of the people she once cleaned for. Hoppo's older brother, Lee, couldn't—or wouldn't—take leave. Hoppo sits at the front, wrapped up in a duffel coat that seems too big for him, arm in an industrial-looking sling. He has lost weight and looks older. The hospital only released him a few days ago. He is still returning for physio.

Gav sits in his wheelchair beside him and Cheryl on the pew the other side. I take a seat behind them, next to Mum. As I sit down, she reaches for my hand. Like she used to when I was a boy. I take it and hold tight.

The service is short. Which is both a mercy and a timely reminder of how seventy years on this planet can be condensed into ten minutes of summary and a few unnecessary wafflings about God. If anyone mentions God when I die, I hope they burn in hell.

At least, with a cremation, once those curtains have swished closed, that's it. No slow shuffle out to the churchyard. No watching the coffin being lowered into a gaping grave. I still remember that all too well from Sean's funeral.

Instead, we all file outside and stand around in the garden of remembrance, admiring the flowers and feeling awkward. Gav and Cheryl are holding a small wake at The Bull, but I don't think any of us are really up for it.

I talk to Gav for a bit then leave Mum talking to Cheryl and sneak around the corner, primarily for a quick cigarette and a sip from my hip flask but also just to get away from people.

Someone else has had the same idea.

Hoppo stands near a row of small headstones marking where ashes have been buried or scattered. I always think the headstones in the crematorium garden look like shrunken versions of the real thing: a miniature model graveyard.

Hoppo looks up as I walk over. "Hey?"

"How are you, or is that a stupid question?"

"I'm okay. I think. Even though I knew this was coming, you're never really ready."

No. None of us is ever really prepared for death. For something so finite. As human beings, we're used to being able to control our lives. To extend them, to an extent. But death brooks no argument. No final plea. No appeal. Death is death, and he holds all the cards. Even if you cheat him once, he won't let you call his bluff a second time.

"You know the worst thing?" Hoppo says. "Part of me feels relieved that she's gone. That I don't have to deal with her anymore."

"It's how I felt when Dad died. Don't feel bad about it. You're not glad she's gone. You're glad the illness is gone."

I take out my hip flask and offer it to him. He hesitates, then accepts it and takes a sip.

"How are you doing otherwise?" I ask. "The arm?"

"Still not much feeling, but the docs have said it will take time."

Of course. We're always giving ourselves time. Then, one day, it just runs out.

He offers the hip flask back. Even though I feel a tug inside, I gesture for him to have some more. He takes another sip and I light my cigarette.

"What about you?" he asks. "Ready for the big move to Manchester?"

I plan to work as a supply teacher for a while. Manchester seems a suitable distance away to get some perspective on things. A lot of things.

"Just about," I say. "Although I have a feeling the kids will eat me alive."

"What about Chloe?"

"She's not coming."

"I thought you two . . . ?"

I shake my head. "I thought it would be best to stay friends."

"Really?"

"Really."

Because, nice as it might be to imagine that Chloe and I could have some kind of relationship, the fact is she doesn't see me that way. She never will. I am not her type, and she is not the right person for me. Besides, now I know she is Nicky's little sister, it just feels wrong. The pair of them need to build bridges. I don't want to be the one to blow them up again.

"Anyway," I say, "maybe I'll meet a nice northern lass."

"Stranger things have happened."

"Isn't that the truth?"

There's a pause. This time, when Hoppo offers the flask back, I take it.

"I suppose it really is all over," he says, and I know he doesn't just mean the chalk men.

"I suppose."

Even though there are still plot holes. Loose ends.

"You don't look convinced?"

I shrug. "There are still things I don't understand."

"Like?"

"Don't you ever wonder who poisoned Murphy? It never made

any sense. I mean, I'm pretty sure Mickey let him off the lead that day. Probably because he wanted to hurt you, like he was hurting. And the drawing I found was probably Mickey, too. But I still can't see Mickey *killing* Murphy. Can you?"

He takes a long while to reply. For a moment, I think he won't. Then he says, "He didn't. No one did. Not intentionally."

I stare at him. "I don't understand."

He looks at the hip flask. I hand it back again. He upends it.

"Mum had already started getting a bit vague about stuff, even back then. She would misplace things, or put things in the wrong place entirely. Once I caught her pouring cereal into a coffee mug and then adding boiling water."

That sounded familiar.

"One day, maybe a year or so after Murph died, I came home and she was making Buddy's dinner. She'd put some wet food in a bowl, and she was adding something from a box out of the cupboard. I thought it was his dry food. And then I realized—it was slug pellets. She had mixed the boxes up."

"Shit."

"Yeah. I stopped her giving it to him just in time, and I think we even made a joke about it. But it got me thinking: what if she had done the same thing before, with Murphy?"

I consider this. Not deliberate. Just a terrible, terrible mistake.

Never assume, Eddie. Question everything. Always look beyond the obvious.

I laugh. I can't help it. "All this time, and we had it so wrong. Again."

"I'm sorry I didn't tell you before."

"Why would you?"

"Well, I guess now you have your answer."

"One of them."

"There's something else?"

I drag harder on my cigarette. "The party. The night of the accident. Mickey always said someone spiked his drink?"

"Mickey always lied."

"Not about that. He never drank and drove. He loved that car of his. He would never risk pranging it."

"So?"

"I think someone *did* spike his drink that night. Someone who wanted him to have an accident. Someone who really hated him. But they didn't count on Gav being in the car as well."

"Someone like that would be a pretty poor friend."

"I don't think that person was any friend of Mickey's. Not then. Not now."

"Meaning?"

"You saw Mickey when he arrived back in Anderbury. The first day. You told Gav he'd spoken to you."

"So?"

"Everyone assumed Mickey wandered into the park that night because he was drunk, thinking about his dead brother, but I don't think so. I think he intended to go there. To meet someone."

"Well, he did. A couple of teenage muggers."

I shake my head. "They're not being charged. Not enough evidence. Plus, they deny being anywhere near the park that night."

He considers. "So perhaps it's like I said right at the start—Mickey was drunk, he fell in?"

I nod. "Because 'there are no lights along that stretch of the path.' That's what you said when I first told you that Mickey had fallen in the river and drowned. Right?"

"That's right."

My heart sinks, just a fraction.

"How did you know where Mickey fell in? Unless you were there?"

His face slackens. "Why would I want to kill Mickey?"

"He finally found out it was you that caused the crash? He was going to tell Gav, put it in the book? You tell me."

He stares at me for a little longer than is comfortable. Then he hands me back the hip flask, pressing it hard into my chest.

"Sometimes, Ed . . . it's better not to know all the answers."

TWO WEEKS LATER

It's strange how small your life seems when you are leaving it behind.

After forty-two years, I imagined my space upon the earth would be bigger, the dent I have created in time a little larger. But no, like pretty much everyone else, most of my life—at least, the material part of it—can be safely accommodated in one large removal van.

I watch as the doors slam shut, the last of my earthly possessions safely boxed up and labeled inside. Well, almost the last.

I smile at the removal men in what I hope is a jovial and matey kind of way. "All done, then?"

"Yup," the older, more weathered of the team replies. "Sorted."

"Good, good."

I glance back at the house. The SOLD sign still glares at me accusingly, as if telling me that I have somehow failed, admitted defeat. I thought Mum would be unhappier about me selling, but actually I got the sense she was relieved. She has insisted on not taking a penny of the profits.

"You'll need it, Ed. Set yourself up. A new start. We all need those at times."

I raise a hand as the removal van drives away. I am renting a one-bedroom flat, so most of my things are going straight into storage. I walk slowly back into the house.

In the same way that my life feels smaller now that my possessions have been taken away, the house, inevitably, feels larger. I hover a little aimlessly in the hallway, then trudge up the stairs to my room.

There's a darker patch on the floor, beneath the window, where my chest used to stand. I walk over to it, kneel down and take a small screwdriver out of my pocket. I wedge it under the loose floorboards and lever them up. Only two items remain inside.

I carefully lift out the first: a large plastic container. Folded up underneath is the second: an old rucksack. Mum bought it for me after I lost my bumbag at the fair. Did I mention that? I liked the rucksack. It had a picture of the Ghostbusters logo on and it was both cooler and more practical than a bumbag. Better for collecting things, too.

I had it with me when I cycled out to the woods that bright, bitter morning. Alone. I'm not sure why. It was still really early and I didn't often ride out to the woods on my own. Especially not in winter. Maybe I just had a feeling. After all, you never knew when you might find something interesting.

And that morning, I found something very interesting.

I literally stumbled over the hand. After the shock subsided, and a bit more searching, I found her foot. Then the left hand. Legs. Torso. And finally, the most important piece of the human puzzle. Her head.

It rested on a small pile of leaves, staring up at the canopy of trees. Sunlight filtered down between the bare branches. It pooled in golden puddles on the woodland floor. I knelt down beside her. Then I reached out a hand—trembling slightly with anticipation—and touched her hair, brushing it back from her face. The scars didn't look so harsh anymore. In the same way that Mr. Halloran had softened them with the gentle strokes of his paintbrush, death had softened them with a cool caress of his skeletal hand. She looked beautiful again. But sad. And lost.

I ran my own fingers over her face and then, almost without thinking, I lifted her up. She was heavier than I thought. And now

I had touched her, I found I couldn't let go. I couldn't leave her there, discarded among the rusty leaves. Death had not just made her beautiful again, it had made her special. And I was the only one who could see it. The only one who could hold on to it.

Gently and reverentially, I dusted off some of the leaves and placed her in the rucksack. It was warm and dry and she didn't have to stare up into the sun. I didn't want her staring into darkness either, or bits of chalk getting in her eyes. So I reached in and closed her lids.

Before I left the woods, I took out a piece of chalk and drew directions to her body, so the police could find her. So the rest of her wouldn't be lost for too long.

No one spoke to me or stopped me on the way back. Maybe if they had, I would have confessed. As it was, I reached home, took the bag with my precious new possession inside and hid it beneath the floorboards.

Of course, then I had a problem. I knew I should tell the police about the body right away. But what if they asked me about her head? I wasn't a good liar. What if they guessed I had taken it? What if they sent me to prison?

So I had an idea. I took my box of chalks and I drew chalk men. For Hoppo, for Fat Gav, for Mickey. But I mixed up the colors to confuse things. So no one would know who had really drawn them.

I drew my own chalk man and pretended—even to myself—that I had just woken up and found it. Then I cycled out to the playground.

Mickey was already there. The others followed. Like I knew they would.

I TAKE THE lid off the container and stare inside. Her empty sockets stare back at me. A few strands of brittle hair, fine as candyfloss, cling to the yellowed skull. If you look closely, you can still see small grooves in her cheekbone where the metal from the Waltzer sheared right through her flesh.

She has not rested here all this time. After a few weeks, the smell in my room became unbearable. Teenage boys' rooms smell bad, but not that bad. I dug a hole right at the far end of our garden and kept her there for several months. But I brought her back. To keep her close. To keep her safe.

I stretch out my hand to touch her just one more time. Then I glance at my watch. Reluctantly, I close the lid, place the container in the rucksack and walk downstairs.

I put the rucksack in the boot of the car and pile several coats and other bags on top of it. I'm not expecting to be stopped and questioned about the contents of my car, but you never know. It could be awkward.

I'm just about to climb into the driver's seat when I remember my house keys. The estate agent has a set, but I meant to post mine back for the new owners before I left. I crunch back across the driveway, take out the keys and slip them through the letter . . .

I pause. The letter—?

I try to grasp for the word, but the more I try, the faster it slips and slithers away. The letter—? The damn letter—?

I picture my dad, staring at the door handle, unable to find that obvious yet elusive word, his face a picture of frustration and confusion. *Think, Ed. Think.*

And then I find it. The letter . . . *hole.* Yes, the letter hole.

I shake my head. Stupid. I panicked. That was all. I'm just tired and stressed about the move. Everything is okay. I am not my dad.

I shove the keys through the door, hear them land with a clunk, then walk back to my car and get in.

Letter *hole.* Of course.

I start the engine and drive away . . . toward Manchester, and my future.

ACKNOWLEDGMENTS

Firstly, thanks to you, the reader, for reading. For buying this book with your hard-earned cash, for taking it out from a library or borrowing it from a friend. However you got here, thank you. I am eternally grateful.

Thanks to my brilliant agent, Madeleine Milburn, for plucking my manuscript from the slush pile and spotting its potential. Best. Agent. Ever. Thank you also to Hayley Steed, Therese Coen, Anna Hogarty and Giles Milburn for all their hard work and expertise. You are a fantastic bunch of people.

Thanks to the wonderful Maxine Hitchcock at MJ Books for our conversations about toddler poo and for being such an inspiring and insightful editor. Thanks to Nathan Roberson at Crown US for the very same things (minus the conversations about toddler poo). Thanks to Sarah Day for the copy edit and to everyone at Penguin Random House for their support.

Thank you to every single one of my publishers worldwide. I hope to meet you all in person one day!

Thank you, of course, to my long-suffering partner, Neil, for his love and support and all the evenings he spent conversing with the back of a laptop. Thanks to Pat and Tim for so many things, and to my mum and dad—for everything.

Almost there, I promise . . .

Thanks to Carl, for listening to me witter on about my writing when I used to be a dog-walker. And for all the carrots!

Finally, thank you to Claire and Matt, for buying our little girl such a great present for her second birthday—a bucket of colored chalks.

Look what you did.

READ ON FOR AN EXCERPT FROM C. J. TUDOR'S NEXT NOVEL

"Razor-sharp writing and masterful plotting drive this dark story about a small town, buried secrets, and ghosts from the past. Witty and compelling all at once, *The Hiding Place* is a must-read page-turner!"

—Wendy Walker, bestselling author of *All Is Not Forgotten*

CROWN
NEW YORK

AVAILABLE WHEREVER BOOKS ARE SOLD

1

Never go back. That's what people always tell you. Things will have changed. They won't be the way you remembered. Leave the past in the past. Of course, the last one is easier said than done. The past has a habit of repeating on you. Like bad curry.

I don't want to go back. Really. There are several things higher up on my wish list, like being eaten alive by rats, or line dancing. This is how badly I don't want to see the craphole I grew up in ever again. But sometimes, there is no choice except the wrong choice.

That's why I find myself driving along a winding road, through the North Nottinghamshire countryside, at barely seven o'clock in the morning. I haven't seen this road for a long time. Come to think of it, I haven't seen 7 a.m. for a long time.

The road is quiet. Only a couple of cars overtake me, one blaring its horn (no doubt the driver indicating that I am impeding his Lewis Hamilton–esque progress to whatever shitty job he simply must get to a few minutes sooner). To be fair to him, I do drive slowly. Nose to the windshield, hands gripping the steering wheel with white, peaked knuckles slowly.

I don't like driving. I try not to whenever possible. I walk or take buses, or trains for longer journeys. Unfortunately, Arnhill is not on any main bus routes and the nearest train station is twelve miles away. Driving is the only real option. Again, sometimes you have no choice.

I signal and turn off the main road onto a series of even narrower, more treacherous country lanes. Fields of turgid brown and dirty green sprawl out on either side, pigs snuffle the air from rusted corrugated huts, in between tumbledown copses of silver birch. Sherwood Forest, or what remains of it. The only places you're likely to find Robin Hood and Little John these days are on badly painted signs above run-down pubs. The men inside are usually more than merry and the only thing they'll rob you of is your teeth, if you look at them the wrong way.

It is not necessarily *grim up north.* Nottinghamshire is not even that far north—unless you have never left the hellish embrace of the M25—but it is somehow colorless, flat, sapped of the vitality you would expect from the countryside. Like the mines that were once so prevalent here have somehow scooped the life out of the place from within.

Finally, a long time since I've seen anything resembling civilization, or even a McDonald's, I pass a crooked and weathered sign on my left: ARNHILL WELCOMES YOU.

Underneath, some eloquent little shit has added: TO GET FUCKED.

Arnhill is not a welcoming village. It is bitter and brooding and sour. It keeps to itself and views visitors with distrust. It is stoic and steadfast and weary all at the same time. It is the sort of village that glowers at you when you arrive and spits on the ground in disgust as you leave.

Apart from a couple of farmhouses and older stone cottages on the outskirts, Arnhill is not quaint or picturesque. Even though the pit closed for good almost thirty years ago, its legacy still runs through the place like the ore through the earth. There are no thatched roofs or hanging baskets. The only things hanging outside the houses here are lines of washing and the occasional St. George's flag.

Rows of uniform sooty-bricked terraces squat along a main road, along with one dilapidated pub: the Running Fox. There used to be two more—the Arnhill Arms and the Bull—but they shut down a long time ago. Back in the day (my day), the landlord of the Fox—Gypsy—would turn a blind eye to some of us older kids drinking in there. I still remember throwing up three pints of Snakebite, and what felt like most of my guts, in the filthy toilets, only to emerge to find him standing there with a mop and bucket.

Next door, the Wandering Dragon fish-and-chips is similarly untouched by progress, fresh paint or—I'm willing to bet—a new menu. One glitch in my total recall: the small corner shop where we used to buy bags of penny candy and Wham bars has gone. A Sainsbury's Local stands in its place. I suppose not even Arnhill is completely immune to the march of progress.

Except for that, my worst fears are confirmed. Nothing has changed. The place is, unfortunately, exactly as I remember it.

I drive further along the high street, past the run-down children's play area and small village green. A statue of a miner stands in the center. A memorial to the pit workers killed in the Arnhill Colliery Disaster of 1949.

Past the village's highlights, up a small hill, I see the gates to the school. Arnhill Academy, as it is called now. The buildings have been given fresh cladding, the aging English block, where a kid once fell from the very top, has been pulled down and a new seating area put in its place. You can roll a turd in glitter, but it's still a turd. I should know.

I pull into the staff parking lot around the rear of the building and climb out of my worn-out old Golf. There are two other cars in parking spaces—a red Mini and an old Saab. Schools are rarely empty during the summer holidays. Teachers have lesson plans to write up, classroom displays to organize, interventions to supervise. And sometimes, interviews to attend.

I lock my car and walk around to the front reception, trying not to limp. My leg is hurting today. Partly the driving, partly the stress of being here. Some people get migraines; I get the equivalent in my bad leg. I should use my cane, really. But I hate it. It makes me feel like an invalid. People look at me with pity. I hate being pitied. Pity should be saved for those who deserve it.

Wincing slightly, I walk up the steps to the main doors. A shiny plaque above them reads: "Good, better, best. Never let it rest. Till your good is better and your better is best."

Inspiring stuff. But I can't help thinking of the Homer Simpson alternative: "Kids, you tried your best and you failed miserably. The lesson is, never try."

I press the intercom beside the door. It crackles and I lean forward to speak into it.

"I'm here to see Mr. Price?"

Another crackle, a piercing whine of interference, and then the door buzzes. Rubbing at my ear, I push it open and walk inside.

The first thing that hits me is the smell. Every school has its own individual one. In the modern academies it's disinfectant and screen cleaner. In the fee-paying schools it's chalk, wooden floors and money. Arnhill Academy smells of stale burgers, toilet blocks and hormones.

"Hello?"

An austere-looking woman with cropped gray hair and spectacles glances up from behind the glass-fronted reception area.

Miss Grayson? Surely not. Surely she'd be retired by now? Then I spot it. The protruding brown mole on her chin, still sprouting the same stiff black hair. *Christ.* It really is her. That must mean, all those years ago, when I thought she was as ancient as the frigging dinosaurs, she was only—what?—forty? The same age I am now.

"I'm here to see Mr. Price," I repeat. "It's Joe . . . *Mr.* Thorne."

I wait for a glimmer of recognition. Nothing. But then it was a long time ago and she's seen a lot of students pass through these doors. I'm not the same skinny little kid in an oversized uniform who would scurry through reception, desperate not to hear her bark their name and rebuke them for an untucked shirt or non-school-regulation trainers.

Miss Grayson wasn't all bad. I would often see some of the weaker, shy kids in her little office. She would apply bandages to scraped knees if the school nurse wasn't in, let them sit and drink juice while they waited to see a teacher, or help with filing, anything to provide a little relief from the torments of the playground. A small place of sanctuary.

She still scared the crap out of me.

Still does, I realize. She sighs—in a way that manages to convey I am wasting her time, my time and the school's time—and reaches for the phone. I wonder why she's here today. She isn't teaching staff. Although, somehow, I'm not surprised. As a child, I could never picture Miss Grayson *outside* of the school. She was part of the structure. Omnipresent.

"Mr. Price?" she barks. "I have a Mr. Thorne here to see you. Okay. Right. Fine." She replaces the receiver. "He's just coming."

"Great. Thanks."

She turns back to her computer, dismissing me. No offer of coffee or tea. And right now my every neuron is crying out for a caffeine fix. I perch on a plastic chair, trying not to look like an errant student waiting to see the headmaster. My knee throbs. I clasp my hands together on top of it, surreptitiously massaging the joint with my fingers.

Through the window, I can see a few kids, out of uniform, messing around by the school gates. They're swigging Red Bull and laughing at something on their smartphones. Déjà vu swamps me. I'm fifteen years old again, hanging around the same gates, swigging a bottle of Coke and . . . what did we hunch over and giggle about before smartphones? Copies of *Rolling Stone* and stolen porn mags, I guess.

I turn away and stare down at my boots. The leather is a little scuffed. I should have polished them. I *really* need coffee. I almost give in and ask for a damn drink when I hear the squeak of shoes on polished linoleum and the double doors to the main corridor swing open.

"Joseph Thorne?"

I stand. Harry Price is everything I expected, and less. A thin, wrung-out-looking man somewhere in his mid-fifties in a shapeless suit and slip-on loafers. His hair is sparse and gray, combed back from a face that looks as though it is constantly on the brink of receiving terrible news. An air of weary resignation hangs about him like bad aftershave.

He smiles. Crooked, nicotine-stained. It reminds me that I haven't had a cigarette since I left Manchester. That, combined with the caffeine craving, makes me want to grind my teeth together until they crumble.

Instead, I stick out a hand and manage what I hope is a pleasant smile in return. "Good to meet you."

I see him quickly appraise me. Taller than him, by a couple of inches. Clean-shaven. Good suit, expensive when it was new. Dark hair, although rather more shot through with gray these days. Dark eyes that are rather more shot through with blood. People have told me I have an honest face. Which just goes to show how little people know.

He grips my hand and shakes it firmly. "My office is just this way."

I adjust my satchel on my shoulders, try to force my bad leg to walk properly and follow Harry to his office. Showtime.

"SO, YOUR LETTER OF RECOMMENDATION from your previous head is glowing."

It should be. I wrote it myself.

"Thank you."

"In fact, everything here looks very impressive."

Bullshit is one of my specialties.

"But . . ."

And there it is.

"There is quite a long gap since your last position—over twelve months."

I reach for the weak, milky coffee that Miss Grayson eventually slammed on the desk in front of me. I take a sip and try not to grimace.

"Yes, well, that was deliberate. I decided I wanted a sabbatical. I'd been teaching for fifteen years. It was time to restock. Think about my future. Decide where I wanted to go next."

"And do you mind me asking what you did on your sabbatical? Your CV is a little vague."

"Some private tutoring. Community work. I taught abroad for a while."

"Really? Whereabouts?"

"Botswana."

Botswana? Where the hell did that come from? I don't think I could even point to it on a frigging map.

"That's very commendable."

And inventive.

"It wasn't entirely altruistic. The weather was better."

We both laugh.

"And now you want to get back to teaching full-time?"

"I'm ready for the next stage in my career, yes."

"So, my next question is—why do you want to work here at Arnhill Academy? Based upon your CV, I would have thought you have your pick of schools?"

Based upon my CV, I should probably have a Nobel Peace Prize.

"Well," I say, "I'm a local boy. I grew up in Arnhill. I suppose I'd like to give something back to the community."

He looks uncomfortable, shuffles papers on his desk. "You are aware of the circumstances in which this post became available?"

"I read the news."

"And how do you feel about that?"

"It's tragic. Terrible. But one tragedy shouldn't define a whole school."

"I'm glad to hear you say that."

I'm glad I practiced it.

"Although," I add, "I do appreciate you must all still be very upset."

"Mrs. Morton was a popular teacher."

"I'm sure."

"And Ben, well, he was a very promising student."

I feel my throat tighten, just a little. I've grown good at hardening myself. But for a moment it gets to me. A life full of promise. But that's all life ever is. A promise. Not a guarantee. We like to believe we have our place all set out in the future, but we only have a reservation. Life can be canceled at any moment, with no warning, no refund, no matter how far along you are in the journey. Even if you've barely had time to take in the scenery.

Like Ben. Like my sister.

I realize Harry is still talking.

"Obviously, it's a sensitive situation. Questions have been asked. How could the school not notice that one of their own teachers was mentally unstable? Could students have been at risk?"

"I understand."

I understand Harry is more worried about his position and his school than poor dead Benjamin Morton, who had his face caved in by the one person in life who should have been there to protect him.

"What I'm saying is I have to be careful who I choose to fill the position. Parents need to have confidence."

"Absolutely. And I completely understand if you have a better candidate—"

"I'm not saying that."

He hasn't. I'm bloody sure of it. And I'm a good teacher (mostly). The fact is, Arnhill Academy is a shithole. Underperforming. Poorly regarded. He knows it. I know it. Getting a decent teacher to work here will be harder than finding a bear that doesn't crap in the woods, especially under the current "circumstances."

I decide to push the point. "I hope you don't mind me being honest?"

Always good to say when you have no intention of being honest.

"I know Arnhill Academy has problems. That's why I want to work here. I'm not looking for an easy ride. I'm looking for a challenge. I know these kids because I used to be one of them. I know the community. I know exactly who and what I'm dealing with. It doesn't faze me. In fact, I think you'll find very little does."

I can tell I've got him. I'm good in interviews. I know what people want to hear. Most important, I know when they're desperate.

Harry sits back in his chair. "Well, I don't think there's anything else I need to ask."

"Good. Well, it was a pleasure meeting—"

"Oh, actually, there is just one thing."

Oh, for fuck's—

He smiles. "When can you start?"

ABOUT THE AUTHOR

C. J. Tudor is the author of *The Hiding Place* and *The Chalk Man*. She lives in England with her partner and their daughter, where she is hard at work on her third novel.